From: Delphi@oracle.org
To: C_Evans@athena.edu
Re: demolitions expert, Lucy Karmon

Christine,

I think we've cornered Arachne. With the information from Diviner's computer hacks, we've pinpointed a potential home base in Cape town, South Africa. It's tricky politics down there, but Lucy Karmon has what it takes for this mission. Your recommendation was spot on.

Not only does she know the land and the people from her years in South Africa with her mother, but she's got a history of breaking the rules, especially when she feels the end is justified. This is one of those times. As you know, we'll do anything to take down Arachne's web.

I'll make contact with Lucy today.

D.

D0992916

Dear Reader,

What a blast it was writing such an exciting, nonstop, action-adventure as *Flashpoint*. The story had a fluid movement that kept me glued to the keyboard, and the words just flowed. When it came to the ending, I actually suffered a week of depression, because I didn't want to let Lucy or Nolan go.

It was so exciting to watch their love story unfold amid the danger they both faced. And what a neat setting for them to fall in love! Africa, with its unforgiving harshness and its alluring beauty. It truly is a melting pot of all cultures, and that's what made researching Cape Town so special to me. There is no other place on Earth quite like it.

I can never do Africa the justice it deserves—no written word can—but I hope I've painted enough mental pictures to pique your interest. Maybe one day you'll journey to Cape Town and think of Lucy and Nolan during your own adventures.

Hope to see you there!

Best wishes and happy reading,

Connie Hall

Connie Hall

FLASHPOINT

Silhouette®

ATHENA FORCE

Published by Silhouette Books

America's Publisher of Contemporary Romance

SILHOUETTE BOOKS

ISBN-13: 978-0-373-38980-3
ISBN-10: 0-373-38980-9

FLASHPOINT

CONNIE HALL

Award-winning author **Connie Hall** is a full-time writer. Her credits include six historical novels and two novellas written under the pen name Constance Hall. She's written two action-adventure novels, *Rare Breed* and *Flashpoint*. Currently, she is working on *The Guardian* for Silhouette Nocturne. Her novels are sold worldwide.

An avid hiker, conservationist, bird-watcher, painter of watercolors and oil portraits, she dreams of one day trying her hand at skydiving. She lives in Richmond, Virginia, with her husband, two sons, and Keeper, a lovable Lab-mix who rules the house with her big brown eyes. For more information, visit Connie's Web site at home.comcast.net/~koslow or e-mail her at koslow@erols. com.

Special thanks to Natashya Wilson, Stacy Boyd
and all the editorial staff at Harlequin,
all Bombshells in their own right.
As ever, thanks to Anne and Camelot.
Couldn't live without you guys. And to
Norm and the boys, for your support and for never
complaining about the number of hours I spend at
my computer. You'll always be my heroes!

Prologue

The icy cold of the operating room soaked through the flimsy sheet, oozed through the hospital gown and bled right down to Jan Strafford's bones. Her teeth chattered from the cold. Odd thing was, she was sweating all over. Must be a case of nerves.

Muzak played from a speaker in the ceiling. Was it Beethoven? She'd hate "Für Elise" for the rest of her life. She could see windows in the ceiling and an observation gallery beyond the windows. Was it empty—no, wait. A shadow loomed across one window, but she couldn't see the person. The person must have been sitting in the last row of the gallery, beyond her view. She felt like a specimen being opened for a biology lab, for one special student.

The smell of disinfectant clung to her nostrils like a cloying fog. Why had she agreed to this? Why had she watched that HBO documentary on plastic surgeries gone bad? She could end up maimed, or worse. The doctor had reassured her facial reconstruction was a breeze, an outpatient procedure. But it wasn't him lying on the table, shivering, sweating every second. The hell with it. She was desperate. She owed several powerful men large sums of money. This was her way out.

A door opened and the nurse anesthetist entered the room carrying a menacing-looking tray. Overhead fluorescent lights gleamed off the glass drug vials and syringes. The end of a rubber tourniquet hung over the tray's edge. The nurse wore a clinical blank face, a lot like her white coat. Not a hint of compassion in her expression.

Jan felt her palms sweating as she dug her fingers into the sheet covering. The gold charm bracelet she had insisted upon wearing during the operation clanked against the metal gurney, the Victorian ornaments rattling like bones. She'd had the bracelet since her twelfth birthday and never took it off. It was her talisman, her good luck charm. Boy, she needed it now.

"I must see both arms, *por favor.*" The nurse looked at the veins on the inside of her arms, then the backs of her hands. She grunted under her breath, grabbed Jan's right arm and tied a tourniquet around her bicep.

"Relax, *señorita,* just a little stick," the nurse said.

Jan glanced up at the shadow above her head. It seemed to grow darker and larger, a monstrous thing, many legs spreading all across the observation windows.

Just as the shadow began to emerge in the gallery window, she felt the prick of the needle, the metal forcing its way into a vein. Her last coherent thought was she'd never look the same again. Then searing fire coursed through her mind.

Chapter 1

Puerto Isla

Lucy Karmon, still clutching the remote detonator, stared through the special fiber-optic scope at the burning meth lab below her. Pieces of the structure mushroomed into a spectacular cinder cloud, two hundred feet of it, masking the night sky.

On the ground, the rebels responsible for supplying Puerto Isla with everything from black tar heroin to Jamaican sinsemilla ran for their lives. Some men, their clothes aflame, dove into a stream at the bottom of a ravine.

Mesmerized, she watched the symphony of destruction opening up before her. This is where she thrived, in the middle of uproar, mayhem, a world on the brink; a world she created and controlled. It touched a chord within her, an odd inner peace, a place that she desperately craved. Her mind settled into the calm and grew still. She observed the fallout, the wind shift, the added perk that she'd taken out the van and old Pontiac Bonneville parked near the building. Mission accomplished. Target annihilated. But what could she have done better? Less fallout, perhaps. That equaled less C-4. Maybe she should have used Danubit or Semtex explosive. But she'd been correct in avoiding TNT. Too volatile and subject to the high humidity on the island.

She always questioned her work. Dissect, assess, moderate and estimate: DAME. She had perfected DAME at the Athena Academy for the Advancement of Women, a highly specialized college prep school for young women. Lucy could still hear Mrs. Warren, her junior year demolitions instructor, saying, "Strive for excellence. Anyone can destroy with explosives, but can you raze the target without loss of life? Can you tear down the ant hill without harming the ants? Refinement of the art, ladies, that is the key. DAME will help you not only in demolitions but in any aspect of your life. Remember the old dame well and she will always come through for you." Mrs. Warren's voice would always be a ghost in Lucy's head, one of many.

A real voice piped into her ear. "Viper to Chaos, copy?"

"Copy, Viper," Lucy whispered into the bone mic resting against her chin.

"Nice job, Chaos. It's Fourth of July up here." Tommy Jefferson, aka Viper, spoke over the sound of chopper blades. An ex-test pilot, he could fly anything with wings. He also owned a locksmith and security business, priding himself on being the world's best safecracker. He chewed gum at the moment, his words clipped off by each chomp. "Ready for pickup in two, over."

"Roger that." She heard the Mojave helicopter pass overhead as she stuffed the detonator into a pocket of her ghillie suit and began running toward a grove of coffee bushes. "Madonna, you copy?" she asked, watching a rabbit she'd flushed dart out in front of her, turn and run off into the night.

"Copy, Chaos. Roger that. By the way, kick-ass job. Wish I had a burger to grill." Betsy LaFave's thick Georgia accent came through loud and clear.

Betsy, a top-notch sniper and black belt, had taken up a position on a higher elevation of the mountain. Lucy wouldn't want anyone else covering her back. Like her, Betsy was ex-army, special ops. They had both left at the same time for different reasons, Lucy's much more tragic.

Lucy ran as she spoke, her voice breathy as she called the last person in the team. "Chaos to Dragon, copy?"

"Copy, Chaos." Cao Sun Tzu, the fourth member of the team, answered her, his Chinese inflection sometimes hard to follow. He was a defector from the People's Republic's Central Security Regiment Unit. There wasn't a computer Cao couldn't mine, or a code he couldn't scramble. That he was a master of disguise and dabbled in inventing new electronic devices didn't hurt, either. "That burger might get a little burned, over."

"Not for me," Betsy said. "I like my meat well done, over."

"Give me a big steak, baked potato and a Corona Light the size of a Jeep, over," Lucy said, feeling the tension that always built in her gut with each assignment, still there, still writhing, even though all team members were present, breathing and accounted for. Now to leave the island with no casualties.

"See you guys on the flip side, over and out." Lucy stuffed the detonator into her backpack, along with twenty-five feet of detonating cord, four fuses and six two-inch hand grenades she'd made out of plumbing pipe. Traveling light on this mission, she thought, grinning.

She zipped up the backpack, threw it over her shoulder and

drew her Colt .45 from the shoulder holster. She ran along the edge of the coffee plantation, toward an open field, her eyes constantly scanning for uninvited drug dealers.

Her backup weapon, a .45 Colt Commander, rested securely on the right side of her left combat boot in an ankle holster. One of her mottos: never go on a mission without at least one Colt. If the first one didn't stop the enemy, the second one would.

She reached the clearing just as Tommy lowered the chopper. Blade turbulence hit her full force, tearing at her ghillie suit, whipping her bright red hair from the tight knot at the back of her head, thrusting against the skin on her face and making it feel as if it would rip from her skull at any moment.

Like well-oiled machine cogs, all three team members emerged into the clearing at the same time. They had worked as a team for two years and it showed. She crouched-ran beneath the whirling blades. Cao reached the chopper first. Betsy, point man—in this case woman—covered them with a Sokolovsky .45 automatic, while holding the case for Sugar, her .308-caliber Remington 700 bolt-action rifle. Custom-built. It shot five match-grade 168-grain boattail hollow-point bullets. Betsy had let Lucy shoot Sugar once. Only once, after much coercing and a gift certificate to Starbucks. No one touched Sugar but Betsy.

When Lucy and Cao were on board, Betsy left her spot and Lucy covered her as she ran for the chopper. In one smooth movement, Lucy grabbed Betsy's hand and helped her up into the cargo hold. At five foot eleven, Lucy was almost a head taller than Betsy and outweighed her by thirty pounds. She kept her body lean and prided herself on lifting as much as most men her size.

"Goodies on board," Lucy said, the loud throbbing of the blades forcing her to speak over the mic to Tommy, though she could see the cockpit and the back of his blond head from where she sat.

"Roger that. Rock and roll."

Lucy felt the vibration of the motor deep within her chest as Tommy throttled up and the chopper lifted off. She shoved the Colt inside the holster, set down the backpack, then plopped down and pressed her back against the wall of the cargo hold. The adrenaline rush slowly left her, her heart slowing, the familiar pulsing of the chopper like a soothing glass of wine.

Relax. Breathe. Another mission down. One they could be proud of, and one they'd be very well paid for by Puerto Isla's new democratic government. The new president was intent upon cleaning up the drug trade on the island. The team had been more than happy to oblige. That's what they did. International mercenaries for hire.

Betsy moved past Lucy, clutching Sugar's rifle case. Camouflage paint covered Betsy's bronze skin and short bleached hair, but her beautiful Halle Berry face was still evident. Lucy wished she had such great skin and near perfect features. She had fair skin, freckles and brown eyes, gifts from her father. Chromosomes could be so cruel.

Betsy saw Cao watching her. She ignored him, plopped down next to Lucy and dropped the rifle case next to her leg with an impulsive thump. Betsy seemed to realize she had set the case down too forcefully so she ran her hands over its aluminum exterior as if to make sure it was okay.

Lucy pushed the strands of hair out of her face and saw Cao's expression fall. She suspected Cao had a crush on Betsy. It seemed her instincts were on target. He was well above average in the male department, with his round face, dark intelligent eyes and straight black hair worn in a ponytail. Why didn't he make a move? At least if Betsy wasn't interested, he could stop with the calf eyes and the underlying tension that stirred between them. The romantic in Lucy decided to help them along.

"So, what've you guys got planned for R and R?" she asked.

Betsy spoke first. "Heading for Baton Rouge. My grand-mama's sick. You going home?"

Lucy wished she could go home to her dude ranch in Montana to unwind. She grimaced as she said, "Ethiopia for me."

Cao looked at Betsy, his mood changing, the stern mask softening, his caring side revealed in his eyes. "Sorry about your grandmother."

"She's been sick a while." The pain of impending loss flashed across Betsy's face; then as if the emotion were too raw, she turned to Lucy, which caused a crestfallen look in Cao's eyes. "Your mom in Ethiopia now?" Betsy asked.

"Yeah, she's kinda settled in there at a clinic. Been there for over a year and half now. A long time for her," Lucy said, thinking of her mother. Dr. Abby Karmon contracted work for the World Health Organization.

"Is she going to stay there a while?"

Lucy shrugged. "I don't know. When wanderlust strikes her, she'll move again."

"What about your father?" Cao asked, shifting so his elbows were on his knees, chin resting on his hands. "Is he back from China?"

At the thought of her father, Lucy narrowed her brows in a frown. Roy Karmon, an engineering specialist, built bridges, tunnels and dams. He had been hired to work on the engineering miracle of the twentieth century, the Yangtze River Three Gorges Dam project in China. "That's why I'm going to Ethiopia. Mom says he's coming for a visit."

Lucy hadn't spoken to her father in a year. And she wasn't looking forward to this visit. She could have invented an excuse not to go this time, but she had heard the pleading in her mother's voice and she couldn't disappoint her.

"Your mom cool with that whole long-distance relationship thing?" Betsy's eyes squinted slightly as if she were baffled.

"It's always boggled my mind, but it seems to work for them."

Betsy grinned. "Conjugal visits twice a year isn't for me. If I'm going to marry a man, his ass better be in my bed at night keeping my feet warm."

"I'm with you on that." Lucy thought of her parents' unconventional relationship. It wasn't for everyone. She'd decided long ago it wasn't for her, either. If and when the right guy came along, she wanted more than the casual connection that had kept her parents' marriage together for the past thirty-two years. She had suspicions that her mother's wanderlust was a coping mechanism for the loss of her husband's presence, but Lucy had never questioned her for fear it might bring up resentment and emotions best left buried. "But there is a highlight to the trip. Val will be there. She's stopping by on her way to the States."

"Y'all have been friends forever, haven't you?" Betsy asked.

"We have," Lucy said proudly.

They'd been friends forever, or so it felt like. Their friendship had begun as pen pals. Val had already been attending the Athena Academy. Her glowing descriptions of the school and the challenges it posed in her letters had intrigued Lucy. There had been restlessness in her, even at fourteen, that she could hardly control. "Rebel Lucy" is what her mother had called her when her tutors complained about her lack of attention. Lucy just hadn't felt challenged. Monotony was her enemy. She had always found her father's work more than interesting and she had invented her own engineering designs just to keep from dying of boredom.

By age eleven, she could design and place explosive charges to bring down either a whole structure or simply a wall within that structure. It hadn't seemed to impress her father, though.

In several letters, Val had suggested Lucy write to Christine Evans, the principal at the Athena Academy, and apply. Lucy thought getting accepted into the academy might please her father since nothing else ever had, so she took Val's advice.

She had described her fledgling engineering designs and the knowledge she had gained from her father. She had been a ninth grader at the time. Most students entered the Academy in the seventh grade, like Val, so Lucy figured getting into the school had been a long shot. But to her surprise, she had received an acceptance letter.

She considered her years at AA the most important of her life. The Academy had taught her wilderness survival, martial arts, how to focus her physical and intellectual energies and find what she excelled at: demolitions. Somewhere along the way they also taught Lucy self-worth, confidence, and to achieve new heights to please herself—not her father. She didn't know where she would be at this moment if the Academy had not been a driving force in those critical teen years. At the Athena Academy, she had become a part of something remarkable, made lifelong ties that could never be broken. Such as Val, fellow alumna and Lucy's dearest friend, a sister in every way but blood.

"Where'd you say she worked again?"

"The U.S. Consulate in Egypt." Lucy couldn't tell anyone about Val's real job, as a CIA operative. The consulate was her cover. Some Athena grads did internships for the FBI, CIA and NSA, and went to work for those agencies. Lucy had interned with the army's special ops demolition division. Thoughts of her short stay in the army made her quickly change the subject. "So, Cao, what will you do?"

"Training." He glanced longingly toward Betsy as if he wanted to ask her to go with him.

"For what?" Betsy asked.

"A triathlon."

Betsy cut her eyes at him. "Sounds like torture."

"It's a challenge." He looked over at her from beneath his long dark lashes. "But too much for some."

Betsy stiffened. "You saying I can't keep up with you?"

Cao smiled placidly, but the smug look in his eyes was unmistakable.

"You're on, Jocko. When and where?"

"Sun River, Oregon." He held up a finger. "One month."

"I'll be there."

Cao's smile widened. "I'll be the one at the finish line."

"I'll be the one already there, waving at you."

Lucy glanced at Betsy and wondered if she knew she'd just been manipulated into spending time with Cao. He was good, but Cupid had his work cut out with these guys. She tried once again to give him a helping hand. "Hey, you two, we never do anything just for fun. Let's meet in New York in a couple of weeks and do the town. All of us. Sound like fun?"

Tommy spoke up. "Wait a minute, no one asked me what I was doing. Am I invited to this party?"

"Absolutely," Lucy said, almost forgetting Tommy had been listening to the conversation through the mics.

"I'm in," Betsy said. She pointed at Cao. "But I doubt Jack LaLanne there can make it. He's got to train."

Cao straightened at the challenge, his dark eyes glowing. "All work and no play makes Jack a dullard. I accept."

The gauntlet had been thrown and picked up. By the toxic gleam in both their eyes, Lucy wondered if she should have suggested a less populated place, like Area 51.

Thoughts of seeing her father again made her wish she were heading to Area 51, the Mojave Desert, New Zealand, even the South Pole. Anywhere in the world but the same room with Roy Karmon. There wasn't a room, a house, a castle or a country big enough for the both of them. Talk about pyrotechnics. At least her mother would be there to run interference and put out the blaze. Hopefully.

Pincer Industries, Cape Town, South Africa

"I've hired someone for the new chief of security position."

Miranda N'Buta stared at the woman who'd just spoken in a raspy deep voice. The woman's image passed through a webcam and onto the monitor on Miranda's desk. Only a portion of the woman's slender torso showed in the background, the webcam situated so her face and lower limbs were hidden. She always wore black and today was no different. Her breasts barely filled out a black silk shirt, and she sat in a wide modern chair that looked like something from the bridge of the Enterprise. Electronic keys covered both chair arms. Her right hand was close on the Web camera and magnified, filling the foreground. Slender fingers with long black painted nails held a cigarette. Smoke spiraled up past a large spider-shaped ring. Eight gold legs fanned out over three fingers. What looked like a five-carat diamond sat in the middle. Gaudy in the extreme, in Miranda's opinion. Still, she felt a tinge of jealousy at the size of the diamond.

"You hired someone without consulting me?" Miranda stared blankly into the webcam directly in front of her, seething inside, yet appearing at ease on the outside. She'd spent years hiding her true feelings—animosity and pure loathing—for the woman on the monitor.

"I decided to screen the applicants myself."

"I don't know why we need the position at all. I oversaw security here—"

"You need what I say you need," the image snapped back.

Miranda stiffened. The charms on her bracelet clicked,

striking the room's silence like nails hitting steel. Irritation churned in her stomach, and she had to swallow a scathing reply.

"You have enough to do. Security shouldn't be your concern," the witch's voice mellowed to a patronizing tone. "I created this new position to help you."

"Giger will be upset that you hired someone other than him. He's handled security matters for us for years."

"Don't tell him right away about the position. Let him learn about it on his own." The witch took a drag off her cigarette. She blew a cloud of smoke at the webcam. The thick cloud filled the monitor and blurred her black silk blouse to gray. "And have Giger meet our new employee at the airport. He arrives on British Airways, Flight 451, at 10:00 a.m."

"Who is this man?"

"Nolan Taylor. I'll send you his résumé. He's perfect for what I need."

It was always about what the witch needed. What about what was best for the company? The witch thought the whole world revolved around her. One day, she'd discover it didn't.

"Why is he perfect?" Miranda asked.

"He's hungry for money and eager for a quiet position in security where he can avoid certain aspects of his life." A snide smile slithered through the witch's tone.

"Is he wanted?" Miranda arched a brow.

"Wanted by the wrong people. At least three contracts are out on his life."

"What's he done?"

"Let's just say he made some enemies in his old line of work." She paused to take a drag on her cigarette. "No, I'm sure our Mr. Taylor will be eager to please and make a good impression. See that he is made comfortable and kept in the dark until we're certain we can trust him. Keep me informed of his progress." The hand reached toward the webcam, the spider's diamond winking, then the picture went blank.

Miranda made a nasty face at the blank screen, then picked up her phone and dialed Giger's extension. "I need to see you right away."

Minutes later, a knock sounded on her door.

"Enter."

Giger Anfinson walked inside and closed the door. He was a Scandinavian giant, towheaded, blue-eyed. His massive chest and arms could crush a man with little effort. He wore brown pants, white shirt and a tweed sport coat, the left side bulging from a side holster and handgun. Miranda's office always felt small with Giger in it.

He walked toward her desk and paused, towering over it. "What do you need?" A Norwegian lilt marked his words and they had sounded like, "Vat do you neet?" The words also held an undercurrent of jaded ruthlessness, as if he'd do anything she required of him, however unseemly.

Miranda felt a familiar vibration of nerves around him. Though Giger was as loyal as any hound and had worked for Miranda and the witch for ten years, she had always wondered what he'd do if he were double-crossed. He wouldn't be too happy when he found out the chief of security position had been created and someone else had been hired for the job. If Giger threatened her, Miranda could blame it on the witch and save her own skin. Giger wouldn't dare retaliate against the witch. In many ways, they were both the witch's captives.

She kept the edginess from her voice as she said, "We're expecting a new employee. You're to pick him up at the airport." Miranda told him the flight number and time.

"What position is he filling?" An underpinning of suspicion swam through his words, while he gazed at her in that direct, brutal way of his.

Miranda hesitated, weighing her options. She could lie as the witch asked her to do and deal with Giger's anger later when he found out. Or she could tell the truth and direct his anger at the person who deserved it, the witch. Why not be honest and lay the blame where it should go? Why should the responsibility fall on her shoulders when the witch was the real culprit in this drama? And if Miranda were being honest, she was sick of being under the witch's tyranny.

Miranda drummed her fingers on her desk. "To tell you the truth, our superior has filled the chief of security position."

Giger gritted his teeth, the veins in his thick neck bulging and pulsing. His pale complexion transformed before her eyes, getting redder and redder by the moment. His body tensed and shook with rage. He slammed his fist down on the edge of Miranda's desk and made her jump. "I wanted that position. The bitch knew that. She did this on purpose."

"I wish I could help you, but my hands are tied on this. She hired this man without my knowledge." Miranda poured it on.

"We'll see about this. Nobody passes Giger Anfinson over." Giger stalked from the office, his hand resting on the pistol beneath his jacket.

Chapter 2

Jijiga, Ethiopia

Lucy rode in the passenger seat, clutching her purse, feeling her insides being jarred loose.

Her father drove the Hummer over another unusually large rut.

Lucy grabbed the dashboard and glanced over at the driver's seat. Was that a hint of a smile on her father's face? He'd found every hole from here to the airstrip. Lucy refused to acknowledge that his lousy driving was getting to her, so she held the dash and braced her feet on the Hummer's floor.

Beyond a curt hello, they hadn't spoken, and the tension in the Hummer had turned into a thick wall that she dared not climb. Why had her mother sent him to pick her up? What was she thinking? Quality father and daughter time? Yeah, right.

She glanced out the window. Up ahead, the Karamara hills looked like a massive python with rolling humps that met plains and river valleys as far as she could see. In the middle of this wide expanse, the mud and grass huts, tin shacks and markets of Jijiga looked like scattered Tinker Toys. Jijiga was a reasonably large city for the region, an aid coordination center for Ethiopia. A city born out of need, where people came to get food and medicine to survive the drought-stricken area.

The rain gods had been kind to the area. The flat plains that were usually clouds of red dust were now verdant. Even a coiffure of green covered the hills. Streams coiled out across the plains. She could see a group of Amhara women washing clothes in a nearby brook.

Silence stretched between them, the tension solidifying by the second. Lucy felt it pulsing against her, drenching the air. When she found it hard to breathe any longer, she said, "It looks like they've had rain here." The weather was a safe subject.

"Your mother says it's a blessing for the area. The nomads are going back to the countryside to graze their herds. It'll mean less starvation and people will be able to survive," he said, his words forced through his lips, uttered with stilted formality. He didn't glance at Lucy, but stared straight ahead at the road. A muscle twitched in his right cheek.

She had brought up a subject. His turn now. She waited. Nothing.

She watched as they passed two men on camels and asked, "So, how is China?"

"Just as I left it."

She stared at this man who'd always been a stranger to her, yet in many ways a mirror of herself. Both independent, both stubborn, and both apparently feeling the strain of dealing with an alter ego.

For a man of fifty-seven, her father was still in good shape.

Well-defined muscles showed below his short-sleeve safari shirt and matching shorts. He wore a fedora that covered his short, red, wavy hair. Since the last time she'd seen him, he'd grown thick muttonchops that sliced across his ruddy cheeks and almost touched the corners of his mouth. That wasn't the only change in him. More wrinkles crept out from the corner of his brown eyes, and the freckles on his face had multiplied, unlike her own that only dotted her nose. She stared at the large hands clutching the steering wheel, the veins protruding on his muscular freckled forearms. She couldn't remember the last time she had felt them hug her. Had her father ever hugged her?

"So…"

Lucy almost jumped at the sound of her father's confident voice. "So," she parroted back, knowing she must have sounded like a voice recorder.

A pregnant silence hung between them as if neither of them could think of one safe subject.

He shifted in the driver's seat and stretched out his left leg, rubbing his knee. Was that arthritis bothering him? Somehow he'd aged without her realizing it. God, she wished things were different. She fidgeted in her seat, pulling at the seat belt.

Finally he said, "So, how is this latest venture of yours going?"

His emphasis on the word *venture* made her grit her teeth. He seemed unable to say the word, so she supplied it for him, "You mean the *team?*"

"Yes, that."

"It pays the bills."

He paused as if trying to control his emotions. It didn't last long as he said, "You put your life in danger to pay bills?"

"You have a lot of room to reproach me. You work in Third

World countries where you need a full-time security force to protect you."

"I don't risk my neck like you—"

"Don't you? The only difference between us is that you blow up mountains. I blow up targets. And have you forgotten you're the one who got me interested in demolitions?"

"I didn't know you'd make a career of it."

"Ah, come on, Dad. You were the one who taught me how to make gunpowder before I was eight. Most girls my age were playing with dolls. I was designing bombs. Admit it. You were grooming me."

"Not for taking the kind of chances you do."

"Don't talk to me about chances." In her heart Lucy always knew her father had wanted a son. Tough. He'd gotten her.

"I'll talk all I want. I never thought you'd use that knowledge in a mercenary capacity." He sighed as if part of his soul was escaping through his lips. "You could have worked with me, done something constructive with your life."

Here we go. Do not pass Go. Do not collect two hundred dollars. Go directly to emotional jail. She forced her voice to stay even. "That's right, but I'm happy with my life."

"You should have finished engineering school."

"Wasn't for me." She hadn't been able to tame the restlessness in her long enough to get an engineering degree.

"Premed didn't suit you, either. You destroyed your mother's hopes of you following in her footsteps."

"It doesn't bother Mom half as much as it bothers you."

"And it'll bother me all my life. If you had—"

"If could'ves and should'ves were candy and gold, yeah, yeah, yeah." She dug her fingers into the brown leather of her purse.

"You didn't even stay in the army."

That one was below the belt. "I chose to leave."

"Because you're too damn hardheaded to follow orders."

"That's not the reason I left." Lucy squeezed her purse into her chest, seeing the whole tragedy unfold in her mind. It tore at her insides. She had never told anyone why she left the army.

"So, enlighten me." He'd raised his voice, his face bloodred.

She blurted out, "I saw a friend get his head blown off, all right?"

The silence of stunned disclosure settled in between them.

Finally her father said, his tone softer, "I'm sorry, but you knew when you joined the army it wasn't going to be all peaches and cream."

She and Jack Kane had been good friends. One night in a bar, Jack had come clean about his attraction to her. They had decided to start dating. Two days after their first date, she'd had to watch a forensic team pick up pieces of him off a field. She wrung her hands in the strap of her purse. Her voice shook as she said, "Peaches and cream, Dad? How callous can you be?"

"That's not callous, that's practical. He shouldn't have been in demolitions if he didn't know what he was doing."

"He was following orders, going by the book."

"There's a right way to do things. Casualties happen. You join a man's world, you have to take it like a man. I thought I taught you that."

Lucy's brows narrowed at her father. She had just poured out the nightmare that had changed her life forever and all he had to say was, "…take it like a man."

It made her lose control and raise her voice. "Yeah, Dad, there's the take-it-like-a-man, by-the-book, blow-your-guts-out-way, or the logical way." The Athena way, she thought. "So you're right. A soldier's life may be dispensable to a general sitting two hundred miles away giving orders from some secure command room, but every life in the field counts with me. And if too damn much red tape gets in my way and I see a better way to go about a mission, you better believe I'm taking it."

"That's your trouble. You've taken your own road your whole life. And look at you, floundering around with a group of mercenaries. The only worthwhile thing you ever did was that Athena Academy. I thought it would turn your life around."

Lucy wanted to tell him that it had turned her life around, and the irony was she still felt closer to her instructors and Athena classmates than she did to her own father.

She couldn't stand another moment of this so-called bonding, so she grabbed the door handle. "Let me out. Now."

Her father jammed his foot on the brake. The Hummer skidded to a halt. He stared straight ahead.

Lucy flung open the door, rolled out of the seat and slammed the door. Trembling all over, she stood firm as the Hummer's spinning wheels spewed dirt and dust all over her. She watched the white vehicle dripping and running into gray behind her tears. Why was it always like this between them? Why couldn't he just accept her and be proud of her? Maybe by the time she reached her mother's home, they both would have calmed down and been able to stay in the same room together. Maybe.

She blinked back the tears, slung her purse over her shoulder and strode down the road. The red clay soil felt like spongy crust beneath her sandals. Afternoon sun beat down on her head. She took off the white scarf from around her neck and tied it around her head. Thank goodness she'd worn a long white linen peasant dress. At least she wouldn't be so hot.

The morning heat swirled up the inside of her legs as she walked. Her shoulder bag thumped against her right hip, her .45 adding to the weight. Over the years, the sensation of a weapon close at hand made her feel secure. At the moment, it didn't give her any refuge, her father's words still smarting.

She grew aware of her lucky charm thumping against her

sternum. She pulled out the .25 caliber casing. The small empty brass cylinder dangled from a gold chain. When she was little, her father would take her to the range. When they were done shooting, they always picked up the spent casings and reloaded them with gunpowder. This was the first casing her father had taught her to reload. She hadn't been able to part with it. It made a lump form in her throat and she dropped it back inside her dress.

One of her two cell phones rang. One connected to the team only. The other was a secure line, chipped for international use and connected to AA.gov, an Athena Academy network overseen by the Department of Defense. She had done courier assignments for AA.gov in the past, and if this was another assignment it would be a welcome interruption to her dad hell.

She reached in her purse, found the phone and popped it open. An encrypted text message scrolled across the LCD screen. She hit a button and the encryption scrambled into English:

Lucy,
A contact named "Delphi" wishes to hire you and your team to go after a target in Cape Town, South Africa.

She narrowed her eyes at the moniker Delphi and typed back:

I've never worked for a contact named Delphi before.

The response:

This is a legitimate assignment. It's tied to recent threats against the Athena Academy, including the kidnapping of two students. Athena alums have been targeted, as well. You could be in danger, so if you accept this assignment keep your own Athena alum status on the QT. Do you accept?

Lucy read the message again, intrigued by what she was told and what she was *not*. Like who had been kidnapped, and was this target in South Africa behind these threats. She typed:

Will accept.

Another line appeared:

Stand by for verbal briefing with Delphi in two minutes.

She slapped the phone closed and waited for the briefing. Thoughts of breaking the news of her shortened visit to her mom made her grimace. She hated disappointing her, but she'd make up for it later. Maybe ask her to vacation at her ranch. Her father, well, he'd probably wish her gone. What about Val? She was to arrive at the end of the week. Lucy truly missed her friend. They'd just have to reschedule.

Lucy watched two women, balancing full laundry baskets on their heads, stride past her as the phone rang again.

She answered, eager to speak to this Delphi. If she was going to risk her life and the team's lives, she wanted to directly communicate with this person. And she wondered how Delphi was tied to the AA.gov network.

Cape Town, Africa

Nolan Taylor followed the red line that led to the porter's booth on the walk of Cape Town International Airport. When he reached the end, he paused, the toe of his black wingtips an inch from the end of the line. He set down his suitcase and glanced behind him.

The big bloke was still following him. He had paused, going through the motions of buying a newspaper from a vending machine. Sunglasses covered the fellow's eyes, but his head was turned Nolan's way. He looked about thirty, his pink fair-skinned scalp showing through his crew-cut white hair. His fairness hinted at a Scandinavian descent. He was burly, tall, about six foot three but still three inches shy of Nolan. From the bulge under the bloke's tweed sport jacket, Nolan suspected a concealed weapon. Nolan hadn't wanted to suffer yards of red tape to bring his own Ruger revolver into South Africa, but he wasn't completely helpless. He had his fists and a T-shaped push knife hidden in his belt buckle.

Nolan quickly stood. He'd made a lot of enemies ferreting out terrorists. It was the main reason he'd left England. At least two terrorist organizations had a price on his head. Was this bloke an assassin? An alarm went off on his watch. Exactly 10:00 hours. He had two hours before his interview at Pincer. Enough time to deal with Viking. With a flick of his finger, he snapped the alarm off.

He handed the porter a five-pound note and spoke to him in Afrikaans, or "Cape Dutch," a West Germanic language spoken mainly in Cape Town. *"Praat U Engels?"*

The porter nodded. *"Ja."*

He switched to English. "Be a good chap and get me a taxi."

The line of taxis, ten cars deep, stretched along the walkway, comprised of every make and model of car, mostly older models. He even saw an ancient Checker Cab; thoughts of London and home stabbed him. He missed his parents until there was an ache in his chest. But he couldn't contact his family and put them in danger. No, he was on his own.

The porter blew a whistle and motioned toward the taxi at the front of the line. The taxi sped forward. Another cab pulled out from the back of the line and floored it. The taxis raced toward him, headlights to headlights. The driver on the left overtook the one on the right, cutting him off, almost colliding. Brakes screeched as the winner stopped at the curb in front of him.

The loser shook his fist at the winner and yelled an expletive in Afrikaans. Taxi wars amused Nolan. Capitalism at work.

He waited until the porter threw his suitcase in the trunk, then slid inside, his knees touching the front seat.

The Crown Victoria smelled of stale cigarettes, body odor and filth. He leaned forward to speak to the driver, a small man with dreadlocks. *"Praat U Engels?"*

The driver bobbed his head. "Ya, boss."

"Excellent. There's a big chap in a tweed sport coat in front of us—don't look. He's getting into a black Taurus sedan in the valet area. He's been following me. You'll get a twenty-pound tip if you lose him."

"Ya, boss, lose him." The man nodded, whipped the taxi out into the flow of traffic.

Nolan memorized the license plate number: 1267PR as they passed the Taurus.

The taxi driver zipped around a double-parked bus, taking his tip seriously.

Nolan kept the Taurus in view as it sped up, and Viking bullied his way into the traffic behind them. The sporting part of him, the part that enjoyed a good game of rugby, made Nolan grin.

Jijiga, Ethiopia

"Hello, Lucy," an electronically altered voice said.

She hadn't expected the disguised voice and it raised her suspicion. "Look, if this is some game you're playing—"

"For safety reasons I protect my identity. I assure you I want to hire you. We are working on the same side."

"Convince me. Name a person on your side."

"Lucy, this is Allison Gracelyn speaking. This is a conference call."

"Allison?" Lucy knew Allison Gracelyn. She was the daughter of Marion Gracelyn, the founder of the Athena Academy. Allison was a fellow Athena alumna and a consultant to the board of directors. Lucy trusted Allison.

"It's me. Delphi thought you might need some convincing, so I was allowed to participate in this briefing."

Yep, that was Allison's voice. It was all the convincing Lucy needed. "Okay, I'm in."

Delphi's creepy altered voice said, "You probably know that House Representative Bryan Ellis is under arrest for fraud and attempted murder of Athena alum Francesca Thorne."

"I heard about it on the news." When Lucy had seen the report that Ellis had tried to kill Francesca, she had wondered why. The report hadn't gone into much detail. "Why did he try to kill her?"

"She was instrumental in his arrest."

"Oh."

"What you probably don't know is that fellow Athena grad Nikki Bustillo recently captured a computer hacker, Martin Slobojvic, a Kestonian wanted in a dozen countries for corporate espionage and spying. We found out he's been working for Bryan Ellis—"

"In what capacity?"

"Someone was blackmailing Ellis, and Slobojvic was helping him track the blackmailer. Slobojvic traced the blackmailer through the regular electronic fund transfers taken from Ellis's account. With Slobojvic's help, we've tracked the blackmailer's trail to a safety deposit box in a Swiss bank. We believe the blackmailer has a home base near Cape Town and has been conducting business through this bank. You are to retrieve any records within the box and the name behind the account."

Lucy suspected she wasn't getting the whole briefing and she waited, silence stretching between them on the line. She listened to Allison clear her throat, then Delphi's hesitant breaths as if what was about to be said was highly classified.

Finally the altered voice said, "You should know this international blackmailer has been on all U.S. intel-gathering agencies' radars for years. In Russia she's known as Madame Web. Weaver, Spider, Webcrawler and Arachne are just a few of her other personas. Not only the U.S. but nations across the globe have a price on her head. She's managed to avoid capture by staying one step ahead of us. We're certain her wealth figures into the equation."

"Like how wealthy are we talking?"

"Billions."

"Jeez, that's a lot of extortion." Lucy couldn't imagine the number of lives this blackmailer had destroyed.

"You don't know the half of it."

"So you believe Arachne is behind these kidnappings and threats to Athena grads." Lucy watched two young boys riding a camel pass her on the road.

"Yes, and we're trying to locate her before she strikes again. All the information you need, as well as your fee, is being forwarded to you by courier and will arrive at a safe house in Cape Town. Proceed there and wait for the courier. You can rendezvous with your team there as well. The house's address will be texted to you, along with the keypad entry code."

"Fine."

"And Lucy, Arachne is, above all, a killer. If she's cornered, your life, as well as your team's lives, could be in the balance. Be careful."

"I will."

"Keep me posted on your progress at Delphi@oracle.org."
Click.

"Goodbye, Lucy," Allison said, "and good luck."

"Goodbye."

The dial tone sounded in Lucy's ear.

She stared at the phone. Why was Arachne targeting
Athena Academy alumnae? What did she hope to gain from
the kidnappings? The very notion that someone was trying to
harm the Athena Academy and its grads awakened Lucy's pro-
tective instincts and caused them to roar to the surface. Anger
stirred in her breast as she thought of Arachne. One thing Lucy
was good at was destroying a target, and Arachne was now in
Lucy's crosshairs.

The Flats, Cape Town

"Listen, mate, leave my suitcase at the Waterfront Arabella
Sheraton." Nolan handed the taxi driver the fare, keeping one
eye on the Taurus as it pulled in behind a bus. He knew his
suitcase might not make it, so he added, "There'll be another
twenty in it for you if you come back for me in half an hour."

"You sure you want to get out here, boss?" The driver
motioned to gang drug dealers standing on the corner.

When the driver hadn't been able to lose Viking, Nolan had
directed him through the city to the low-lying Cape Flats,
southeast of the city. From memory, Nolan could have drawn
a complete map of the Flats and Cape Town proper. He'd been
here before and he never entered a city without knowing the
quickest exits and entrances, the airports and the bus and train
terminals. And the most dangerous areas.

Shantytowns melded into each other in the Cape Flats and
gangland violence contributed to the highest murder rate in
the world. Known as "apartheid's dumping ground" of the

1950s, the area became home to people the apartheid government designated as "non-White." Race-based legislation made
it illegal for those people to live in "White" areas. So they were
forced into the Flats, an area scarred by apartheid's influence.
And an ideal playing ground to deal with Viking types.

"Absolutely," he said, pulling his long legs out of the cab.

He tapped the top of the hood, to let the driver know he
was clear, then the taxi sped off as he walked in the other direction. The air was redolent of suntan lotion and dirty sand.
The beach, only a block away, heightened the water's glare
and forced him to squint.

He strode past bleak metal and wooden sheds, made of
lumber, tin and plastic scraps. Lean-tos and metal shacks
served as pool parlors, coffeehouses and *shebeens,* a local
word for bars. Sidewalk vendors sold cheap beach towels,
sunglasses, sunscreen and woven hats. He passed some gang-
bangers selling coke on a corner. He might have stopped and
forced them to move on, if he didn't have a more pressing
matter behind him.

Several hookers waved at him from a doorway. One wore
a string bikini, the other a halter top and short shorts that left
nothing to the imagination.

"Hey, boss, a discount you," Halter Top said to him in
broken English.

"Hmm, baby, baby you're a big one. I like 'em big," Bikini
called out in Afrikaans, touching her breasts suggestively.

"Not today, ladies." Nolan winked at them, handed them
a twenty-pound note and said, "Get off the streets."

They purred a thank-you.

He knew they'd still be there tomorrow and kept walking.
He glanced behind him.

Viking still followed. He stared directly at Nolan, all
pretense of stealth gone. His lips thinned in a threatening smile.

Nolan grinned back, silent code that he accepted the challenge.

Nolan broke into a jog.

Viking followed.

Chapter 3

Fish Hoek Village, False Bay, South Africa

Lucy stood looking out on the balcony of the safe house, polishing off a glass of sangria. She'd just finished eating a meal of *bobotie,* a kind of shepherd's pie made with a lightly curried mince topped with savory egg custard, served on a bed of turmeric-flavored rice with a dab of chutney. Lucy loved the pungent spices. The dish, a local favorite, came from the Cape Malay cuisine, a blending of early European Dutch and Malay fare.

The July wind gusted and whipped Lucy's hair against her face. South Africa's winters ran from June to October, so different from America's. She set down her glass on the railing and zipped up her sweatshirt. The wind hadn't stopped blowing since she'd arrived, and she'd quickly learned that she hadn't packed enough warm clothes. She'd had to make a run to the local market to buy another sweatshirt.

The safe house was in Fish Hoek Village, about thirty minutes from Cape Town. The village faced the Indian Ocean side of the Cape Peninsula and, like most of the Cape, the winds tore at the shore, molding the beaches to its will. She'd since learned that the wind blew constantly here, sometimes at twenty knots. Monster thunderstorms were known to rise up without notice. Even now dark clouds gathered to the west. She watched a janitor emptying a trash can on the beach, struggling to corral the plastic bags, paper cups and empty soda cans. A bag got away from him, flitted across the beach, smashed into the sea froth and was swallowed by the thick lengths of black kelp that chopped against the shore. The kelp was so thick, two surfers in wetsuits fought it to paddle away from the beach.

She looked out at the horizon and saw whale-watching boats bob and list in the wave swells. Miles up the beach, penguins guarded eggs, cavorted in the surf and wobbled up and down the beach like stiff wind-up toys.

The three-story safe house itself was shaped like a Far Eastern pagoda with a curved smiling roof, wide pillars standing tall across the front. A balcony wrapped around the top floor, providing awesome vistas of the Cape. Behind the house were the sharp jagged peaks of Simonstown Mountains. Mountain ranges seemed to cover the western coast of South Africa. Jagged escarpments coughed up pristine white beaches, creating spectacular seascapes.

The violence and savagery of the wind here drew her. She enjoyed the unrestrained feeling of it pushing against her, thrashing her shift against her legs, bits of sand stinging her lips. It stirred her almost as much as the African bush. She had seen a lot of Africa traveling with her mother and nothing could compare to the wildlife and wilderness of the bush, but Cape Town was by far the most beautiful city on the continent.

Inside the house, retro modern furniture and thick mahogany tables were paired with an oriental theme. A windowless basement ran the length of the house and held a lab with enough explosives and weapons to keep an anarchist happy for a couple of years.

She felt her hair stinging her cheeks as the wind lashed it against her face. Uncertainty tugged at her. She'd been here a whole day and no courier had arrived. The team should be here in a couple of hours. No one complained about the change in plans. Flexibility was essential in their line of work. Tommy was flying Cao and Betsy over in the Cessna he used for his security business. She had taken a chartered flight in from Jijiga.

A knock on the door brought her out of her seat. She stepped through the open patio doors and paused near the security monitor.

The heart-shaped face and short brunette hair she spotted made her smile. She pressed the intercom and screamed, "Oh my God!" Her jaw fell open. "Val!"

"Hey, girlfriend, open the door. I'm growing warts here."

Lucy grabbed the knob and flung open the door. She almost leaped into Val's arms, but the cupcake and burning candle her friend held made her pause.

Val broke out into a smile. "Thought I'd forget? Happy birthday, McGill."

Lucy grinned at the sound of her old nickname. McGill stood for McGillicuddy. Louise Benson, Lucy's archrival at the Athena Academy, had dubbed Lucy with the name because of her red hair resembling Lucille Ball's. The name had stuck. Lucy hadn't liked the pet name at first and she had paid Louise back by putting Elmer's Glue in her hair conditioner. Louise had walked around for a week with chopsticks for hair.

Louise hadn't known it at the time, but she'd done Lucy a big favor. The nickname had made Lucy buckle down, rein in her restlessness, strive harder in her classes so she wouldn't live up to her *I Love Lucy* namesake. She had graduated with honors, and if she were brutally honest with herself, it was partially owing to Louise's spite.

"Oh, no! I forgot yours," Lucy said. They shared the same birthday and had always tried to celebrate it together. She wondered if her mother had planned a surprise party for both of them. Knowing her mother, she probably had. She'd have to make it up to her.

"Okay, so I win the better friend medal today." Val strode inside, sporting an Ann Taylor white pant suit, matching shoes and purse. Sleek white sunglasses to match. When Val made an entrance, heads turned.

Lucy stared at her own jade-green shift, Nikes, and white tourist sweatshirt with Cape Town, South Africa silk-screened on it. She felt a little dowdy around Val, who always looked like she'd just stepped out of a Neiman Marcus window.

Lucy closed the door and Val held out the cupcake. "Make a wish for both of us."

Lucy filled her cheeks, closed her eyes and blew.

"Still got enough hot air for both of us, I see." Val thrust the cupcake at Lucy, pushed her sunglasses up on her head, and glanced around at the luxury surrounding them. "Can you find a knife in this dump?"

Lucy laughed until her eyes glistened with tears. God, she had missed Val. "Share some dinner with me, then we'll eat the cupcake."

"Lead the way. I'm starving."

Val followed her into the galley-style kitchen. "So what are you doing here? How did you find me?"

Val wiggled her fingers like an evil conjurer, her bright

green eyes glistening. "We Khaosians have ways of finding out things."

Lucy thought of the Khaos mentor group Val and she had belonged to at the Athena Academy. The group had been named after Khaos, the primeval Greek goddess of air. Her name actually meant "gap," the space separating heaven and earth. They went hot air ballooning and sky diving, and on special occasions put on fireworks displays. The group activities had been a blast, but Lucy had taken the most pleasure in setting up the fireworks.

"Come on, spill the beans," Lucy said.

Val pulled a manila envelope from her backpack and handed it to Lucy. It looked like any business envelope, innocuous enough. She must have breezed through customs.

"You're the courier?" Lucy asked, staring at the envelope in disbelief.

"Delphi must have known we were friends and asked me to drop it off."

"I just found out about this Delphi person. I was skeptical at first."

"Delphi is one of the good guys. You shouldn't have any reservations about accepting an assignment from that quarter." Val hesitated for a moment, then said, "Delphi thought you might have some questions and said I should brief you on the Oracle network."

"What is Oracle?"

"All I know is that it's a secret network that monitors intel from U.S. intelligence-gathering agencies, and Delphi oversees it."

"So you work for Oracle, too?"

"I do assignments when I can."

"We're both Athena grads. Does that mean Oracle gets its recruits from the Athena Academy?"

"I don't know if all the operatives who work for Oracle are AA grads. I have my suspicions that a lot of them could be. And I know they often use resources from AA.gov."

"Do you know who Delphi is? That altered voice creeped me out."

"You, too?" Val grinned. "You get used to it."

Lucy had a feeling Val was avoiding the question so she said, "Okay, so who is it?"

Val shrugged. "I'm not sure, but I believe it's someone connected to the Athena Academy. I don't even know who any of the other Oracle agents are. I only knew about you because Delphi gave me your name as my contact. We're not even supposed to be discussing it. Pretty hush-hush stuff."

"Oh, okay." Lucy let it drop, but she was still curious about Delphi's identity.

Val pointed to the envelope. "By the way, you're not to open that until I'm gone."

"So you're not here for long?" The excitement dropped from Lucy's voice. She set the package on the counter and pulled out a plate and fork and knife for Val.

"Sorry." Val checked her Rolex. "We got two hours, then I'm on a flight for the States."

"CIA biz?"

Val nodded as she picked up the take-out container and shoveled the rest of the rice onto a plate. "What did you wish for?" she asked.

"Can't say. Bad luck and you know it."

"Remember that silly vow we made our sophomore year?"

"I'd almost forgotten about it."

Val shrugged and shook her head. "Falling madly in love by our thirtieth birthday and turning down at least five marriage proposals. Hard to forget."

They both smiled at each other, their expressions turning somber, pensive.

A strange sadness tugged at Lucy. Maybe it was the lost closeness they had shared at the academy, a youth that had slipped by all too quickly. Or it could be the vow that still nagged at the back of her mind, a whispered uncertainty that she might not ever fall in love. She certainly hadn't turned down any proposals. Thoughts of Jack Kane surfaced, but she hadn't really loved Jack in that breathless, love-ever-after way. They'd only gone out on one date before he died. But if they'd had more time…. Jack might have been the one. She forced memories of Jack back into that dark place she refused to enter.

"Remember," Val said, her voice faraway, "I wanted twin boys that looked like—"

"Johnny Depp." Lucy finished for her. "And I wanted a girl—"

"Without red hair and freckles who didn't look like an extra from the cast of *Annie*," Val said, grinning. "Although, you know, all the Khaosians envied your red hair."

"They did?" Lucy stared at her in disbelief.

"Sure, why do you think everyone kept calling you McGill? Nothing but jealousy, girlfriend."

"Well, if we're coming clean, I've always wanted your hair—anyone's hair color but my own." Lucy grinned.

"So we didn't get a family and we didn't get the hair color we wanted, but we got kick-ass careers…" Val's words trailed off, her tone slightly sulky. Her brows narrowed as she poured herself a glass of wine from the open bottle of sangria Lucy had left out. She gulped down a large swig.

"What?" Lucy looked expectantly at her.

"I'm just…I don't know."

"Lonely," Lucy supplied for her.

"Yeah. Even in a singles bar, hunks all around me, hitting

on me with their goofy lines, and I still feel like I'm alone on the planet."

"So fall for a line."

"I'm tired of one-night stands. I don't think there's anyone for me. Don't you ever feel that way?"

"Sure, but I haven't given up yet." Lucy hadn't really been on the prowl for a man. There'd been a few meaningless nights, when she hadn't been able to face an empty bed and another night alone, with guys whose names she couldn't even remember. But no one serious. And she wanted to keep it that way.

"Oh, you're a hopeless romantic." Val waved her empty glass at Lucy.

Lucy realized she might have been a romantic at one time. God, she wanted to feel that way again.

At Lucy's silence, Val said, "Remember that time you made me watch *An Affair to Remember* six times?"

"You cried. I saw you. Admit it."

Val rolled her eyes.

"Talk about tired movies. What about your Steven Segal fests?" Lucy pointed at Val.

"I thought you liked them, all the explosions."

"Only my *own* explosions." Lucy grinned. "Too much overkill and fallout in Hollywood."

"You're right. Let's do an indie weekend, get in some serious angst and melancholy with a little black humor thrown in." Val grinned at Lucy, then looked at her watch. "And we'd better plan it quick. One hour and fifty minutes and counting."

Lucy gulped back the tightness that had suddenly swelled in her throat. She wanted more time with Val. She glanced at the envelope sitting on the counter, and it felt as if minutes were traveling at light speed. An overwhelming restlessness within her wanted to reach out and grab time, force it to be still. Suddenly a foreboding gripped her, one that told her she'd better enjoy this fleeting moment with Val because she might never get another one.

Cape Flats, Cape Town

Nolan fought the wind hitting his face and darted into the throng of an open air market. He weaved his way past farmers hawking melons, grapes, fava beans, coffee and spices from crates and wheelbarrows. He dodged sari-clad women, dragging packages and children behind them. He knew his height made him an easy target to follow, so he crossed to the market's higher-end side and zigzagged his way through the covered stalls. Vendors sold everything from ostrich-skin wallets to zebra-hide cushions. The strong smell of body odor, animal hides and incense made him grimace. He could barely make out Viking's footfalls over the market's noise.

When he neared a rug seller, he darted in between several lines of hanging carpets. The vendor, a thin man wearing a turban, watched him with wary eyes as if street violence and people being chased was the norm.

The carpet line ended near an abandoned metal shack. Beside it, knee-high grass covered a small area. Nolan ducked beneath the last Karabakh carpet, and pressed his back against the metal, the heat of it burning his spine. He waited.

Viking's footfalls grew closer.

Nolan watched his progress below the carpets. Viking's feet came to the end of the line and halted.

A carpet wall separated them.

Nolan listened to Viking's heavy breathing and could almost hear his indecision: lift the carpet or not. Make the leap or be safe. Be the clever intimidator or the wimpy sod. Nolan had learned early on in his life that muscle-bound thugs liked testing their strength on bigger chaps. And since he'd always been in the top percentile for height and weight, he'd fought every bully at school and in his neighborhood before he'd turned six. It was no different in his later life. He was actually looking forward to facing this sod.

Nolan didn't move, breathing through an adrenaline rush.

As Nolan had planned, Viking stepped around the carpets, the barrel of his gun coming first. Nolan drop-kicked the gun from Viking's hand.

It landed in the grass and discharged; the report seemed to echo for miles.

Viking faced him, pulled a switchblade, his face like that of a cat with its prey. "How you like this?"

"The question is, do you have the bollocks to use it?" Nolan circled him, his arms out in a wrestling stance.

Viking lashed out at him.

Nolan easily avoided the knife, grabbed Viking's arm and twisted it behind his back. Nolan caught the man in a headlock. "Sorry, mate, you'll have to do better than that."

Viking cursed in Norwegian and struggled in Nolan's arms. But Nolan was bigger, stronger and had the upper hand.

"Move again, and I'll break your bloody neck."

Viking growled in frustration and stopped struggling.

"Better. Now, who do you work for?" Nolan asked, his tone pleasantly composed.

No answer.

Nolan turned Viking's head within a millimeter of snapping his neck. Color bled into Viking's pale cheeks. The patient quality left Nolan's voice. "I'll ask again, but this is the last time."

"Myself," Viking ground out.

"What have I ever done to you?"

"My job…"

"Your job?" Nolan narrowed his brows at him.

"She gave you my job. It should have been mine."

"You work at Pincer?"

Viking ground out, "Yes."

"It's all very clear now." Relief washed over Nolan. At least the terrorists hadn't discovered his whereabouts—if this bloke was telling the truth.

Instead of breaking Viking's neck, Nolan applied pressure to his carotid artery. Too long and the lack of oxygen to his brain would kill him. Just enough and he'd be out for a while and wake up with a bloody headache. Nolan chose the headache.

Viking went limp in his arms. He patted the sod down, pulled out his PDA. He pocketed the handheld computer, then grabbed Viking's arms and pulled him toward the abandoned building. He wasn't certain Viking had been telling the truth. Jealousy could make a person do just about anything, and Viking seemed like the type to even scores at any cost. Nolan hoped the PDA might contain information that could confirm Viking's story.

Fish Hoek Village, False Bay, South Africa

"Plus Suisse Worldwide Depository is our target?" Cao asked, frowning at Lucy across the dining table. He sat nearest the open balcony doors, and a breeze rustled the shaggy black hair protruding from beneath his black sun visor. He wore a black matching warm-up suit.

"Yes." Lucy squinted at the schematic on the computer screen. It was part of the info Delphi had sent her on a flash key. She'd also received the history of the PSWD, a twenty-four-hour, fully automated *Geldschrank* bank. They maintained offices not only in Switzerland, but all over the world. Criminals and terrorists could hide stolen bonds, accounts, art treasures, passports. Just about anything they wanted to keep from law enforcement. Ambiguity was PSWD's ultimate profit source: electronically untraceable computer source code escrow accounts. *Anonyme lager,* otherwise known as anonymous drop storage boxes. Digitized international transferable accounts. All high-tech blankets of privacy. Accounts were by numbers only. No names. No faces. The bank's very anonymity policy could be its downfall. It might be its only one.

She studied the building's twelve floors, six of which were underground bank vaults, buried beneath thousands of tons of concrete and steel. It really looked like a rat-maze fortress.

"You say there are three electronic readers we have to get through to get inside?" Betsy asked, reaching for the bag of potato chips. She chomped one down, then chased it with a sip of sangria. Betsy had on red biker shorts that looked poured over her small hips. The straps of her sports bra peeked out from the top of a red sweater that hugged her flat stomach.

"Yes." Lucy peered at the schematic Delphi had supplied for them. "One in the underground parking deck. Two on each vault floor."

Tommy gazed at Betsy's glass of fruity wine, tasting it with his eyes. He'd been a recovering alcoholic since he was sixteen. He picked up his can of Pepsi, frowned at it like an old friend who annoyed him, then said, "How many guards on duty?" He settled against his flight jacket that rested on the back of his chair and sipped his soda. The slogan, Pilots Do It Better, blazed across his T-shirt.

"One at the lobby desk," Lucy said. "Three manning the security cameras."

"Better than ten." Tommy rubbed his finger around the top of the can.

"I can get us past the readers and the metal detectors," Cao said in his quiet, serene voice, all the while looking at Betsy as if he were imagining what lay beneath her sweater and bra.

He reached in a briefcase and pulled out something that looked very similar to a hotel pass key, but had a metal casing.

"What is it?" Betsy asked, narrowing her eyes at the gadget.

"A microprocessor wireless modem. My design." He grinned, looking pleased that she had questioned him about it. "You just insert it into the electronic reader and I'm in their computer."

Betsy frowned at the invention as if it were a new brand of bullet that she'd never used before. "You sure it will work?"

"Of course." Cao shot Betsy an indignant glance.

"Won't they have filters that scramble a foreign signal?" Tommy asked.

"I'll break them before the alarm goes off." Cao paused, seeming to be at war with an emotion for a moment, then said, "There's one drawback."

"What?" Lucy asked.

"This device has to stay in the electronic card reader and cannot be taken out. Preferably the reader in the parking deck. Inside the bank, the wireless signal will be blocked."

"It's only got to get me inside and to the strongbox. So will it work…here?" She pointed on the schematic to the security gate that opened into the underground parking deck.

Cao nodded.

Betsy reached for another chip. "We have to make sure it's not spotted by a guard or another customer."

"We'll deal with them." Tommy chugged the rest of his Pepsi and burped.

"You'll have three minutes between the entry doors," Cao said.

"Okay."

"What about the strongbox's password?" Cao asked. "No way I can find out that info."

"I got the password right here." Lucy pointed to a pea-size piece of C-4 she had stashed in a pillbox.

Tommy leaned back in his chair, the glint in his green eyes turning apprehensive. "There's another hitch—the carbon monoxide delivery system in the vaults. Get caught in there and your ass is grass."

Cao spoke up. "It only takes a concentration of .04% to be fatal. At 1.28%, you're dead in less than three minutes."

Betsy frowned at him. "You're a regular book of creepy facts."

Cao cocked his head at her. "I designed a gas chamber for North Korea once." He didn't sound proud of the fact, but he still met her eyes without blinking.

Betsy winced. If he had meant to shock her, it had worked.

Lucy said, "So will a gas mask work?"

"Not with CO," Cao said. "It absorbs all available oxygen, and with a mask you're filtering and breathing in the stuff that comes out of your car's tailpipe, but more deadly."

Tommy spoke up. "You can use a portable oxygen mask. That'll keep you alive until you can get to an oxygen source."

Their conversation drifted into a heavy silence that mixed with the sound of the breaking waves outside the door.

Lucy stared at the glowing schematic on the screen. It radiated with an eerie liquid blue glow. Was she looking at the blueprint of her own coffin?

Pincer Industries, Cape Town, South Africa

Nolan Taylor drummed his fingers on the arm of the chair. What was taking so long? He had arrived promptly, not a minute before or after, twelve hundred hours. He lifted the heavily starched French cuff of his white shirt and read his watch: 12:10. Was punctuality too much to ask?

The hum of a computer on the sleek modern desk across the room began to irritate him. He looked at the webcam turned in his direction. Was he being observed? Nervous energy got the better of him and he stood and walked over to the windows that ran floor to ceiling in the high-rise office, out of the webcam's sight.

From his fifteenth-story view, the vast microcosm of humanity that was the metropolis of Cape Town spread out before him. Cape Town had evolved from a refueling outpost for Dutch ships in the sixteen hundreds to what it was today, a diverse city with 2.9 million people, one of the busiest shipping corridors in the world. This made it a perfect place for smugglers and terrorists.

He could see the N1 Freeway curving around the fringes. White beaches and blue water met the Atlantic seaboard side of Camps Bay and Bantry Bay. Along the waterfront were the old Dutch docks that had been converted into Victoria and Alfred Waterfront, a tourist's dream of shops, bars and cinemas. Part of this area, the Sea Point Promenade, included the Muslim district and the notorious "red light" district. He'd tracked down terrorists in the Muslim district before.

High-rises stacked the city proper like building blocks. Down the street from Pincer Industries, the historical yellow sandstone walls of City Hall gleamed in the sunlight. Farther on the Botanical Gardens formed a lake of green. Table Mountain towered in the background over the whole seaside city, its plateau looking just like the natural UFO landing pad in *Close Encounters of the Third Kind* with a few extra hills on either side.

His gaze moved southeast of the city to Cape Flats, where its white beaches looked pleasantly beautiful, innocuous enough from this distance. His brows furrowed as he remembered what he'd left there only two hours ago.

A side door to the office opened. He straightened his tie, then turned to face the CEO of Pincer Industries.

Downtown Cape Town

Lucy drove a rented Corolla down St. John's Street. She had rented six vehicles for the stay in Cape Town: the Corolla, three Jeeps and two vans, all at different rental places, all fees paid with cash, and all under assumed names. She tugged at the short black bangs of a wig, making sure her auburn eyebrows were covered. Cao had her disguised with a Roman nose, black glasses, and sideburns. She'd wrapped her breasts so they wouldn't show beneath the male pin-stripped suit she wore. She was just tall and muscular enough to pull it off, with the help of shoulder pads. How did men get used to all these layers of tight clothing?

She glanced in the rearview mirror. The white van carrying the rest of the team cruised several car lengths behind her. It reassured her, but it didn't stop the adrenaline strumming her veins.

She neared the target, Plus Suisse Worldwide Depository, a monolith of steel and glass that shadowed half a block.

She approached the cement-lined ramp to the underground parking deck and slowed. "Okay, going in," she spoke into the bone mic.

"Passing you," Tommy said as the van eased past her.

"Turning."

Cao, Betsy and Tommy all wished her luck, and she heard the worry in their voices. Tommy pulled the van into an alley across the street, next to a sleek modern law office. Cao slid a tiny portable dish onto the roof.

She paused before the electronic podium and gate. An LCD screen spewed out directions in Afrikaans, French, Dutch, German, English, Xhosa, Zulu, Sesotho, Setswana, Muslim, Hindu…and the languages kept rolling.

She spoke more than ten languages, a necessity from

having lived in many impoverished Asian and African provinces with her mother, so she had already pulled out the mini modem.

"Okay, in we go." She slid it in. It fit perfectly. No alarm went off. Always good.

Would it work? Her faith in Cao had never wavered until this moment. She counted the seconds by the steady pulse in her temple.

Waited. Held her breath.

Chapter 4

Pincer Industries, Cape Town, South Africa

Nolan gazed into the woman's face, an unremarkable face, the type that once you passed it on the street it was forgotten. A conservatively tailored black suit hugged her thin figure. She approached him. Her black designer heels whispered on the thick white carpet. She smiled with Cheshire cat teeth.

"Ah, Mr. Taylor." She spoke with a nondescript American accent.

Usually he could pinpoint any American accent. This one eluded him. California, maybe?

She checked him out from head to toe, neither disapproval nor approval showing in her expression. She released his hand. Her voice stayed guarded as she said, "So nice to finally meet you. I'm Miranda N'Buta."

"Quite, we spoke on the phone." He used his best elocution. He'd worked hard to rid himself of his cockney dialect, and he knew the effort made him sound just a tad stuffy at times, so he cleared his throat and said, "Very pleased to meet you."

She shook his hand, the gold charms of her bracelet clinking. "Please sit." She pointed to the chair he had just vacated, directly in front of the cam.

"I was admiring Cape Town," he said, struggling to smile at her, feeling as if he were being put on electronic display.

"It is beautiful. I've grown fond of it myself." She sat behind the desk, tapped on the computer keyboard, the gold charms creating a discordant symphony. "Ah, this shouldn't take long as I reacquaint myself with your résumé." Her gaze moved back and forth across the screen. Her face remained coolly polite and unemotional.

He smoothed down his tie again and said, "I thought we had discussed my background on the phone when you hired me."

"Yes, well," her lips moved in a hint of a smile, "my days can get hectic here at Pincer." The lips hardened into dry putty. "So, you grew up in London?"

"Yes." He watched her reading, probably that he was raised in Tower Hamlets, one of the poorest boroughs in London. A stigma he had tried to rise above his whole life. He wondered if this interrogation was more than just a memory refresher. Had she somehow found out he'd had to leave England because of attempts on his life?

"Ah, you attended Sandhurst Academy. Graduated with honors. And received a lieutenant's commission in two years. All before age thirty. Impressive."

"Thank you, madam." Did he detect authentic praise in her voice? She hadn't praised him during their phone conversation. Perhaps she was absentminded and his first impression of her had been too harsh.

"You were in the Intelligence Corps, I see."

"The Terrorists Division."

"Forgive the forwardness, but why did you leave?"

He had already answered this question over the phone and he made an effort to keep the impatience from his voice. "Money issues, madam. The Corps doesn't pay as well as the private sector." He stuck with the first lie he had used.

She closed the file with a flick of the Delete key. "Did we speak about salary?" She studied him for an answer as if she couldn't remember.

"You told me I'd be well pleased and you'd make it worth my while to move from England."

"I have to be honest with you, Mr. Taylor. The chief security officer's position you were hired for is newly created. I haven't really set a salary for the position yet."

"I see." Right now, he didn't care how much his salary was as long as he found work.

"Let's start you at a hundred thousand pounds per annum. Raises are based on merit. Does that meet with your approval?"

"Of course." He nodded, hiding his surprise and delight. The pay was more than she had quoted him over the phone. A small fortune. He thought of Viking. "If you don't mind my asking, why was this position created?"

Her eyes flashed for a second, then turned opaque again, unflinching. "We've decided to beef up security."

"I saw the state-of-the-art security system you have here. Laser grids in the floors and walls." He looked at the security outlets that ran along the base of the walls in her office.

"Yes, well." She looked pleased that he was observant. "It will be part of your responsibilities to maintain them and modify them if necessary. I've laid out security protocol for the company that must be followed to the letter." She handed him a thick binder. "Acquaint yourself with them."

He took the ring binder. "I'm a stickler for rules, myself."

Her lips thinned in a plastic grin. "No doubt you are, coming from a military background."

"I suppose—" he studied his fingernails for a moment, then cocked a brow at her "—I should confess something."

Her face turned to polished marble, a vein ticking in her tense neck. For a moment she vacillated, her eyes turning to pinpoints as if trying to read his mind. Finally she spoke, "What, Mr. Taylor?"

"One of your employees threatened me." He imagined it could get a little awkward meeting Viking in the hallways.

"Yes, well, I'm sorry you had to deal with the inconvenience. He wasn't happy I hired from outside." She let out a long-suffering sigh. "Unfortunately, I didn't feel he was chief of security material. You understand?"

"Quite." He scrutinized her face, wondering why she'd hire a bloke like that to begin with.

"You needn't worry he'll bother you again. He's been terminated."

"No need to fire him on my account."

"We don't want firebrands working here." She smiled as if a safety pin had just been inserted into the quick of a fingernail. "I'm sure we won't have that trouble with you. Now, you need to know you'll be on a probationary period for six months."

"Understood."

"You'll have to sign a security agreement, be fingerprinted and submit to a DNA test—" she paused "—as a precaution."

Why so many hoops for a private sector company? It wasn't unheard of for defense contractors to be anal about security, but Pincer wasn't in defense. At the salary Pincer was paying him, he wouldn't ask questions. He found himself nodding and saying, "That's quite all right with me."

"We're done here, then." She turned and punched an

intercom line on the phone, her bracelet clicking. "Belinda, please come up. Mr. Taylor is ready for personnel." She glanced at him. "After you are processed, you'll be shown to your new office."

Just like that, he was in. Why didn't he feel elated? Probably because Miranda N'Buta hadn't bothered to inquire after Viking's current physical condition. For all she knew, her employee could be in an intensive care unit.

He was good at reading people, but he hadn't been able to get a sense of her character. She appeared to be made of cold professional granite, on the inside as well as on the outside. Later he'd get to know her, he promised himself.

On his way out of the office, he turned and said, "You can find your employee in the Flats." He gave her an address.

"I know." There was no warmth in her voice and her fingers tightened into white-knuckled fists.

He felt the camera's lens watching him. For a second, the back of his neck tingled as if he'd just backed into a spider's web. Momentary doubt stabbed him, then he let it go and walked out of the office.

Miranda watched Nolan Taylor leave her office, his head almost touching the top of the doorjamb. She kept the muscles in her face like weights, cold, unresponsive clay, hiding any emotion. She had worked for years to school her expressions and prided herself on how well she had progressed.

She touched a button and connected instantly to the webcam site. The silhouette of the witch's dark shadowy figure filled the screen. "Did you observe all that?" she asked.

The witch raised the cigarette out of view, then Miranda heard her take a long drag. She blew out the smoke in a snake-like stream, then she said, "Of course I did, you fool."

Miranda kept her face marble solid, but inside she wanted

to scream at the witch who had ruled her life for years, who had spoken to her as if she were beneath contempt. One day, she promised herself. "I think the situation with Giger has been defused."

"It surprised me that Giger took matters into his own hands." The witch's fingers moved, the spider ring branching out over the whole monitor. "I wonder how he found out about not getting the position so soon."

Miranda schooled her features. "I have no idea."

The witch said nothing, her silence worse than any words she could have used. It pressed on Miranda until she felt it filling up her lungs. Finally Miranda said, "I personally don't like Mr. Taylor. There's something about him that I don't trust."

"I didn't ask for your opinion."

Miranda came back with a deadpan, "I'm sorry."

"I happen to like Mr. Taylor." An abrasive wheezing breath came from another cloud of smoke. "We'll keep him. If anything, he'll amuse me."

Miranda was certain having Nolan Taylor inside the company was a bad idea, but she knew better than to express her opinion again. "Very well. And you're going to handle Giger?"

"I'll deal with his punishment. I've always had a soft spot for him." A pale, bony, long-fingered hand moved toward the keyboard.

Long black nails and the gold spider ring expanded and swelled as the hand came toward the screen. The spider seemed to wink at Miranda as the screen went blank.

Plus Suisse Worldwide Depository, Downtown Cape Town

Finally the steel gate whooshed up.

Lucy let out the breath she'd been holding and spoke to the bone mic. "Had me going for a sec, Dragon."

"A blip. Won't happen again." Cao spoke over the frenzied tapping of his fingers on a keyboard.

"Counting on it." Lucy checked her watch.

Two minutes and forty-five seconds to get to the next reader.

She drove past the gate and descended the steep drive. Sunlight no longer penetrated the area and only artificial lights illuminated her way. The smell of stale car exhaust and moldy air seeped through the Corolla's air-conditioning vents. Shadows grew thicker as a suffocating, closed-in sensation wrapped around her.

She breathed through it and zoomed into the customer-only parking deck on the first floor. No cars occupied the other nine parking spots. Tuesday morning wasn't a busy banking day.

"Entering second cave."

"On it."

After grabbing her backpack, she hopped out of the car. The wind met her and whipped the lapels of her jacket up toward her chin. She didn't bother to fix them, just kept walking. Four security cameras followed her progress. She headed directly into the eye of one of them, offering a straight-on view of her male disguise.

She paused before the main security door. Minicameras above her head buzzed as they swept her. She pretended to slide in the gold hotel key card palmed in her hand and waited, her pulse ticking off the seconds.

A buzzer clicked.

Second obstacle down.

"Out of ears in two. On the flip side." Lucy stepped inside, hearing the expected dead quiet of her mic. Like Cao's device, it couldn't receive inside this tower of metal.

Thunk. The heavy door closed behind her.

She walked through tall metal detectors without a glitch, then took in the small lobby, all granite and gray marble.

Green palms softened the hard edges. A black and gold carpet sliced across the lobby. Universal transportation signs and Braille directed her to follow the carpeted path. The rebel in her refused to be led by a banking institution's orders, so she walked along the outside edge of the carpet.

A guard looked up from the desk. He acknowledged her with a nod but didn't speak. Anonymity at its best.

Lucy returned the smile and kept moving, stepping into a hallway. It angled directly down, the walls twenty feet of solid steel. No windows, just sleek steel sides and recessed fluorescent lights. No way out.

She checked her watch. Two minutes to the last electronic reader.

A computer animated voice began a litany, opening with Afrikaans, "Welcome to Swiss Worldwide Depository account number 1456HRT. Our automated system is currently locating your box for your convenience. We hope your stay is pleasant. Please proceed to the main elevators."

Pleasant. The word echoed in her mind. Just get out alive, how about that? Butterflies flitted in her gut as she walked along the inclined hallway. Signs led her to the main elevator. The sterile smell of polished metal and freshly cleaned carpets wafted through her senses. Security cameras hummed as they watched her progress. Time throbbed against her chest, the beat of her heart counting seconds, milliseconds, nanoseconds.

Her backpack thumped against her side, the weight of her .45 inside it comforting her. She had strapped the Commander to her forearm, the jacket's long sleeve covering it. Four mini grenades, that she had made in the safe house lab, were taped to her back, hidden by her jacket. A mini oxygen tank also weighed down the bag. Her fingers tightened protectively around the backpack's strap. Salvation in a bag.

She reached the elevator. Open doors met her. She stepped inside. No buttons to push, only a speaker and an overhead recessed light.

Come on, come on. The doors seemed to take forever to shut. Two minutes before Cao opened the last door.

An electronic voice again, "Please hold the railing until the elevator comes to a complete stop. Thank you."

She barely felt the elevator's movement. Only the weightless feeling in her legs and stomach made her aware of it. It stopped and the doors opened.

"Vault Two. Proceed ahead to the viewing area."

Outside the Plus Suisse Worldwide Depository

Betsy listened to Cao's fingers pounding the keys. A fine sheen of sweat glistened on his brow from the stress he was under, and his right cheek twitched slightly from his clenched teeth. He usually annoyed her, watching her with those brown prying eyes all the time, but right now she admired him. Miracles never ceased.

"Damn," Tommy said.

She glanced through the rearview mirrors at a Porsche heading straight for customer parking. "A determined customer?"

"Yeah, he'll take out the device," Tommy said.

"I'm on it." Betsy hopped out of the van's side door and crossed the street in seconds. She felt the Sokolovsky riding in her shoulder holster as she pulled an ID from her pocket and held up her arms in a Stop gesture.

She reached the Porsche twenty feet from the entrance. She waved him to a halt. The driver was a man with dark skin, graying cropped hair and chipmunk cheeks. A cell phone headset rested on his right ear.

She held up the false FBI ID. "Sorry, but this block is closed and so is the bank."

"Closed?" He spoke to her in English and glowered at her.

"A security drill. Can't be too careful nowadays."

"When I opened my account I was told the bank never closes. It's automated. That's why I bank here."

"Sorry. Take it up with the board." She shrugged.

He eyed her black jogging suit, then her gun. He seemed to want to argue, but thought better of it. "Okay, I'll come back later."

She saw the driver watching her pistol as he picked up his cell phone and dialed a number.

"Try to give some folks the benefit of the doubt and see what happens," she muttered, lunging for the driver's door.

She was inside, smashing her fist into his face, before he knew what had happened. He slumped over the wheel.

She grabbed the headset and listened to a woman's voice saying, "One-one-two emergency cell phone dispatch. May I help you?"

"Sorry, wrong number."

"Wait, I was just speaking to a gentleman."

Betsy hit the End button.

"We may be screwed," she said into the mic. "Big-time."

Inside Plus Suisse Worldwide Depository

Lucy stepped off the elevator and traversed a hallway as long as the first, but level this time. She reached another security door and the lock clicked just as she went through the motion with the card in her hand. Thank goodness for Cao.

An airlock hissed as the door closed behind her.

The empty air filled her throat and lungs and hung there as if she'd breathed in gelatin. She glanced around her. Shiny metal walls covered the vault's sterile viewing room. A few seascape paintings and a table in the middle of the room added to the sleek modern decor. In the center of one wall was a cavity about five feet by five feet. Before the opening a weight-sensitive pad lay on the floor. In the pad's center were two printed black footprints. The whole building was a technological, computer-animated marvel.

She stepped onto the black grids, carefully, keeping her feet within the footprint parameters. She felt as if she were standing in place for an X ray.

"Please wait until the viewing door opens before stepping off the pad." Another direction from the computer.

She stood there in dead silence, waiting, her heart pounding, her fingers tight around the backpack handle.

After what seemed like a week, there was a slight thump, then the small portal door whooshed up. The safe deposit box sat in the middle of the alcove where two robotic arms had placed it. She couldn't see the mechanical appendages, but she knew they were hidden by an upper panel in the recess.

She stepped off the pad and walked to the safe deposit box. She dropped her backpack in the alcove. To the security camera in an upper corner of the room, it looked as if she'd nonchalantly set it down anywhere, but she had set it in a spot that blocked the camera's eye. The square box, about a foot wide, had been placed with the lock and the LCD password screen toward her for easy access. A twelve-digit keypad, designed like that of a phone, sat below the screen. A tiny cursor on the screen blinked at her, waiting for the password.

Lucy pulled the pillbox out of her pocket and reached inside for the pea-size piece of C-4 and a one-inch piece of detonation cord. Her hands flew as she packed the C-4 and det cord inside the hole in the lock. She lit the cord with a piezoelectric device that looked like a pen. It worked by magnetic dipoles aligned near piezoelectric quartz crystals. Mechanical stress, such as pressing a button, caused a charge to flow between the electrically charged dipoles and the electrically neutral crystals, which ignited the wick. She needed something that burned clean and wouldn't set off the fire alarms, so she had built the device inside a pen casing.

Confident that she'd used just enough plastique to only open the box with the least amount of fallout, old DAME at work, she kept her position so the flame was blocked by the camera. She pretended to enter a number on the keypad. Three, two, one… She counted the seconds to detonation.

The lock opened with a firm splat, a sound much like a book dropping on the floor.

She manufactured a coughing fit that masked the noise, then reached for the lid.

What was in there? How was it connected to Arachne? And would it lead Delphi to the person behind the threats against Athena women? This was the first thing Lucy had touched inside the bank, and she felt the layers of high viscosity superglue Cao had applied to the tips of her fingers to mask her fingerprints. With a slight tremor in her hands, she opened the lid…

Pay dirt. A social security card for Miranda N'Buta. Five driver's licenses in five different countries, America included, all with different names on them. Passports with the same names. Documents that looked like real estate titles. Bearer bonds. A ledger. But no computer files. She didn't take the time to look closer, she just stuffed everything inside the backpack, closed the zipper, then turned and walked back to the pad.

"Thank you for banking with us."

The sentence kept rolling in forty-thousand languages as the door to the recess closed.

Now to get out of here. She checked her watch. Thirty-eight seconds before Cao opened the vault door.

She reached the door and went through the motions of inserting the pass key into the electronic reader. The door was taking forever to open.

Thirty-five seconds. Twenty-five. Twenty.

Had Cao forgotten her?

Finally, the lock buzzed.

Lucy slipped through and picked up her stride going down the hall, heart pumping, tension tightening every muscle in her body. Each weighted second kept time with her heartbeat.

Almost home free. One more door and she was out of there.

She felt her body relax a tiny bit as she hurried up the long hallway to the elevator.

Abruptly she heard:

"Security breach. Security breach," a computerized voice roared in between the sonic alarm blasts.

Click.

She glanced up just as the hidden vents opened in the ceiling. An invisible gas spewed into the hallway, the hiss of it sounding deadly. The alarm shouted in Lucy's ears as she felt the gas pouring from the vents. She could feel the useable oxygen being sucked out through a tiny air exchange vent near the floor. The gas had no color, no odor.

The semiconductor carbon monoxide monitor Cao had made for her in the lab came to life on her wrist. A high-pitched alarm whined in her ears. The tiny meter, no bigger than a pack of matches, was attached to her belt. Cao had explained that thin wires of tin dioxide, a semiconductor, were connected to an insulating ceramic base, which provided an integrated circuit. When CO was present in the air, it reduced the resistance in the semiconductor and allowed a current to trigger a watch alarm.

She held her breath, running for the elevator, and pulled the mask for the portable oxygen tank from her backpack. She placed the mask over her face and switched on the tank. It would buy her five minutes.

She saw a steel door, a foot thick, coming down to seal off the elevator. It was the only way out.

She dove and rolled. The steel door crashed down as she yanked the backpack inside.

She lay on the elevator floor, feeling the vents spewing CO. It hit her face and eyes, and she groped at the mask that covered her mouth and nose. *Control your breathing or you'll run out of air.*

She forced her diaphragm to slow, remembering her basic training in the army where she'd had to hold her breath underwater for a full three minutes. Her drill sergeant had tormented her and the other ten women in the platoon the whole time she was at boot camp. Just to piss him off, she'd held her breath longer than anyone. She'd broken a record. He'd called her a troublemaker and made her walk back to camp from the lake. It was the finest thirty minutes of boot camp.

She went into that tranquil place, where only bright white light existed, where time didn't count, where she controlled everything. Her breathing slowed as she glanced upward at the light in the elevator's ceiling. It was a long rectangle, two feet by six feet. A milk glass cover fit snugly over two fluorescent bulbs. The schematic had shown an elevator safety hatch behind the light. God, she hoped the schematic was correct.

She tried to get the light cover off, but it was bolted down. She stood, took out the oxygen tank and clipped it onto her belt, then swung her backpack as hard as she could at the light cover.

The glass cover cracked but didn't give way.

She glanced down, closed her eyes, and hit once more.

A loud pop. Glass crashed down on her, hitting her neck, head and shoulders.

She shook it off and saw the trapdoor between the broken jagged bulbs. She leaped up, grabbed the latch and pulled.

The tiny door swung open.

She tossed her backpack through the opening, then chin-upped her way through the tiny portal. The oxygen mask fogged up from the exertion.

The elevator shaft was not airtight like the vault and the CO alarm had stopped buzzing. In one quick yank, she pulled off the oxygen mask and tank and dropped them on top of the elevator. She craned her neck and peered up the shaft. The top floor looked miles away. She was still five vault stories away from ground level. All she had to do was make it to the first floor.

She put the backpack on, leaped over to the shaft's service ladder and began climbing.

Almost to the first floor doors.

Abruptly the doors opened and she stared into the faces of two guards, their Heckler & Koch MP5 machine guns four feet away, pointed straight at her.

Front of the Plus Suisse Worldwide Depository

Betsy heard the sirens in the distance. They sounded like they were headed directly toward the bank. "Trouble's on the way," she spoke into the mic. "Look alive, boys."

She pulled the driver out of the Porsche and deposited his limp body behind a hedge of palm trees. She hopped into the car, buckled her seat belt and sped toward the bank's underground parking deck. In seconds she was in the deck.

"Cao, can you get me through the door with the alarm activated?"

"Don't toy with my intelligence."

"Don't take all day."

"Do I ever?"

Smart-ass, she thought, as she heard his fingers flying over the keyboard. She left the car running, leaped out, drawing her Sokolovsky from the shoulder holster. The door clicked before she reached it.

"About time," Betsy said.

"Ingrate. And Betsy?"

"What now?"

"Don't make me have to come in there and rescue you and Lucy," Cao said, all the humor gone from his voice.

"I second that," Tommy said.

"You boys don't know what Southern women can do? Watch and learn." She held the Sokolovsky, cupped in her palms, close in, as she swept the lobby for the security guard.

Running footsteps to her left.

She darted right, crouched behind a palm, and watched two security guards run past her, carrying shotguns. Betsy followed them down the hall, knowing they'd lead her to Lucy.

Chapter 5

Plus Suisse Worldwide Depository, Elevator shaft

"Move and we shoot," a guard spoke to Lucy in Afrikaans.

She gripped the ladder rung, feeling the smooth cold metal beneath her fingers. Her gaze stayed locked on their eyes. The men were ready to mow her down, their fingers bent on the triggers.

She spoke back to him in the same language. "What do you propose? That I stay here forever."

"You have two choices. We shoot you, or you hand over your backpack, then we help you out."

Lucy wasn't parting with the backpack. Instinct told her it was the only thing keeping her alive at the moment.

She ground out, "Okay. I'm taking off the backpack."

She held on to the ladder with one hand and with the other

hand reached as if to take off the backpack. That's when she flicked her wrist and the Commander dropped into her palm. She fired at the oxygen tank below her.

The almost-empty tank exploded, mixed with the CO coming up through the elevator's escape hatch and torched a flash of blue flame up the shaft.

The guards leaped back.

Lucy jumped off the ladder, dove for the opening, firing the Colt.

Fire licked at her back through the open doors, the heat singeing her neck. Bullets pinged around her as she hit the floor.

She aimed at the guards' kneecaps, rolled between the two men as they fell and was up on her feet. She kicked their guns down the burning elevator shaft and ran.

The men screamed behind her. She glanced over her shoulder and saw them grabbing at their bloody knees.

As she wheeled around, she skidded to a halt. Two more guards coming straight at her with HKs. They fired.

Lucy hit the floor. Bullets whizzed over her head and plunked into the walls and floor. She started to fire back, but Betsy appeared behind the guards. With a dropkick and two throat chops, the guards went down.

"Come on, let's get outta here."

Lucy was never so glad to see anyone in her life. "What took you so long?" She was up on her feet, running beside Betsy.

"Little problem. Cops are on their way."

They ran toward the lobby, their guns up and ready to fire. They reached the security door and it was already buzzing to be opened. Cao was on his game today.

When they ran out into the parking deck, police sirens screamed, dozens of them. Red lights flashed. They were surrounding the building.

"Cavalry's here," Lucy said.

"This way." Betsy ran for the Porsche.

"Nice ride." Lucy followed her.

"Ain't it, though."

"Call the wheel."

"Shotgun for me." Betsy hopped in on the passenger side.

Lucy already had a hand grenade palmed as she drove with one hand.

They made it to the end of the drive. Two more security guards greeted them. Lucy and Betsy ducked to avoid a barrage of bullets.

"I got this." Betsy took aim out the window and fired at the security guards' kneecaps. Two bullets apiece. Dead on. One thing about Betsy, she didn't like wasting good bullets. They went down in unison, groaning and holding their legs.

Lucy sped around them and out into the street.

"Damn," Lucy said, noticing two police cars in front of them. Her rearview mirror revealed two behind them. Trapped. Maybe.

"Seat belts." Lucy snapped her own.

"All right." Betsy's chunked into place.

Lucy lowered her head, her eyes narrowed on the police cars' front bumpers. They were closing in fast. She could see the reflection of the Porsche in the Fiat's chrome bumper, getting larger and larger.

Determined, Lucy held her course, foot to the floor. Forty-five…fifty…sixty.

The cops weren't moving.

She wasn't veering.

They were feet from each other….

The cops swerved.

"Got the rear." Betsy turned, hung the Sokolovsky out the window, sighted and fired.

Lucy watched the action in the rearview mirror. The police

cars' front tires seemed to shrivel before her eyes. The cars swerved in different directions. One veered and hit the row of palms on the bank's lawn, the other somersaulted and landed upside down on the opposite sidewalk.

Lucy sped around the corner onto Bouquet Street, glancing in her rearview mirror for cops....

None.

She hung a quick left, then a right onto Roeland Street, whipping the Porsche into the flow of traffic. Sirens screamed through the city as cops sped toward the bank, but they were well away from the action.

Lucy let herself relax. Restaurants, dry cleaners, jewelry shops and *shebeens* twined the street's edge. Prostitutes crowded the bar doorways, flirting with patrons. People walked along the sidewalk, arms laden with bags.

"This handles like a dream. I'm buying one of these when I get home," Lucy said, looking at the windshield cracked and littered with bullet holes.

"Me, too," Betsy said.

"Maybe we should get one with bulletproof glass."

"Might be a good idea."

Lucy and Betsy looked at each other and grinned.

Pincer Industries, Cape Town

Nolan stood with Miranda N'Buta beside him. She had called all the security personnel into her office to introduce Nolan. Six security officers stood before him—Giger wasn't one of them.

He noticed all the guards were dressed in green short-sleeved uniforms and standard-issue Glock .45's hung from leather hip holsters.

Miranda walked past the first man and stopped. He was a

thin African with a drawn face and perceptive eyes. "This is Salim Cummay. He works the graveyard shift."

Salim gave a stiff salute and made quick eye contact with Nolan. "Hello, sir." He spoke in proper English.

Nolan sensed Salim Cummay's military background right away. He also noticed that Salim kept his gaze away from Miranda and he gripped his fingers into a fist at her closeness. He could almost smell the fear on him. Why was Salim so afraid of the CEO of Pincer? He'd question him later. He also had questions about why she would need to keep a thug like Giger around.

Miranda introduced the rest of the men. They too kept their gazes on the floor. When the introductions were over, she waved them out of her office. "That will be all."

Nolan and the guards filed out and into the hallway. Miranda's secretary, Belinda, sat at a cubicle directly opposite Miranda's office. She glanced up from her keyboarding. She looked about nineteen, an energetic brunette with come-hither eyes. She had flirted with him when she'd taken him down to personnel. Now she ran her tongue over her red lips and smiled at him.

He returned the smile. Later, he'd ask her to tea and ply her for office gossip, the best source for insider information. He turned his attention back to the guards and followed them to the elevator.

He grabbed Cummay's arm before he stepped on. "A word, Mr. Cummay."

The other men gave Cummay a collective warning look, then the doors closed.

Cummay's nervousness increased. He stuck his hands in his pockets and jingled the change there. "Yes, sir."

"First of all, I must tell you I require honesty above everything."

"I will always be honest with you, sir."

"Quite. Then you won't mind answering my questions.

Tell me what you know about Giger Anfinson." Nolan had learned Viking's name from his PDA.

At Anfinson's name, Cummay stopped jangling the change and nodded. "He works exclusively for Ms. N'Buta," he said, his voice strained. "I don't know what his position entails."

"What do you mean?"

"He's rarely in his office." Cummay paused, looked torn, then said, "May I speak bluntly, sir?"

"Of course."

"He's the brunt of the gossip at Pincer. He has no title, just an office. We call him," Cummay lowered his voice, *"vivu ng'ombe dume."*

Nolan didn't recognize the language and said, "Pardon?"

"Sorry, sir. I speak Swazi. It means lazy bull."

Cummay appeared so uncertain of the consequences of his disclosure that Nolan gave him a slight smile to put him at ease. "Where is his office?"

"In the basement, sir. Near the mailroom."

"Basement," Nolan repeated.

Cummay looked uncomfortable and said, "Is that all, sir?"

"One more question, Cummay. Why are you so afraid of Ms. N'Buta?"

"She holds my job in her hands."

"It seems like something more than that." Nolan eyed him and stepped closer, looking down on him. He'd learned long ago how to intimidate using his height.

"It's not, sir." Cummay backed away from him and kept hitting the elevator button. "I really have to go home now and sleep. Ms. N'Buta called me in to meet you, so I came. I work nights." Cummay didn't wait for the elevator and darted to the stairwell door and slipped through.

Nolan scratched his chin, watching the door close. Something wasn't right about Pincer. Hired thugs. Employees deathly afraid of the CEO. What kind of company was this?

He headed for the basement.

Fish Hoek Village, False Bay, South Africa

Lucy sat at a computer desk in the basement of the safe house, working on the state-of-the-art computer equipment provided for her. The broadband they received was encrypted and scrambled and completely secure.

Cao's fingers tapped on his own laptop. He sat at a lab bench behind her. Partitioned off by sections, the basement looked like an industrial lab. One area contained Bunsen burners, test tubes and a safety hood for dealing with toxic chemicals or biological agents. Another station was for working with metal. Welding and soldering equipment lined shelves, along with sterile trays of electronic circuitry. Another area was designed for nanotechnology and held an electron microscope and cabinets filled with bottles and slides. A hermetically sealed vault that contained the explosives took up one whole corner. Cao had oohed and aahed when he'd seen it. It was a phenomenal place. She couldn't believe this safe house was only for Oracle agents. Other intel agencies must have a hand in its upkeep. She knew from her intelligence-gathering classes at Athena Academy that all American intel agencies have an I'll-scratch-your-back-if-you-scratch-mine relationship, and it wasn't uncommon to share safe houses.

She could hear Tommy and Betsy's footsteps overhead as they made dinner. Cao could hear them, too, and scowled up at the ceiling every now and then. The tension between Cao and Betsy was still sharp enough to pierce body armor. Lucy would have broached the subject, but she knew it would make him uncomfortable. Better to wait out his reserve and let him find his own courage.

She gazed back at the bright light of the scanner as it moved over a document she'd taken from the bank. It was one of the last items she'd scanned in the long list of bearer bonds, Swiss account passbooks, passports for countries all over the world—the U.S. included. The same woman's picture was on every passport; only the name changed. There were forged birth certificates, a U.S. social security card, driver's licenses and a thick bookkeeping ledger with columns of financial figures. Identities in a box.

Lucy turned to Cao. "You got anything?"

"Almost. Have a hit on one of the names. Miranda N'Buta. She's local. I'm downloading a newspaper article on her."

A tangle of excitement pulled at Lucy as she looked at the name Cass Overton, typed on a passport she laid on the scanner. "I wonder why she hasn't tried to conceal her identity. How long before you get it?"

"Wait, I got it." Cao's eyes lit with excitement.

"And what does it say about our lucky contestant?" Lucy wanted to peer over Cao's shoulder, but she had to wait for the passport to finish scanning.

"She's CEO of Pincer Industries, a local company in Cape Town. It's a conglomerate that deals with shipping and mining. They're the largest exporter of gold in Africa. Pincer also got in on the ground floor of the cell phone industry in South Africa. It says here they own two wireless networks."

"Hmm, if you're an international blackmailer that might be convenient."

"More than convenient." Cao went back to reading. "Miranda N'Buta started Pincer Industries twenty years ago. She came to South Africa from America. Says here she's civic-minded and volunteers at AIDS fund-raisers."

"There's a picture of her but it's not very good. This press release is over eight years old." Cao turned the computer around so Lucy could see the picture.

Lucy grimaced. It was a black-and-white outdoor picture. The woman wore an impeccably tailored suit and a matching designer hat, the broad brim slashing across half her face. Wide sunglasses covered her eyes. The only thing visible on her face was a Teflon smile for the camera as she cut the ribbon on Pincer's first cell phone tower.

"You're right. This is a lousy picture."

"I'll try to find a better one." Cao searched again.

"Did the article say where in America she was born?"

"Didn't mention it."

"Can you see if the social security number on the passports is real?"

"Give me a minute." Cao typed furiously, his face shifting through a myriad of expressions. After a few minutes, he said, "The number exists but it's attached to someone named Clarence Jones who lives in Wichita, Kansas."

"Interesting."

"I can't find another photo of her," Cao said.

"Miranda N'Buta is a ghost." Had they found Arachne? Lucy felt her heart race. "Can you e-mail that info to this computer's address?"

"Sure." Cao pushed a button and sent it to the safe house's e-mail account.

Lucy watched the file pop into the e-mail. She typed all the information Cao had found out about Miranda N'Buta and attached the scanned files and e-mail. She hit the Send button to Delphi@oracle.org.

Lucy hadn't told the team about Delphi or the Oracle Network. The team only knew they were working for a private agency that wished to remain anonymous.

Abruptly a pop-up flashed across the screen:

WARNING, E-MAIL HAS BEEN INTERCEPTED BY AN OUTSIDE SOURCE. DATA MINER DETECTED. WARNING... WARNING.

"Damn it! Cao, look at this." Lucy leaped up and let the computer master have the helm. "Can we retrieve it?"

"Sorry, the minute you pressed the button it was in cyber-space."

"Did it get to the intended address?"

"The original did, but a copy was forwarded. I might be able to track it, though." Cao's fingers flew over the keyboard. "Give me a minute."

Who had tapped into the secure connection? Delphi had received the information, but so had someone else. Who? If Arachne was on to them, then it could put the whole team in danger. Not to mention compromise her mission. She watched Cao, heart pounding, dread creeping into her.

Pincer Industries, Cape Town

Nolan breezed past the mailroom. Through the glass enclosure surrounding it, he could see several employees sorting mail. He nodded to them and kept walking. He avoided the security cameras and found the office. A cheap plastic placard on the door claimed it as Anfinson's space.

Nolan made sure the hallway was clear and then tried the door.

Locked.

He pulled out a lock pick set from his shirt pocket and in seconds had the door open. He slipped inside.

The walls were bare, save for a poster of a busty woman

surfing. A sofa and desk packed the tiny room. The smell of stale marijuana lingered in the air, along with the musty odor of the basement. He walked across to the small desk. The drawer was locked so he again used his picks.

Inside he found several boxes of bullets, condoms, a hit of cocaine, a switchblade and brass knuckles. Nice combination. Get them high, shag them, stab them, beat them, then shoot them. A mark didn't have a chance against this guy. An oily feeling at being in Giger's office oozed over Nolan. This guy was more than hired muscle. How much more, he wondered?

He moved to the computer and woke it from sleep mode. Windows sprang to life. It asked for a password.

Nolan flicked on the PDA. The computer picked up the wireless connection, and a computerized voice said, "Good day, Mr. Anfinson."

Nolan was in. He downloaded every file on the hard drive. Loud voices came from behind the door and drew close. He dove behind the desk. It was so small he wasn't sure it covered all of him.

The door opened and he heard Miranda N'Buta's voice:

"I'm asking you not to cause a scene. You need to leave. She'll be in touch with you."

"Just like that you fire me for taking what should have been mine."

Nolan recognized Viking's accent.

"You shouldn't have attacked him. I told you only to pick him up."

"I wasn't going to let him have my job. That's the thanks I get. All these years of service. All the shit I've cleaned up. You'll pay. Both of you."

"Don't do anything rash."

"You haven't seen rash." Giger's angry footsteps pounded down the hallway.

Nolan heard a cell phone click open, then Miranda's voice, "Yes, it's me. We've got a problem. A big one."

Miranda N'Buta closed the door and Nolan couldn't hear the rest of the conversation.

He let out his breath. That was close. And who was Miranda N'Buta calling about her problem? Was it the same "she" Giger and Miranda had mentioned? It sounded like there was another person over Miranda who called the shots. The intrigue inside Pincer just got better and better. Or worse and worse, depending on one's point of view.

He had hoped to find refuge at Pincer. A place to save some money, build a little retirement, send a few pounds home to his parents and lie low. All his well-ordered dreams were fading fast.

He should cut his losses and find a new situation, maybe in Canada. But he'd gone to a lot of trouble and expense to move here and he didn't have the blunt to decamp until he received a couple of paychecks. With his meager military salary, he hadn't been able to put money aside and help his parents with their rent. They barely got by, even with his assistance. His father had been ill for seven years with heart disease and his mother cleaned houses for a living. They had both scrimped and saved so their only son could attend the Royal Military Academy Sandhurst, and he would never forget what they had sacrificed for him.

Nolan could still hear his father bragging to Nolan's uncle, "My lad goes to Sandhurst. Right up there with the best of them. He'll make officer one day. You watch. My lad will make something of himself." Nolan's father came from a long line of bricklayers, and he'd always desired more for his son.

Both his parents had made certain Nolan never wanted for anything at school and that he fit in with the other, richer kids. He hated taking pocket money from his folks, so he had started playing cards and relieving the wealthy cadets of their allowance. The profit from his moneymaking ventures had lasted him two or three months at a stretch, and he'd even made enough to give some back to his parents.

All Nolan had ever wanted was to make his parents proud of him. He'd studied hard, graduated with honors and fit perfectly into the military. He enjoyed running to ground terrorists and seeing the world while doing it. Even now he found himself missing the discipline and rigor that was so much a part of it. And he had stayed in the corps as long as he could. But when the murder attempts began and he realized whole terrorist networks wanted revenge—on him—he'd been forced to leave everything. Selling out had broken his parents' hearts, but they knew he had no choice.

At the thought of never seeing his parents again, he felt a familiar empty ache deep in his chest. He'd said goodbye to them for the last time. The tears he'd seen in his father's eyes still haunted him. But he could never return to London, not unless he wanted to put them in danger. And he'd never do that.

No, he'd have to stay at Pincer for a while and handle their security. He wasn't one to duck and run at the first sign of trouble, anyway. In fact, he liked overcoming obstacles. They made life interesting. Working for Pincer would be a breeze compared to staying in England and dodging bullets. He'd just sniff around while doing his job. It never hurt to be prepared for the next bolt in the crank waiting to shake loose. And he was certain there were a few bolts at Pincer that definitely needed tightening.

Fish Hoek Village, False Bay, South Africa

Cao's face fell and he slumped over the keyboard. "I can't trace it any farther. The trail stops in Hong Kong. Sorry."

"You did your best." Lucy touched his shoulder. "I'll relay this information to our employer."

"I'm going to rest," Cao said.

"You're not going to eat dinner with us?" Lucy asked, listening to Betsy and Tommy's footsteps in the kitchen above them as they made sandwiches.

"Not hungry."

Lucy watched him walk up the steps, his feet seeming to drag. Cao didn't take defeat well. No one on the team did. She had suddenly lost her own appetite.

An instant message popped up and caught her attention:

LUCY,
RECEIVED YOUR MESSAGE ABOUT DATA MINER AND WILL FOLLOW UP LEAD IN HONG KONG. AS A PRECAUTION, DO NOT E-MAIL ANY INFORMATION TO DELPHI@ORACLE.ORG UNTIL THE SITE HAS BEEN SECURED. LAY LOW AND SEE WHAT YOU CAN FIND OUT ABOUT PINCER AND MIRANDA N'BUTA. I'LL LET YOU KNOW WHEN YOU CAN SEND INFORMATION AGAIN.
DELPHI

How had Delphi known Cao had traced the data miner? Lucy hadn't e-mailed that information yet. Delphi must have been monitoring the system.

Uncertainty ate at her. What would Miranda do next? Lucy powered down the computer and decided on her own next move.

Long Street, Cape Town

Giger Anfinson walked through the doors of the Velvet Arms, one of the nicer Long Street clubs in the City Bowl District. It was too techno for Giger. He liked jazz, and he rarely came here. If he wanted to pick up a piece of ass, he combed the bars in the Flats. True, the hookers there were full of VD and AIDS, but he could use them the way he wanted.

He thought of the last whore he'd paid. He'd left her with a face and body so swollen she was unrecognizable as female. He knew exactly when those feelings to hurt something came on him. It was like being caught in a strong undertow that he couldn't swim out of, and in order to breathe and survive he needed the release. He had felt it coming after Miranda told him he was fired. The bitch! Did she think kicking him out of the company would work? After all the dirt he had on her and the big boss, all the hits he'd made for them. Miranda had no idea how much pain he could cause her.

He would have showed them, too, if the boss lady hadn't agreed to pay him hush money. He planned to take the cash and retire to Norway.

She had said she was bringing the money herself. He'd never met her in person, only taken orders through text messages or the webcam. He didn't even know her name. When he had first started taking direct orders from her and doing jobs for her outside of company business, he'd been surprised to learn that Miranda wasn't the head honcho. She was just a figurehead, a queen with no kingdom, a puppet. And he had enjoyed reminding Miranda of that in his own little way. He was meeting the real string-puller tonight. He actually looked forward to the encounter.

Through a haze of smoke he scoped out the place. Techno music boomed and thumped inside Giger's throbbing head. The crowd on the dance floor swayed, bobbed and gyrated to the beat. Lighted sculptures of African art glowed along the walls. Four guys shot pool in the back.

He scanned the people at the bar. A hooker with dyed white hair propositioned her next john. An overweight guy on the verge of a stroke sucked bourbon and smoked a cigar. Two African gays shared a mug of beer.

A set of dark booths lined the back of the room. He headed that way, shouldering a path through the crowd. He picked a booth where he could watch the door and the customers who came through it. He lit a joint and waited.

A thin waitress in a short skirt and a strapless top paused near the table. She looked bored as she yelled over the music, "What'll you have?"

"Bottle of beer. Not that African piss. German. The darkest you got."

"I'll see what we have." She turned and sauntered to a table near the dance floor to take a couple's order.

Giger glanced at the door in time to see a beautiful woman step inside. She looked about twenty, short blond hair framed her petite, tanned face. Black leather pants and matching vest covered her lithe body. A white shirt opened down the front of her chest to her navel, showing the rise of tempting high-tipped breasts. She'd captured the attention of every guy in the bar.

"Hello," Giger whispered, his eyes zeroing in on her. He felt his body tighten. He'd have her after his business was over.

Her vivid green eyes scanned the room as if looking for someone. A guy came up to her and spoke. She shoved him aside with a swipe of her hand. The guy leaped back from her as if she'd bitten him, a strange look on his face.

She spotted Giger and strode toward him, her body moving with the liquid grace of a cat. She paused at his table and leaned across it so he could get a good look at her breasts. "You must be Giger." She spoke in a deep raspy voice that purred softly.

"And this must be my lucky night." There was something about her that didn't fit the person he'd communicated with via the webcam. But, of course, he'd never seen her face. He looked for the spider ring, but she wasn't wearing it.

"What if I said it was?"

"Then I wish we'd met a long time ago." He eyed the bronze nipples of her breasts and he was past caring if she was the boss lady or not.

"So now we meet." Her lips stretched in a smile.

"You have the money?" He had looked for a briefcase and hadn't seen one.

"I don't ever carry a million dollars on me. It's not safe. It's in my limo." She ran a finger along the base of his chin.

Her careful stroking felt like velvet brushing his skin. She knew just how to touch a man to turn him on. "Let's get it."

He left a bill on the table for his beer and slid out of the booth. He followed her, watching the lights play along the shiny leather of her pants, enhanced by the sexy sway of her hips. He licked his lips, almost tasting her. He'd get more than just his money tonight.

Chapter 6

Pincer Industries, Cape Town

Lucy sat in a Jeep, listening to a BBC report on a new terrorist attack in Saudi Arabia, watching the Pincer building, a megalith of glass and steel. It occupied half a city block on Adderley Street. She counted fifteen floors. Pretty impressive for a blackmail queen.

She'd parked at an angle to the building, so that the employee parking lot was directly across from her and she could watch both entries, the one in front and the rear shipping entrance. Earlier she'd gone into the lobby and taken pictures of the laser grid security system with her mini cell phone camera. After the guard had shooed her out, she'd come back to the Jeep and placed a call to Miranda N'Buta's office under the guise of a chairwoman raising money for a local orphanage. Luckily, the secretary had been lax at screening calls and eagerly put Lucy directly through to Miranda N'Buta. When Miranda answered, Lucy hung up. She only wanted to confirm Miranda was in her office.

Lucy had also scoped out the parking lot for the CEO's spot and found a big sign: RESERVED FOR MIRANDA N'BUTA. A shiny black Mercedes took up the space. That had been two hours ago. Lucy hated stakeouts. They were boring, and she really didn't have the patience. She drummed her fingers on the telephoto lens of the digital 35 mm camera she'd borrowed from the safe house basement. She hoped Miranda N'Buta wasn't one of those conscientious workaholic CEO's that didn't leave the office until eight o'clock. Then again, a CEO of a blackmail empire might do her best work late at night.

She wondered how Betsy and Tommy were doing on their assignment. They had gone to search Miranda's home, while Lucy came to Pincer to get a traceable photo of her and any other suspicious-looking employees. Also, she wanted to scope out the building to see what hurdles awaited her when she came back later to search Miranda's office. Lucy had left Cao scowling at his laptop screen, typing heatedly. He couldn't believe he'd lost the signal in Hong Kong, and the Internet puzzle was driving him crazy.

Lucy watched as a group of men and women exited through the front doors. None of them approached the CEO's parking spot nearest the door.

The team's cell phone rang. Lucy looked at the caller ID, switched off the radio and said, "Hey, Viper."

"The house is clean," Tommy said.

"Nothing about her family or past?"

"Nada. But her shoe closet puts Imelda Marcos to shame. She's also got two Dobermans guarding the place and a pretty

nice security system. Someone gave her good advice."
Tommy always admired and critiqued any security system he
had to overcome.

Lucy heard Betsy in the background, "Tell her I hate attack
dogs and that she owes me a new pair of jeans."

Lucy smiled and said, "I heard that. Was Betsy bitten?"

"Her pant leg was."

Betsy said, "I told you they were not totally out yet. But
no, you wouldn't wait. Now I'm down a pair of jeans."

"So sue me," Tommy said.

Lucy wondered who was having a conversation with whom
and she broke in, "How'd you deal with the dogs?"

"Gave 'em a couple of Betsy's sleeping pills."

Betsy piped up in the background, "I wanted to give 'em
the whole damn bottle."

"Will they wake up before she gets home?" Lucy asked.

"They should wake up in about half an hour, feeling no
pain. She won't know anyone's been here."

"Good. Get out of there."

"Ten four. How're you making out?"

"No action on this end, yet."

"Betsy wants to know if dinner's on you tonight."

Lucy thought Betsy would play the dog card somehow.
"Sure, I'll pick it up on my way back. That is, if my target
ever leaves and I get a clear shot at her."

Suddenly a well-dressed woman emerged from the front
doors. A tall hunk of a man followed her. He looked about thirty
with short, sandy blond hair and linebacker shoulders. He was
so tall he towered over the woman. The wind lashed at his black
suit. He jammed his hands in his pockets to keep his jacket from
flapping in the breeze with an annoyed look on his face that
said he didn't appreciate having his suit so abused.

The woman resembled the pictures on the IDs they'd recovered from the bank. She wore a full-length trench coat with a mink collar. She pulled up the lapels to protect her face against the dust that seemed to blow across every street in Cape Town. Lucy heard it blasting the Jeep's windshield as she waited for them to enter the employee parking lot. They headed toward the black Mercedes. Gotcha!

Lucy rolled down the window, picked up the camera. The auto focus hummed as she depressed the shutter. She followed them to the car. The tall guy opened the door. A gentleman. Was he Arachne's lover? He looked a lot younger than the woman.

He closed her door. Then as if sensing the camera on him, he turned his gaze her way.

The telephoto lens magnified his face, and she looked into a pair of glacier-blue eyes.

She'd been made.

A truck and two buses swept past the street in a fog of carbon monoxide and diesel exhaust. She lost sight of him. Lucy tossed the camera on the passenger seat and started the engine.

When the last bus zoomed by her, she glanced across to the parking lot again. Where was he? Miranda N'Buta was standing on the sidewalk, her gaze in Lucy's direction.

Lucy looked in her rearview mirror and saw the guy. He was almost to her bumper.

Oh, God!

Nolan, a foot from the Jeep's door, lunged for the handle. He caught a fleeting glimpse of the driver's profile inside. Large sunglasses covering half a face. Red hair stuffed beneath a baseball cap. The Jeep sped out and came toward him. He leaped aside, the back tire missing his legs by inches.

"Bloody hell." He watched as the Jeep swerved to avoid sideswiping a sedan.

The car screeched to a stop and hit the horn.

The Jeep darted around it and down the street, sped around a corner and disappeared from sight.

Nolan started to run for his rental car, but then stopped. He knew the driver of the Jeep was long gone. When he walked back across the street, Miranda N'Buta was waiting for him, the keys in her hand jingling as she held them.

"What was that all about?" She made a face at him as if it had been his fault.

"Do you have paparazzi following you for some reason?"

"Certainly not," she said, defensive.

What was she hiding? What was Pincer hiding? He had made a point of walking out with Miranda N'Buta so he could gain some points and maybe her confidence. Instead she'd remained her cold and aloof self. Getting to know his new boss wasn't going to be easy, he realized, but he wasn't giving up.

He hadn't found out anything from Belinda, either. They'd spent their break at Captain James' Beanery, a coffee shop half a block away. Nolan had been disappointed. Belinda was a temp who'd only been Miranda's secretary for a week. She said Miranda never kept a permanent secretary. Belinda knew nothing about the company, other than that Giger Anfinson gave her the creeps when he looked at her and she'd stayed away from him. Nolan had left Belinda with a promise to call and arrange a date.

"Would you like me to see you safely home?" he asked Miranda.

"Not necessary, Mr. Taylor." She turned, her coat lapels flapping against her chest, her dark hair blowing around her oval face. She looked drawn, older in the fading outdoor sunlight. Under the office lights she had looked to be in her late forties, but now in the natural light, he could see the lines at the corners of her eyes. She could be in her fifties.

"Good night." After a sidelong glance, she got in her car.

Nolan watched her pull out. He glanced back down the street to where the Jeep had disappeared. He hadn't gotten a good look at the person driving the Jeep, but if pressed he could have sworn it was a woman behind the sunglasses and baseball cap. He sensed she would be back. He definitely wanted to question her. Maybe she and the information he'd downloaded from Anfinson's computer would lead him to the truth behind the shady depths of Pincer Industries.

Fish Hoek Village, False Bay, South Africa

"So, you had any hits yet?" Betsy looked across the table at Cao as she spooned a bite of *waterblommetjie bredie*.

Lucy ate some, too, the distinctive flavor of the lily stems in the stew lingering in her mouth. It was a particular kind of water lily that only grew in the Cape. She watched Cao swallow a mouthful of papaya stuffed with rice and glanced at the laptop opened next to his plate. "I'm still running the search on Interpol."

Cao hadn't found any wants or warrants on Miranda N'Buta. In fact, he hadn't been able to trace Miranda N'Buta past her South African driver's license. Lucy hoped Cao would find something before she e-mailed the photos of Miranda N'Buta and the tall guy to Delphi at her newly secured address.

Lucy asked, "Nothing on the man, yet?" She couldn't forget that tall guy who'd almost jumped into the Jeep. It was a close call. Too close.

"No." Cao shook his head.

Lucy hid her disappointment and forked *breyani* into her mouth. The coriander that laced the spicy rice and lentil dish blended well with the water lily stew. True to her word, she had brought supper home with her. She'd stopped by Madame

Bukhara's, a small restaurant in the Garden District that served take-out Cape Malay fare. It had been her and her mother's favorite restaurant in Cape Town.

Betsy looked over at Lucy. "Did you say you thought he was her bodyguard?"

"Looked that way. I'd like to know who he is."

Betsy scrutinized Lucy for a moment. "You seem mighty interested in this guy."

"He almost gave her a lap dance," Tommy interrupted, as he perused the colorful array of dishes that filled the table. He picked up a *samoosa*. He eyed the meat pastry and gave it the sniff test before sinking his teeth into the fried doughy outside.

Betsy pointed a finger at Lucy. "The question is, did she enjoy it?"

Lucy pulled a face. "I'm not interested in the guy other than knowing if he's going to get in our way."

Betsy said, "From the photo I saw, he could get in my way anytime."

Cao stared hard at Betsy. "Figures."

"What's that supposed to mean?" Betsy punctuated her words with her pointer finger.

"Nothing." Cao shot Betsy a withering stare.

Betsy's lips hardened and she chewed on the inside of her cheek. "I don't know what's gotten your pants in a twist lately, Cao, but I've had just about enough of your sulking." She stood up, arms akimbo. She wore blue jogging pants and a tight long-sleeved T-shirt.

Cao's eyes swept her body before he said, "That makes two of us."

"I'm going to walk off dinner." She looked directly into Cao's face as if she were really going to walk off his curt attacks.

"I am, too." Cao stood.

"Just make sure you walk the other way."

"Why would I want to walk in your direction?"

"Because, without your nose in a computer, you don't know where you are." Betsy turned in a huff and stomped out the front door.

"I've got to find my earplugs." Cao followed her.

Lucy could hear them arguing as Cao slammed the door.

Tommy said, "Whew. They're enough to give me indigestion." He stood up, downed the rest of his Pepsi and burped loudly.

"Me, too." Lucy pushed her plate away, no longer hungry. But it wasn't Cao and Betsy's arguing that had stolen her appetite. Her mind was still on the tall guy and the fact that they hadn't found anything to prove Miranda N'Buta was Arachne.

"We're not going to get any peace around here if those two don't get jiggy with it soon," Tommy said.

Lucy cocked an eyebrow at Tommy for his perceptiveness. "True that."

"Maybe we can lock them in a room." Tommy rubbed his stomach and suppressed a burp. "I like this South African food but it doesn't like me. Is it too much to hope this place has a stock of antacids?"

"Look in my bathroom. The cabinet in there looks like a pharmacy."

"I'll be back to help with KP duty."

Lucy watched Tommy walk down the hall to her bedroom. She wondered if he was dating anyone special. He never spoke about his love life or sexual orientation, and he adroitly avoided questions about it. Lucy had always wondered if he was gay.

Abruptly, Cao's computer dinged a warning.

Lucy pulled it toward her so she could see the screen. She almost flinched when she saw the deep-set penetrating sky-blue eyes. She studied the strong jawline, sharp cheekbones.

Gold highlights striped his short brown hair. His lips were pressed tight in a sardonic manner. It was a military mug shot, only his wide shoulders showing, filling out a uniform.

Lucy read the Interpol dossier on Nolan Montgomery Taylor: a lieutenant for England's Special Air Service. Thirty-two. Six feet six inches. Two hundred and ten pounds. Born in London. Graduated top of his class at Sandhurst Academy. Trained in the Terrorist Division. Awarded the Military Cross for a mission he'd led in Afghanistan. He'd paid out of the service two months ago.

Nolan Taylor. At least she'd been able to trace his identity. There was no record of criminal activity. He seemed squeaky clean. But that didn't rule out the possibility that he could be working for Arachne. Lucy tapped the screen where his face glowed and said, "For your sake, you better stay out of my way."

Chapter 7

A BBC evening news program squawked on the television while Nolan sat in his hotel room, downloading the contents of Viking's PDA into his laptop. In tracking terrorists, he'd learned that all information should be kept and reviewed. It appeared that what he'd learned in the Air Service would be useful during his job at Pincer. If Giger Anfinson was working for one of the terrorist groups that had a price on Nolan's head, there might be a contact number somewhere in his PDA.

Windows chimed and Outlook alerted him that he had an instant message from his new boss.

Nolan frowned at the message:

Mr. Taylor,

Important personal documents of mine were stolen this morning from the Suisse Plus Bank. I want those documents back at any cost. I believe the thieves work for Pincer's competition and they are trying to blacken my character in order to buy out the company and take it over. I've sent a download of a news clip of the thieves. The documents also had a GPS tracking device in them. I've enclosed the satellite Web site for the tracking device. It should lead you directly to them. Keep me posted on your progress. I can't express to you how important it is that I get those documents back and find out who has hired the thieves.

M.N.

Nolan opened the attachment and a news clip filled the screen.

The camera cut away to a reporter standing in front of the bank. The man's white Muslim robe and headdress was stark against his dark skin. He held the microphone close to his mouth. In the background a tow truck hoisted a police car up onto its flatbed. "This is Saleem Simbel reporting live. Bank robbers struck the PSWD today in a daring robbery attempt. I'm standing here with Captain Mumari and Mr. Wubiset, a customer who witnessed the robbery in progress." The camera panned wide, encompassing the police captain, a short beak-faced bloke. The witness, who stood beside him, had a pronounced twitch in his right cheek.

"Mr. Wubiset. Tell us what happened."

"It was horrible."

"Did you get a look at the robbers?"

Mr. Wubiset smiled for the camera as if he were enjoying the limelight. "A huge man." He spread his arms in an exaggerated width. "We fought. I was winning, too, until he pulled out a gun. He beat me with it, terribly, and left me for dead. I was told later he stole my car. My car…." He grabbed his head for effect.

Captain Mumari leaned into the camera. "We have since located Mr. Wubiset's Porsche, as well as the van used by the perpetrators."

"My car was parked in District Six, ruined. I'd like to know if the city will pay for it. It's not safe in this city."

The reporter stepped in front of Wubiset and focused on the police captain.

"Captain Mumari, do you believe this was the work of bank robbers or terrorists?"

"No terrorist group has come forward to take responsibility for the robbery attempt. We are certain we're dealing with bank robbers."

"How many were there?"

"Three, maybe more."

"What was the robber's target?"

"The second-level vault, but my department stopped them before they could proceed with their plans."

"Do you have a description for us?"

A black-and-white security video of a tall man with black hair flashed onto the screen. He was walking toward the bank's door, a backpack slung over his shoulder.

Nolan narrowed his eyes at the image. To the untrained eye, the person looked like just a regular guy in a suit with a bad haircut. But Nolan had made a living at spotting disguises. The coltish walk with a slight sway in the hips was the first giveaway.

Nolan closed in on the facial features. The brow ridge wasn't prominent. The dimple in the jaw looked male, but it was too delicate and not pronounced enough, and the cheekbones were high but smooth. He was definitely looking at a woman. His gaze shifted to the brand name on the backpack,

Alpine, before the camera cut away to the reporter and Mumari. An itch grew in him to see another clip of the woman. An image sparked in his mind, and he saw the face in the car with the baseball cap. Was it the same woman?

He had a feeling he wouldn't get to the truth until he found and questioned these criminals—particularly the redhead. He also knew this robbery could be tied to the intrigue going on at Pincer. He wondered what was in the documents, but he wouldn't discover that until he found the criminals. A mental image of the disguised woman flashed, and he decided he'd enjoy teaching her the error of her ways. He hit the link to the GPS tracking Web site and found himself grinning.

Fish Hoek Village, False Bay, South Africa

Nolan hid behind a coral tree that was bent almost double from the constant winds blowing in from the sea. He'd parked a rented black Volvo wagon down the street and found an empty beach house diagonally across from the GPS's location. He could watch the front of the house and some of the back from his vantage point.

This wasn't a typical beach neighborhood. The houses along this street were estate size with acres of land around them. These robbers were no nickel-and-dime type. He stood behind a palm in grass up to his knees. A wind-toppled For Sale sign lay several feet from the curb, almost engulfed by the thick scrub grass. He'd been watching the house for two hours now. Lights burned in the windows, and he could see shadows moving behind the shades. Someone was home. He hoped it was his targets.

The temperature had dropped to below forty, and he shivered while he ate the last bite of a Cadbury chocolate bar, a habit he'd acquired in the service during stakeouts. It helped pass the time and kept him awake. He folded the wrapper and stuffed it into his windbreaker pocket, thinking this detail reminded him of his missions in the Service—tracking a target, followed by the arduous hours of stalking, waiting for the right moment to strike.

It was only eight o'clock. He'd have many more hours before the occupants of the house went to sleep and he could do a little recon. He almost sat down by the tree to wait, when he heard a door close and saw a man and two women in jogging suits exiting the back of the house.

He pulled a pair of micro binoculars from his jacket and trained them on the three figures as they stretched and warmed up. One was a stunning, diminutive black woman. The man looked Asian. Nolan zoomed in on the taller woman. She was touching her toes and turned directly into the security spotlights that had come on when they exited. Nolan glimpsed the dimpled chin, the red hair, the full mouth. The same woman from the news clip. He'd stake his life on it.

"You're mine," he whispered to himself.

They laughed at something the Asian said, then started jogging along the beach. Was the house empty?

It was now or never to search the place. He checked the street. All quiet, save for the wind howling through the trees. After dark, most of the beach houses were closed up tight.

He stalked across the street, through tended gardens with shorn silky hakea hedgerows, fan palms, fynbos and circular beds of geraniums and aloes, following the hedged path to the back of the house. When he reached the side that faced the beach, he noticed that the house was two stories. From the street it was graded to look like one story, but on the beach side, the wind had exposed a deep foundation, all bricked. He peeked in through a basement window, no wider than a slit. It had been blackened with paint and he couldn't see inside.

Above him, light glowed out through the patio doors and fanned a sharp ray across the length of the porch. Occasional flashes from a television flitted along the glass and flickered across the steps. Was someone up there? Or had the joggers carelessly left the tele on? It would be a lot easier if the house was deserted.

He was so tall he could reach the porch railing. In seconds he hoisted himself up and over the handrail, inching closer to the glass doors.

A quick peek revealed the profile of a blond bloke, about thirty, sitting on the sofa. He nursed a Pepsi and watched a *Mork and Mindy* rerun with the hypnotic stare of someone who had overdosed on reruns and commercials.

Nolan surveyed the sophisticated alarm system. Sensor wires ran through the door's glass. Red laser beams striped the entrance at one-foot intervals all the way up the door. A high-tech expensive system, with multi-zoned power sources for uninterrupted security. He'd seen these systems before in several sheiks' homes—when they'd been harboring terrorists. These criminals were into more than just robbery. No way in from the outside. That left only one other way in.

On the beach

Lucy inhaled the scent of seaweed, sand, suntan lotion and decayed marine life as she jogged behind Cao and Betsy. She hung back, giving them plenty of alone time. Betsy had insisted Lucy come along. Now Lucy wished she'd jogged the other way and left them alone.

They looked like the perfect couple. Both were short, Cao a head taller than Betsy. Moonlight bathed their sleek forms, and their shadows melted over the waves pounding the beach. Their feet kept time with each other, the rhythm perfect. What could be more romantic than sweating bodies, all that adrenaline pumping in sync? A perfect moment for Cao to make his move.

He remained silent, still brooding over losing the transmission to a data miner.

"Which marathon is the hardest?" Betsy asked, her voice drifting toward Lucy over the pounding surf.

At least Betsy was trying to draw Cao out. Not the most romantic thing to say, but it was a start. She might even cheer him up.

"The Boston Marathon," Cao said absently.

"It couldn't be that hard," Betsy said, teasing him.

"People train for years to enter it," Cao said, growing annoyed and defensive. He didn't take teasing well. "I've trained for years."

"Goody for you, and them," Betsy said, her tone sharpening to match his. "I only took up long-distance running two years ago."

"You have a lot of training to go."

"Who says?"

"I do."

"How about we race right now?" Betsy shot him a saucy, challenging look.

"You're on." Cao brightened.

It was the first hint of pleasure Lucy had seen on his face all afternoon. Lucy watched the reflective stripes on their jackets and pants shifting as their feet pounded the sand. They seemed to have forgotten she was following them. A good thing, because she felt like a third wheel.

"Where we jogging to?" Betsy asked.

"See that bluff up there?" Cao pointed to a jagged cliff overhanging the beach. The black stone glistened gray in the moonlight. It looked ten miles away, or better. "To there. First one back to the safe house wins."

"You're on." Betsy sped up, her legs churning.

Cao followed, keeping beside her.

Lucy gave up and turned back toward the house. Four miles was her limit. Her body told her she'd reached that point five minutes ago. She could smell a storm rolling in from the east. Lightning veined the sky. Thunder boomed like native drums in the distance. Dark clouds scudded behind the mountains and shifted the face of the moon into a grotesque expression. It always amazed her how fast storms moved into the Cape. She hoped Cao and Betsy returned before it rained.

By the time she arrived at the safe house porch, her lungs burned, her calf muscles had cramped from jogging on the sand, and she was dying for a drink of water. She pulled herself up the steps and punched in a code to open the doors.

When she stepped inside, she didn't see Tommy on the couch.

"Hey, I'm back," she called, stepping deeper into the room. "Tommy!" She walked into the kitchen.

He wasn't there.

She stepped back out into the living room and saw an over-turned Pepsi can. The soda had dripped onto the carpet and left a small brown stain. Then she spotted tiny drops of blood leading across the room and toward the hall. Her danger sensors vibrated. She was glad she had decided to jog with a weapon. She eased the .45 from beneath the shoulder holster under her shirt, then headed down the hallway, toward the bedrooms. God, she hoped Tommy wasn't dead.

"Hey, Toms, where are you?" she called, just to throw off the intruder. "Want to share a bag of popcorn? I'm starved after the run."

As she neared the door to her bedroom, a thump sounded inside.

Gun gripped close to her body, heart pounding, she summoned her courage and peeked into the room. She hadn't left a lamp on, and the hallway light cut a jagged edge through the darkness. She scanned the shadows, the bed, the dresser.

Then she spotted a dark figure looming near the chaise lounge, a massive specter lit by the lightning strikes shining in through the window. Was it Tommy?

No way. Too large for Tommy. This prowler was well over six feet. Those bear-size shoulders looked familiar. The guy at Pincer? Had he killed Tommy? Fear and indignation knotted every muscle in her body. The intruder held her suitcase, his big paws riffling through her stuff.

The .45 sighted at his back, she pulled back the hammer on the pistol. It made a distinctive click as only a steel Colt could.

He froze and said, "You don't want to use that." A starched English accent punctuated the whispered words. His deep voice held a silken command that grated on Lucy.

"You're the one breaking and entering and you're giving me orders? I could off you right now. So can that smug tone. Down on your knees. Hands behind your head."

He stepped back from the suitcase and fell to his knees. Even on his knees his head came up to her ribs. How tall was this guy?

"Are you going to kill me?" he asked in a casual tone, not an ounce of fear in it.

"That remains to be seen, doesn't it? How did you get in here?" She thought of Tommy. "Did you hurt my friend?"

"I'm not a killer."

"You better hope you're telling the truth. Where is he?"

"I left him inside the bedroom at the end of the hall."

"Did Miranda N'Buta send you here?"

"Yes. If we're playing twenty questions, it's my turn. Who hired you to steal the bank documents?"

"I have this rule—never play with strangers in my bedroom. And since there's a .45 aimed at the back of your head, it might lengthen your life span to answer *my* questions. You can start with how you found me so quickly."

"I'm a resourceful person. My turn. Why do you want the documents?"

Lucy glanced at her suitcase. She had stashed the documents in a hidden compartment inside the case. If she hadn't come upon him, he might have found them. Had he known they were in there? "I'll ask again. How did you find me so quickly?"

"I don't see how that matters, really. I'm here and we're at an impasse. Are you going to shoot me? If not, maybe we can settle this amicably. You give me the documents and I might let you go." He dropped his hands.

"I don't make deals. Put your hands up."

"I'm sorry to hear that." Suddenly he lunged at her legs and blindsided her.

Chapter 8

Lucy fired the Colt as he tackled her and grabbed the gun. The shot went over his head and hit the wall behind him. They wrestled with the gun as they both plunged to the floor. His strength was unbelievable, and he jerked the pistol from her grasp. It hit the floor with a solid thump.

Before he could pin her to the ground, Lucy jabbed her knee into his stomach and used the momentum of her body to throw him over her head. She did a backflip onto her feet as he hit the floor behind her.

He tried to roll and straighten himself, but she was ready with a dropkick to the face. He smashed into the bedside stand, unfazed.

Lucy attacked with another kick.

He caught her foot and flipped her to the floor, then threw his weight on top of her. She got in a punch to his jaw, but it didn't faze him. He wrestled her hands to the ground and held them there.

She bucked and kicked, but his weight was too much for her. He was larger than any man she'd ever confronted. He must have outweighed her by eighty pounds, a boulder on top of her, squashing her, jamming her lucky charm into her right breast. She could hardly breathe with his iron chest a dead-weight on her lungs. For the first time in her life, she was at a man's mercy. And it made her seethe.

"You're a bloody hellion," he said, his heavy breaths burning her face.

His body heat seeped through her thin jogging suit and burned her as if she wore nothing. She smelled chocolate on his breath and said, "You haven't seen anything yet."

"I'm sure you're full of tricks." He paused and stared down at her.

Shadows covered his face, but she could see the outline of his sharp cheekbones, strong chin, deep-set eyes and short hair. Nolan Taylor, all right. If he weren't irritating the hell out of her, she might think he was handsome. She struggled beneath him, but only hurt her shoulders and hips. "You can't hold me down forever and I'm going to hurt you when I get up."

The outline of his cheeks moved. Was he smiling at her? He pressed his mouth closer to hers, so close she could feel the stubbly whiskers on his chin. "That so?" He bent and sniffed her hair that tangled around her shoulders. "Bloody hell, you smell good. Is that strawberry shampoo?"

"Gunpowder and sweat." She snarled up at him, wishing she could nail him to the wall and use him for target practice.

"Speaking of explosives, I'm not leaving here until I have the documents you stole from the bank today."

"People in hell want ice water." She felt his erection pressing against her abdomen, and it made her aware of how defenseless she was at the moment. Was that another self-satisfied grin on his face?

Lightning flashed outside. Ice-blue eyes blazed down at her, his grin touching them.

Suddenly she heard a door open and Betsy was yelling, "Lucy! Tommy!"

"Help! In here," Lucy yelled, galled that she was at this guy's mercy and had to call for help.

"Wish we could chat longer, love," he said, rolling off of her. "But I'll be back."

As he came up, Lucy drove her fist into the side of his jaw. She owed him at least that.

His head rocked back on his shoulders, but the impact only stunned him for a second. "Bloody hell, we were getting along so well," he ground out.

The next few moments happened so fast it was a chaotic blur.

He leaped to his feet and dove through the window.

Glass exploded in all directions.

The security alarm sprang to life, adding to the pandemonium.

Lucy realized she was in the line of fire and hit the floor.

Betsy emptied a clip and ran to the window. "Damn, damn," she yelled over the alarm. "I hate wasting bullets."

"I'll get him," Cao yelled, running back through the house and out the door.

"Not without me you won't," Betsy said, following him.

Over the ringing in Lucy's ears and the alarm blasts, their footfalls sounded like shovels of dirt hitting a hole. Lucy rose and reached for the wall switch. Light flooded the room. It looked like a war zone. The window was nothing but jagged teeth embedded in the casing, glass everywhere. Bullet holes pocked the wall near the broken window and the chaise lounge. She reached for the security keypad and punched the five-digit code.

The alarm died.

Something bright caught her eye. She stepped over to the window, picked up a silver piece of paper and gently shook bits of glass from it. It was a candy bar wrapper, neatly folded into a perfect square. She sniffed it. Milk chocolate, the same chocolate she'd smelled on Taylor's breath. So he was a sugar freak as well as an overconfident jerk.

She hoped Betsy and Cao caught Taylor. She wanted to question him again, and he might not be so arrogantly defiant this time. He didn't seem like the type easily caught unless he wanted to be. Was he Miranda N'Buta's hit man? Had she sent him not only for the documents but to kill them? If he did get away she knew where to find him: Pincer Industries. She tossed the wrapper on the dresser, then went to look for Tommy. She didn't believe Taylor when he said he hadn't hurt Tommy. She expected to find her teammate dead. Her gut tightened and her chest ached as she walked down the hall.

Nolan sped the Volvo away from the scene, while rain pounded the windshield. He looked in his rearview mirror and saw two blurry figures, the black woman and the Asian man, run out into the street, guns raised. They must have realized he was out of range for they lowered their guns.

His wheels skidded on the wet road as he sped around a corner. He touched his jaw. It ached from the sucker punch. She had a nice right, he'd give her that.

She had more than just a nice right punch. He remembered the shapely body, thin-hipped and lean beneath him. Amazingly long legs. Full breasts that he'd felt against his chest. She'd fit his body in all the right places. The women he'd dated in the past were frail, thin creatures, even Sarah, an old flame he'd left back in England. He'd always worried about hurting her with his bulk. Not Red. He'd slammed his whole weight on top of her and she'd only spit back nasty remarks at him. Bloody hell, that had turned him on more than any woman he'd ever been near. He could still feel his erection.

He remembered her narrowed ginger-colored eyes, oval face, and the flaming red hair that had smelled so damn good. She was a beauty. Not quite in every aspect. Beautiful women didn't go around trying to break a bloke's jaw. She was dangerous and unpredictable; he couldn't let himself forget that.

He'd found the basement and the sophisticated equipment when he'd searched the house, and he was certain these people were more than bank robbers. The big questions were: who'd hired her and what did they hope to gain by taking the documents?

He opened his laptop on the passenger seat. The GPS Web site popped up. A tiny light blinked every fifteen seconds on a map of Cape Town. He hit the Zoom button and plans of the house he'd just left appeared on screen. He zoomed in larger, and a schematic of the house popped up. He moved the cursor to her bedroom and the tracking beam intensified. The documents were somewhere in her room. But where? Soon he'd have them, he promised himself.

His cell phone rang.

"Yes."

"Sir, this is Salim Cummay."

Nolan recalled the name instantly. The night watchman he'd questioned earlier. "Yes, Cummay, what is it?"

His voice pulsed with the uncertainty of a subordinate. "I was making my rounds, sir, checking Ms. N'Buta's office and her computer is—" he gulped loudly "—gone, sir. It's gone. Someone has stolen it. I've looked the building over. I can't figure how they got out with it. No alarms went off. I swear."

Another robbery? Could Red be working with more than three people? Did more of her minions hit Pincer? Red must not have found what she was looking for in the bank documents. Nolan had a suspicion he was being used by Ms. N'Buta, and he was tired of it. But how had the computer gone missing? No alarms, indeed. Must have been an inside job. Then he had another thought. Giger Anfinson could have taken the computer. But why? Too many questions, not enough answers.

"No alarms at all?" Nolan asked.

"No, sir."

Nolan had listened for a lie, but heard only honesty and fear in the man's voice. He spoke over the steady thud of the windshield wipers as he said, "Have you rerun the security cameras?"

"Tried to, sir, but they were blank for about twenty minutes. I know Ms. N'Buta prefers to hear from security personnel directly, but I was wondering…" Another dry gulp. "Could you tell her?"

"Did you call the police?"

"No, no, sir. Standing order. Ms. N'Buta says no police, ever. We're to deal with in-house crimes ourselves."

"Cummay, are you not telling me something?"

"No, sir. Never."

Nolan heard the hard edge of a lie in his voice. "Seal off the top floor. I'll be there as soon as I can."

"Will you tell Ms. N'Buta?"

"Leave it to me." Nolan hung up and decided he'd question Cummay in detail when he got to Pincer. Cummay was hiding something.

Fish Hoek Village, False Bay, South Africa

Lucy paced the length of the great room, listening to rain pound at the roof, tug at the doors, beat against the balcony. She watched her reflection float past the patio doors. Then she turned and faced Betsy as she applied a cold pack to Tommy's broken nose. He lay sprawled on the couch. Cao sat in a chair opposite them, watching Betsy closely.

"I want that sombitch," Tommy said.

"How did he get in?" Lucy asked.

"I heard something outside on the porch. Something hit the house. I thought it was an animal or something. When I went out to see what it was, the sombitch jumped me—ouch, I'll take that." Tommy snatched the cold pack from Betsy's hand and waved her away. Both his eyes were black, his nose swollen three times its size. And his disposition had deteriorated along with his pride.

"Just trying to help," Betsy huffed under her breath.

"That's your problem." Cao sneered at her. "You're too helpful."

"Don't pick on me just 'cause you lost the bet."

Cao didn't answer her. He folded his arms over his chest and looked defeated.

Tommy groaned out loud. "You're both giving me a damn headache. Somebody just get me an aspirin—make that six."

"I've got some, but I don't know why I should share them with you. You're just like him." Betsy thumbed in Cao's direction, then stomped off toward her bedroom.

Cao glared at Tommy. "Now see what you've done."

"Me?" Tommy rolled his eyes.

Lucy stopped pacing and faced them. "Look, we have to focus. How did Nolan Taylor find us so quickly? He knew exactly where to look."

"He could have followed you, or Betsy and Tommy," Cao said.

Tommy lifted the ice pack and made a face. "No way, man. We made sure of it."

Lucy thought of the ride back to the safe house. She'd

driven a circuitous route home, even stopping in a park to make sure she wasn't followed.

Cao sat up straight in his chair, his brows narrowing in thought. "What if we were followed in a different way?"

"What way is that?" Lucy asked.

"Electronically. Think about it. The only thing connecting us to the bank job is the documents."

"Oh my God. You're right." Lucy's fingers tightened into fists. She seethed. Nolan Taylor was probably laughing at her at this very moment.

Lucy headed for her room, Cao followed on her heels, limping.

Chapter 9

Fish Hoek Village, False Bay, South Africa

When Lucy reached the bedroom, she found her suitcase, a present from Val when Lucy had gone into the mercenary business. The case had come in handy on this trip. She threw it on the bed and opened the false shell lining. The documents tumbled out into the case's bottom.

She looked at them closely.

Cao stood beside her and said, "The ledger has the thickest cover."

Lucy grabbed it and tore the black cardboard cover apart. A two-inch-by-two-inch flat circuit board fell out onto the bed. It looked like a motherboard, replete with several red glowing lights.

Cao picked it up in awe. "This is a piece of art. Whoever designed it is a genius."

"Art?" Lucy blurted. "It's compromised our position."

"It could also work to our advantage."

"I see what you're saying." Some of the heat left Lucy's voice. "Where shall we ship it?"

Cao's expression turned devious. "Hong Kong."

"Nice." Lucy grinned at the thought of Nolan Taylor trekking to Hong Kong. She thought a moment and said, "Can we trace the signal before we ship it out?"

He made a face at the device as if it were a puzzle piece. "Depends on two factors. How well it's scrambled and decoded, and if we have access to mainframe search engines set up to receive intelligence data from satellite signals."

"You talking about military intel? CIA, NSA, HAS, that kind of network?"

Cao nodded.

"Can you get into one of them?"

Cao cocked his head at her and thrust out his chin to an insulted angle. "You're looking at the man who used to do it regularly for the CSR."

Lucy gazed at Cao and was glad he had defected to America. He was a dangerous individual to have as a foe. "How long will it take?"

"There's a variable. I broke into computers through the CSR's mainframe. It'll take me a while to gain access to an intel computer. I don't know how long it will take to track the site once I get access."

Lucy thought of Delphi and wondered if he or she could get Cao access. She stared at the blinking circuit, insolently winking at her; then she gazed at the other documents. "Makes you wonder what else is hidden in these, doesn't it?"

"Absolutely."

She gathered them up in her arms and headed for the basement.

Cao followed her, transmitter in hand.

Lion's Head, Cape Town

Miranda N'Buta lay awake. The storm had woken her, but as quickly as it had come, it had dissipated. Now only the winds slashed at the eaves, and she couldn't go back to sleep.

She listened to her two Dobermans, Lani and Lailai, breathing. Their favorite spot was a zebra-hide throw rug at the foot of her bed. She had bought the attack dogs for protection, along with a high-tech security alarm, a must in Lion's Head, the most affluent neighborhood in Cape Town. The neighborhood's mansions dotted the slopes of Table Mountain. She'd bought hers for its dramatic views. And of course, the prestige. She liked looking down upon Cape Town—a throne of wealth that presided over the whole city.

But like every bastion of prosperity in the Cape, it was a target for burglaries. Only last week, thieves had broken into a home down the street and assaulted two servants and the owner before the police apprehended them. She kept a gun by her bed, loaded at all times. But of course, it wasn't simple thieves she feared.

The dogs had seemed unusually lethargic since Miranda had gotten home from work. And they had refused to eat their dinner. She hoped they weren't catching something. It would be another trip to the vet, and she didn't have time for that.

She glanced at the wall clock: 1:45 a.m. She'd never get back to sleep with the thousand thoughts zipping through her mind. Chief among them, the account in her name at the Suisse Plus Bank, about which she knew nothing. If she hadn't worked with the branch manager on an AIDS fund-raising event, she might never have been informed about the robbery. When Miranda had inquired about the contact information on the account, it had been a fax number she didn't recognize. That worried her.

When Miranda had questioned the witch about the stolen documents, the witch had said they were of no concern to Pincer Industries and Miranda shouldn't worry about them. She had even insisted upon handling their retrieval through Mr. Taylor, and all Miranda was to know was: "You're being pursued by corporate raiders—if anyone should question you."

There was only one reason for the witch to exclude Miranda from the retrieval of the stolen bank documents— she didn't want Miranda to know what was in them. But why? And why keep them in a Cape Town bank? The witch had always told Miranda she lived in Arizona. And what would someone want with the papers? Was someone getting close to the witch's empire, and through her to Pincer?

Miranda wouldn't let anything happen to the company. She had been the one to make a success of Pincer Industries. She'd been there at the inception. It was her baby. The witch might have been the financier with contacts in the criminal underground, but Miranda had cultivated those contacts. She'd dealt with depraved individuals who turned her stomach and who, she knew, would slit her throat without thinking. She had done it all for Pincer, and she'd made it turn a profit.

If the press ever found out about the disreputable businesses Pincer was involved in, it would be the end of the company, the end of Miranda's livelihood and a large chunk of the witch's income, as well.

Miranda turned over in the bed, her bracelet tinkled in the room's grimness. If the company went down, Miranda's only consolation was that she'd take the witch down with her. Miranda had recorded hours of their conversations and stored them in her office, payback for all the years of abuse she'd taken. She had edited them, deleting her part in any criminal activities. She'd give them to the police. If they found enough evidence to arrest her, Miranda would swear she was only a figurehead in the business and the witch had threatened to kill her if she didn't do exactly as she was ordered.

She didn't trust this Nolan Taylor. The witch had hand-picked him. Now he was working to retrieve the documents, not even reporting to Miranda. Miranda didn't mind assassins within the company. They served their purpose. But they had always been hers to command. Taylor answered only to Arachne. And there was something in his persona that hinted at duplicity, as if he never let the world see his real face. She knew about such things, because she herself had been doing that for years, hiding behind another face. Taylor, she decided, was dangerous.

A heavy thump sounded in the back of the mansion. The atrium, maybe?

The sound brought Lani and Lailai's heads up. They woofed softly, then turned to her for a command.

"Guard," she whispered.

The dogs padded out of the room, their ears back, their bodies crouched slightly, ready to attack.

Another thump. A window being pried open?

The dogs began to growl and bark.

She looked at the security alarm box in her bedroom. The red light was off. She turned the light on.

The knob clicked in the dark.

Someone had cut the power.

She pulled out a revolver from a dresser drawer and eased out of the bedroom, the gun trembling in her hands, her heart pounding.

Fish Hoek Village, False Bay, South Africa

When Lucy and Cao reached the basement, Lucy searched for two pairs of goggles, while Cao found the UV spectrometer. She tossed Cao a pair as she put on her own and turned off the lights. She flicked on the wand. The documents glowed blue.

"There." Cao pointed to a tiny strip no bigger than the letter J on one of the passport covers.

"What do we have here?"

"I'll look at it under the borescope." Cao took it and picked up the borescope from a shelf. It was rigid, not flexible. An eyepiece was on one end of a four-inch fiber-optic rod and an objective lens was on the other end. A cylindrical LED light source that resembled the otoscope used by doctors to look in their patients' ears was attached to the rod near the eye piece. Cao placed the lens over the microdot and flicked on the light source.

"Hmm, looks like names and addresses of individuals and companies."

"Recognize any?"

"House Representative Bryan Ellis, for one."

"Really. Who else?"

"Dictator Vlados Zelasko of Kestonia. Another guy by the name Juan Mercado Tulio, with a Colombian address. There are account numbers by their names."

Could these be copies of Arachne's blackmail lists? Lucy felt her heart pounding at the discovery. She eagerly combed another passport and found two microdots. It felt like Christmas morning. Hardly able to control her excitement, she set the passport next to Cao. She grabbed the pages of the ledger from which she had torn the cover and slowly swept the wand over them. She found one at the end of each column of added numbers. The money was in euros and went into the millions.

"Jeez, there's a microdot on every ledger page." Lucy kept turning pages.

Glimpses flashed of crime bosses in Boston; some of them she recognized from the news as recently as a month ago.

Shipping companies paired with the name Tulio. Bryan Ellis's name appeared again and stood out next to many of the companies, his shares listed beside each one.

Another page revealed international high-profile companies with key names beside them. It was unbelievable—a limitless web of corruption.

"How does our intruder fit into all of this?" Cao asked without taking his eye from the lens.

For some reason she couldn't get the smell of chocolate out of her mind. Along with something else—Nolan Taylor's erection pressed against her abdomen.

She ground her teeth together until they ached. The inability to forget the experience was almost as frustrating as having been subdued by the oversized galoot. Next time they met, she promised herself, she'd do the subduing.

"I don't know," she said. "I've wondered about it. Nolan Taylor could be involved in Pincer's security somehow. Or he could be Miranda N'Buta's bodyguard. He's a decorated English vet. It's hard to visualize someone with his unsoiled background involved with Arachne."

"There's another possibility," Cao added. "She hired him for that very reason. No one would suspect him."

"True."

"Or," Cao paused for effect, "Taylor could be another undercover intel agent working at Pincer to get close to Arachne," Cao added.

"Maybe." Lucy preferred to think of Taylor as one of the good guys.

"One thing is certain," Cao said. "Everyone wants a piece of Arachne. Even the CSR Unit had a hefty price on Madame Web's head before I left China." His face screwed up in a frown. "Taylor could become a problem."

"If he gets in our way, he'll go down along with her." Lucy

recalled the Englishman saying he wasn't a killer. His word had turned out to be true in Tommy's case.

"Do you think Miranda N'Buta is Arachne?"

"I don't know but we have to find out. Can you scan the rest of these?" Lucy pointed to the coverless ledger.

Cao nodded.

Lucy left him and stood up.

"Where are you going?" Cao asked.

"I'm going to search Miranda N'Buta's office. There might be something there that ties her identity to Arachne."

Lucy took the stairs two at a time and pulled out her cell phone. She had to update Delphi and see how Delphi wanted the microdot information sent. She also needed to ask if Delphi could facilitate Cao's access to an intelligence community computer in order to track the GPS site back to its origin. Arachne's web was getting smaller and smaller, one strand at a time.

Pincer Industries, Cape Town

The recent rain made Adderley Street shimmer like glass in the headlights. Pincer Industries' high-rise looked like a huge dark checkerboard on the tarmac as Nolan neared it. All the lights were out, which was strange. Had the building lost power? He glanced next door at the First National Bank. It had power. So did St. George's Mall a block away.

He turned on to a service road beside the building. As he neared the back delivery entrance, he called Cummay's cell phone number again. He wanted to alert Cummay that he'd meet him at Ms. N'Buta's office. But Cummay didn't pick up. Something definitely didn't feel right.

The innate sense of danger that had kept Nolan alive in the terrorist business and beyond it hummed now. He parked his car in the employee lot and slipped around to the back service entrance. In the dim glow of a streetlamp, he could see the security cameras trained on the heavy aluminum bay doors. A bullet had taken out the lenses.

He pulled out the push knife from his belt and sneaked toward the back entrance beside the bay doors. He tried the doorknob.

Not locked.

He stepped inside.

Lucy parked the Jeep, the front bumper tight against a Dumpster. She scanned the alley behind Pincer Industries. Betsy shifted in the seat beside her as she pulled out her Sokolovsky .45 from a back holster. They'd left Cao and Tommy extracting the rest of the information from the microdots and scanning it. Delphi had given orders to e-mail the info. In Lucy's last conversation with Delphi, it was agreed that Cao would be patched into the NSA's mainframe so he could track the GPS signal. Lucy still wondered in what capacity Delphi was connected to the National Security Agency. Delphi and Lucy had also agreed they should leave the GPS transmitter at the safe house for the time being so Arachne wouldn't be alerted that they were on to her tracking device. Delphi backed up the idea to mail the circuit card to Hong Kong once all the information had been documented and Lucy had overnighted the original documents to a post office box in Maryland. Lucy had left Cao and Tommy to do that. Everything felt as if it was coming into place.

Betsy motioned to the dark windows above their heads. "That ain't good. Looks like they got a power problem."

"Might be someone after the same thing we are. I hope we're not too late."

Lucy pulled the Colt from her shoulder holster and checked to make sure she had a full magazine. Under her sweatshirt she had strapped four grenades to her back—just in case. She pulled a flashlight from a case on her belt.

Betsy and Lucy left the car and crept up to the delivery door by the two bay doors. Lucy silently motioned toward the destroyed security cameras. Betsy acknowledged them with a nod.

Lucy checked the door for laser grids.

Nothing.

"We'll separate. I'll take the stairwell up to her office."

"I'll check for security guards and any other unwanted guests."

Lucy held the Colt in one hand and the pen-size flashlight in the other as she pulled open the door. It creaked eerily in the hollows of the delivery area.

She peeked inside and swept the flashlight over the cement floor of the two delivery bays. A platform ran around the perimeter and up to an office. Pitch blackness covered the whole area except for the backup security EXIT sign above her head. The door on the right looked like the only way into the main building.

Lucy motioned to Betsy that she was going in, then slipped inside.

Betsy pulled a flashlight from her belt and followed on Lucy's heels.

Oil and gasoline fumes permeated the air as Lucy made her way toward the left door. Cautiously she opened the second door. They'd reached the main hallway.

LOBBY signs pointed them straight ahead. They passed a darkened mailroom and an office with the name Giger Anfinson on it.

About twenty feet away, Lucy saw another EXIT sign over a door. She advanced toward it and shined the flashlight through the side glass into a stairwell. She motioned that she was going up.

Betsy nodded, then crept toward the lobby.

Lucy paused, listening for footsteps.

Only silence.

She hurried up the stairs.

Nolan walked down the hallway toward Ms. N'Buta's office. His own rapid breaths sounded like wind hitting sails. EXIT signs cast a globed red haze near the ceiling, the only source of light in the blackness.

He gingerly moved down the hallway. When he neared the office, he could see the door was open, nothing but darkness beyond. He started to step inside, but his foot kicked something solid. It plunked against the wall. He bent and picked up a flashlight, the kind used by Pincer's security force. Nolan had made note of them earlier.

He turned it on. A beam of light hit Cummay's dead face. Nolan froze. A bullet wound oozed blood down the center of his forehead. He'd fallen propped against the wall, his revolver still clutched in his hand. Three feet away was another corpse, lying supine on the floor.

Nolan raised the flashlight. He frowned as he recognized the face.

Viking.

He slowly moved toward them. Viking also held a pistol. He'd been shot through the head in the exact spot as Cummay. It appeared as if they'd shot each other, but Nolan wasn't buying that.

He bent to feel Cummay's neck. His skin felt tepid. He'd probably been killed right after they'd spoken.

Nolan shined his flashlight into the office. Someone jumped him from behind.

He wheeled, but the person had hopped onto his back.

An electrical jolt scorched his neck, slammed through his

nerve endings and bowed his spine. His body shook uncontrollably from the Taser's shock, every muscle contracting. The weight of his attacker and the excruciating pain knocked him to his knees. He felt helpless and couldn't believe he'd allowed himself to be ambushed by this killer. It was the hellion's fault. She had distracted him. Damn her!

"Move and I'll zap you again," a woman's voice purred near his ear.

He felt the pain subside and lifted his arms to fight her, but she hit him again, this time in the middle of his back. His body buckled, jerked, shuddered. He felt as if he'd been immersed in hot grease and was being fried alive.

"I told you not to move." Her arm tightened around his neck, then a knife blade pricked his throat.

He hardly felt it with the pain searing his body. "Shouldn't have stumbled into my work. I'm gonna have to kill you now." The words were like a snake's hiss, a froth of teeming malevolence.

Nolan felt his steely control on his emotions slipping. Fear clawed at his gut. Could he actually lose this fight?

A flashlight beam suddenly hit them. Blinding light spewed from the doorway. At the abrupt interruption, his attacker gripped the blade tighter against his throat.

Nolan had never been so glad to be caught with a woman in a compromising position. He squinted at the blinding light, trying to see who held the flashlight, but he couldn't make out the hazy shadow.

"Any closer and he's dead," his attacker said, her mouth next to his ear, her breath burning everywhere it touched his raw skin.

A voice behind the flashlight beam said, "Go ahead and kill him. Do us both a favor."

Nolan recognized the cocky voice. The hellion. His hope

died a quick death. He gazed into the light, looking into the barrel of the Colt. Bloody hell, he was already dead.

He managed to speak, "How about drawing straws—" He felt the blade of the knife against his windpipe.

The hellion said, "No contest. I'll win."

"You think so," his attacker said as her wrist flicked toward his neck.

Nolan closed his eyes, held his breath, readying himself to die.

Red pulled off a shot. A bullet zoomed so close to his neck, it split hairs. He didn't dare breathe or move a millimeter.

The assassin screamed as the knife fell from her hand. Then she shoved him, catapulting up onto her feet, aiming the Taser directly at Red.

Two dart-like electrodes snaked toward Red. She leaped aside, but one hit her in the abdomen and one in the knee. She collapsed, yelling in pain.

"Later, bitch!" the assassin growled, her wounded, bleeding hand held close to her body. Nolan noticed a ski mask covered her face. A pair of jade eyes flashed in his direction, then she darted out the door.

Nolan couldn't believe Red had saved his life and he prayed she wasn't hurt. He heard the stairwell door open, then the assassin's ruthless laughter reverberating through it as she sped down the steps.

Red didn't seem injured, only stunned, as she jerked out the electrodes and looked over at Nolan. Her voice laced with pain, she said, "Are you okay?"

"I'll live." He struggled to stand, feeling the fire in his nerves subsiding.

"What self-respecting assassin uses a Taser?"

"A shrewd one. She's first-rate, I'll give her that." Nolan went over and managed to help Red stand.

For a moment they both trembled, supported only by their clasped bodies, and stared into each other's eyes. They stood in the beam of the fallen flashlight and Nolan got a good view of her oval face, the long-lashed brown eyes shot with ginger-colored rings, the wide full mouth, brows that seemed to arch at the world, the fine mat of freckles on her nose and cheeks, the proud dimpled chin. Her hair was pulled back in a ponytail. He couldn't exhale for a moment with those amber eyes holding his.

"What's that?"

"What?"

"Shh, listen," she whispered.

Nolan heard the ticking now, and he knew the reason the creature had left them alive. "It's coming from Miranda's office."

"Run!" they both yelled at the same time.

Nolan grabbed her hand and thrust her through the stairwell door.

The concussion of the explosion picked up Nolan as if he were a grain of sand and blew him through the door. Blackness covered him and he let it take him.

Chapter 10

Lion's Head, Cape Town

Miranda pressed her back against the den wall. The dogs hadn't made a sound since she heard the window open in the atrium. Had they leaped out and chased away the intruder? Why weren't they barking?

How long had she been listening? It seemed like hours since she'd flattened her back to the wall. She hadn't moved save for the trembling in her body. In reality it had only been ten minutes or so. Her fingers tightened around the handle of the gun. She couldn't stay like this all night. She pried her body from the wall, arms first, then spine, legs and hips.

The wind knocked at the windows and doors, rattled panes, creaked timbers. Her senses attuned to every sound, she crept across the dark den. Shadows jumped out at her from every direction. A limb scraped the window and sounded like talons scratching crystal. The noise lashed through her and forced her to grit her teeth. She'd fire the gardener for not cutting down the palm as instructed last week. It was too close to the house. No vegetation within ten feet of the foundation. That was her security rule.

A glass breezeway separated the atrium from the house. She could smell the pool's chlorine and the mildewy dampness seeping from the atrium into the breezeway. Clouds had given way to the winter moon, a massive purple ball that reflected a blue glow over the breezeway's clear glass walls and ceiling. It was enough light for her to follow her shifting reflection in the glass. The plasticized face they'd made for her twenty years ago still felt foreign to her. It was like peering out at the world through a mask, her true self swimming and lost behind it.

She hesitated at the atrium entrance. Palms stood on either side. She glanced at the tiled walk around the pool, the chairs, the shadows treading along the pool's surface.

A noise to her right.

A man leaped out of the palm at her.

She raised the gun and fired.

Pincer Industries, Cape Town

It took Lucy a moment to clear the haze from her mind. She'd ended up on her belly in the stairwell landing, her right side pinned against the railing, her back and legs flattened by the Englishman. Darkness covered the stairwell, save for the emergency light near the door. An eerie hollow silence strummed the air.

Her cell phone rang and startled her. Nolan Taylor was deadweight on her legs and back. She managed to free her left arm, reach into her jean pocket and pull out the phone.

"Yeah?"

"You okay?" Betsy asked, worried. "I heard the explosion Was it our target?"

"Yeah, the office and any evidence that proves N'Buta is Arachne is history."

"Got a plan?"

"Yeah, we'll go to her residence and confront her."

"Think she'll talk?" Betsy asked.

"With a little prodding—listen, there's a killer loose in the building. She set the explosive. She's probably gone now, but be careful."

"Got it," Betsy said.

"Meet you at the car."

"Hurry, the cops will be here any minute."

"Got it."

Lucy snapped the phone closed, put it back in her pocke and scooted out from beneath Taylor. She bent over him. He'c pushed her out into the stairwell ahead of him. He'd saved her life. But why? Technically, she had saved his life when the Taser-Queen had held a knife to his throat. Why did she still feel guilty that he'd taken the brunt of the explosion for her? She felt his neck for a pulse.

A steady beat beneath his skin.

She let out the breath she'd been holding. At least he was alive Sirens shrieked in the distance.

Lucy dug around in the Englishman's pocket, found his wallet, a hotel keycard and a cell phone. She pocketed the items and as she did, she felt the foil chocolate bar wrappe that had fallen out in her room. Why had she kept it?

On an impulse, she touched Taylor's cheek, feeling the five o'clock shadow there, and said, "You'll be okay, now. They'l take you to the hospital."

After one more look at his limp figure, hoping he wasn't hurt too badly, she ran down the stairs.

Nolan's eyes fluttered open. His body hurt like hell. The world spun around him. What had the hellion said? Something about Arachne. He'd heard the name mentioned in the service, a legend, really. Arachne was thought to be the paranoid imaginings of intelligence communities across the globe, a phantom able to violate any stronghold, glean all information and use it for blackmail. He'd never believed such a person existed. The hellion was looking for Arachne? At Pincer? The image of Cummay's body and that of Giger Anfinson flashed. Was Miranda responsible for their deaths? Was she somehow involved with this legendary Arachne? It would explain some of the intrigue going on at Pincer. And what about the destruction of her office? Hadn't Red said she was going to Miranda's residence? He had a lot of questions that needed answering and, by damn, he'd get some answers.

He tried to sit up, but his head ached and his vision blurred. He slowly lowered his head to the floor. He remembered something else. The touch of Red's hand on his cheek. Had he imagined that? And...

He felt his pocket.

Empty.

She'd robbed him.

He rarely let his anger loose, but it stirred in his chest, boiling like bad military stew. He grabbed the railing and forced himself to sit up. His head exploded and whirled in all directions. "Bloody hell," he mumbled, then by sheer will he forced his legs into standing.

He'd get those answers, he promised himself as he stumbled down the stairs.

Adderley Street, Cape Town

A vintage Fiat Spyder zoomed down Adderley Street. The driver pulled off the ski mask and watched the barrage of police and rescue vehicles in her rearview mirror, the red lights throbbing across her eyes.

She smiled to herself as she looked at the computer tower she'd stolen from Miranda N'Buta's office. She picked up the cell phone as she whipped around a corner.

"Yes?" a deep gravelly female voice said.

"It's done. I destroyed the files."

"Good. And the Anfinson problem?"

"Done. There was some collateral."

"What kind?" An edge of irritation slipped into the voice.

"A guard, Nolan Taylor, and some woman."

"That is unfortunate. What about this woman?"

"Tall. Redhead. Cocky-ass mouth."

"Could be someone connected to the bank heist. I'll follow up that lead through locals."

"Is Miranda N'Buta history?"

"As far as I know, she's dead. The Cleaner hasn't checked in yet."

"What do you want me to do next?"

"Follow the trail of the documents. They could ruin me."

"I'm on it." She opened a laptop and hit a button. The GPS tracking signal was moving along Settler's Way, the road near the airport. She pulled out a cigarette from a pocket of her black bodysuit and lit it. Its tip glowed eerily in the darkness of the car.

Lion's Head, Cape Town

"I told you, I only got a brief look at the man," Miranda said, impatient to get the two detectives out of her house. A serviceman was working on the power box outside, too. It was like being invaded by ants.

She made a face at the police dusting the atrium door for prints, then leaned forward in the patio chair and petted Lani and Lailai, who stood on either side of her. The intruder had darted them with tranquilizers. She'd found them passed out near the atrium door, the darts still in their sides.

Captain Mumari's beak of a nose wrinkled, his pointed chin arced toward her. He seemed to sense her anxiety and said, "I'm so sorry about these questions, Miranda, but they are necessary."

At the familiar use of her first name, she bristled. She had donated large sums of money to the police force in Cape Town, for bulletproof vests and forensic equipment. It had won her influence and friends in high places and kept the police out of her business. Up until the security company had gone against her specific orders of no police, ever, when the system went down. Now she had this pretentious, insignificant police captain and his crew to get rid of. "How long will this take, Captain?" she asked.

"I assure you, not long." He smiled an elfin grin. "The man, what did he look like?"

"Tall. African. Slender."

"Had you seen him before? Maybe at Pincer?"

"No, never."

"Can you come to the station to give us a composite of his face?"

"I'd be glad to tomorrow." She emphasized the last word hoping he'd get the hint to cut this interview short.

"You say he ran after you discharged your firearm?"

"Yes, like I told you. I didn't make it easy for him. I shot him in the leg. You can see the trail of blood on the tile, Mr. Mumari." Miranda checked her temper.

The captain nodded. "Of course. Do you think this person was a burglar or rapist or…"

"Murderer," she supplied for him.

His thin brows slashed across his eyes in a frown. "Yes."

"I'm sure he meant to harm me, but how or why I don't know. I have a lot of valuable items in my home."

The power came on. Light flooded the atrium. The policeman reached over and turned off several battery-powered halogen lamps.

The captain's cell phone rang. "Excuse me." He snatched it off his belt holder. "Captain Mumari." He nodded, his brown eyes shifting to Miranda.

She began to feel uncomfortable at his straightforward stare.

"Yes, I'm on my way." He slapped the phone closed. "I hate to inform you, Miranda, but there has been an explosion at the Pincer building."

Miranda felt as if someone had grabbed her stomach and was slowly drawing it out through her belly button. "The whole building?" she asked.

"Half a floor." He shook his head. "I'm afraid your office was destroyed."

Miranda felt her face drain of blood and she had to lean back in her chair. The tapes. Gone? Her office bombed. An intruder in her home? What did it mean? Was the witch turning on her? She waved a trembling hand toward the two policemen dusting for fingerprints. "Please, direct all your manpower on my company and forget what happened here."

"Of course." He nodded to the two policemen. "Let's go."

Miranda watched them leave, her nails digging into the wooden side of the front door.

Lucy and Betsy turned onto Lion's Paw Road. Betsy drove, and Lucy glanced out the window. The sun was just starting to touch the dark horizon, leaving swipes of orange and purple and blue. The houses along the street were three, four, sometimes five stories high, embedded on the side of the mountain like pueblo adobes. The yards were landscaped in stair-step fashion. Horizontal rock walls zigzagged along the mountain like drunken lines of notebook paper. The drives that led up to the houses were almost at seventy-degree angles.

Lucy turned her attention back to Nolan Taylor's wallet. She jammed Betsy's flashlight up under her chin, while she searched it. Right away, she found four twenty-rand notes and two condoms—one double-protection ribbed, one green spearmint.

Irritation nagged her at the sight of them. She kept remembering his erection thick and hard against her. Jeez, why couldn't she forget that? "Doesn't that just figure," she said between her teeth.

"What?" Betsy asked.

"Nothing." Lucy chided herself for being annoyed. Why did she care if he kept condoms in his wallet? She took them out and jammed them in her pocket, then moved on to a zippered compartment.

"Hah, what have we here?" She pulled out an ID for England's Special Air Service. Lieutenant Nolan Montgomery Taylor.

She stared at the picture, the deep-set blue eyes, sharp cheekbones, strong chin, short brown hair. She recalled the way his bristly cheek had curved against her palm, the thready pulse in his neck. Guilt stabbed her. She had hated just leaving him there, but she'd had to go before the police arrived. They would have questioned her, may even have figured out she had done the bank job. Was he all right? She hoped so. She couldn't forget the way he'd pushed her through the doorway ahead of him. He didn't have to be so damn noble and smug.

"What'd you find on him?" Betsy asked.

Betsy's voice pulled Lucy back from her thoughts. She looked at the second ID she'd found, a Pincer security ID. "Says here he's chief of security."

"Kinda points to the fact Miranda N'Buta sent him after the docum—" Betsy's words died in her mouth as the sound of sirens came out of nowhere.

Lucy stiffened and instinctively reached for the .9mm strapped to her ankle. She'd lost her Colt in the explosion, thanks to that she-thing that had attacked her and Nolan.

"I see 'em," Betsy said. "Coming out of that drive up ahead."

"Here they come." Lucy inched up her pant leg.

"Not stopping. Not stopping. Going past."

They both let out a loud sigh.

Lucy narrowed her eyes at the gates of the white mansion the police had just left, then at the brass placard on the brick columns in front of the drive. "Hey, there's 102." She paused. The strongbox ID's flashing, the tracking device, the bombed office, the cops coming out of Miranda N'Buta's house. It all came together in a blinding moment of clarity as she said, "I hope we're not too late."

"What do you mean?" Betsy asked.

"I got a hunch, but I don't want to jinx it."

"How we going to do this? Over the wall?"

Lucy saw a power truck in the drive and said, "Looks like she's still got company. Let's go in like everyone else."

Betsy frowned over at Lucy as if she'd lost her mind. "What?"

"Just pull up to the gates. If we get an answer on the intercom, I'll do the talking." Lucy unlocked her seat belt and scooted over to Betsy's shoulder.

Betsy shook her head as if she didn't like the idea, but she gave in with a huge sigh and pulled the Jeep up to the closed gate. A spider monkey on the gate bared its teeth at them, then scampered off into the trees.

The structure's flat roof and two upper stories could be seen above the brick fence. It looked like any modern mansion straight from Mulholland Drive. Lights blazed in every window, making the whole house glow orange in the dawning light.

After a moment, a woman's harried voice said, "Yes."

Lucy leaned in front of Betsy and said, "I need to speak to Ms. N'Buta." She held her breath, hoping that this wasn't a servant.

"This is she," came back the curt reply.

Lucy let out her breath. "We need to talk."

"Who the devil is this?"

"We have the bank documents."

Betsy hit Lucy's arm and her eyes widened in disbelief. Lucy put her finger to her lips to silence her.

After a long pause, the voice said in a resigned snap, "You have ten minutes."

"Thank you."

The security gate clicked, then slowly ground open.

"How do you know she won't call the police?" Betsy asked, creeping the Jeep up the hedged steep drive.

Lucy scooted back over to the passenger side. "Those documents in the safety deposit box could do a lot of damage to her reputation, not to mention her company. The microdots alone could get her convicted of blackmail and extortion. I'm betting she'll do anything to get them back."

"I hope you're right for both our behinds."

Lucy's heart sped up at the anticipation as they parked in front of a circular fountain. A marble gargoyle spit water from its mouth into the pool. A tiny shiver went through Lucy as she stared straight into the gargoyle's open mouth at his pointed tongue.

Chapter 11

Nolan pulled the Volvo over and watched the hellion and her friend standing at the door. His head throbbed as he kept them in sight. He'd give his right leg for a bottle of Tylenol right now. He didn't dare stop at a chemist's shop. He'd heard Red say she was coming here and he knew he couldn't waste time. Why would she approach Miranda? To blackmail her? What had Red been doing at Pincer, before the bomb went off? Looking for information? Had his attacker been looking for information, too, or had she been sent there to destroy the office and its contents? Who were both of them working for? What had been in the office that Red and the assassin wanted? Too many questions. He felt as if he were drowning in the middle of them. He was certain the CEO of Pincer was into something illegal. But what?

He decided to be patient and find out as he eased out of his car and kept low, crouching along the fence. He peeked over it and up the steep yard. Two workers from the electrical company hopped in their van and drove around the fountain and down the drive. He pretended to walk past the house as they sped away.

He heard the front door open and peered over the fence. Ms. N'Buta greeted Red and her friend as if she knew them.

Nolan waited until they were inside, then hopped the brick wall. When he landed, his head ached more. A vervet monkey screamed at him from a banana tree. The little beast scampered higher to take cover in the broad leaves, all the while berating Nolan for frightening him. Nolan gave the primate a look that said he had just as much right to be in the yard, then he crept past the tree.

Keeping low, he followed the landscaping walls until he reached the house. He looked in several windows, and finally found Red, her friend and Miranda. The dogs had a steady bead on Miranda's visitors. He didn't dare try the window or the dogs would be all over him. Miranda and Red seemed to be talking amicably. About what? Ms. N'Buta didn't look to be in danger. In fact, her body language suggested she had the upper hand. He decided to wait and see what transpired.

Lucy felt the hot breath of the Dobermans burning through her jeans as she stood in the sitting room. Sleek modern furniture sat in strategically appointed places to dispel clutter. In fact, the furniture looked nailed to the floor. The gray and white walls made the room feel institutional. It seemed bloodless and colorless and void of warmth, similar to the woman standing before her.

Miranda N'Buta wore all white. Her large overshirt covered tight stretch pants. Her dark hair straggled around a face that lacked makeup, as if she'd been woken from sleep. A pair of black reading glasses rested on top of her head. Her only adornment was a heavy gold charm bracelet that clicked in the suffocating silence.

Without taking her eyes from the dogs, Betsy leaned over and whispered to Lucy, "Look at that glint in their eyes. They want to eat me up."

The dogs growled at her movement.

"Shh, they can hear you." Lucy grinned at Betsy, but she only glowered back at Lucy.

Miranda said, "They'll only rip your throat out if I order them to."

"Thanks for that tidbit." Betsy eyed the dog near her side and made it growl.

"Forgive me for not offering you a seat. It's been a long night." She crossed arms over her chest and tried to look down her nose. But it wasn't working with Lucy, since she was eight inches taller than the woman.

"What exactly happened to you tonight?" Lucy asked.

Miranda lifted her chin to an overconfident angle. "That's none of your business."

Lucy shrugged. "It'd be easy enough to find out."

Miranda eyed Lucy for thirty seconds, her eyes calculating if she could trust Lucy or not. Finally she said, "Well, if you must know, an intruder broke into my house and I shot him." Her eyes narrowed on Lucy and Betsy, a silent warning.

Lucy thought for a moment, then said, "That must have happened at the same time your office was bombed—"

"How do you know about my office? Did you destroy it?" Miranda's eyes blazed at Lucy.

"No, I interrupted the person who rigged your office with a bomb. Is someone out to get rid of you?"

"Why would they?"

"You tell me."

"I have nothing to say to you."

"The documents we have are enough to convict you for a long time—if the police should find them."

Miranda straightened her spine and threw back her shoulders. "You *are* blackmailing me."

"We just want the truth. Are you Arachne?" She saw Miranda's eyes widen the slightest bit at Arachne's name as if she were trying to hide her surprise.

Miranda's expression shifted back to calculating. "No one would willingly admit to that."

Lucy nodded to Betsy, avoiding any sudden movements that might put the Fido killers into attack mode. "Let's go. We're wasting our time here." She had a feeling that Arachne would never have let them this close. Also, she caught glimpses of masked desperation and fear in this woman's face that seemed all too real and vulnerable.

They turned to leave.

"Wait!"

Lucy paused. "The truth or we walk."

"First, I must have an assurance you won't take those documents to the police."

"I give you my word."

"That's not good enough."

"Okay, if you're not Arachne and you help us bring her down, then we'll see that you stay alive and get safely out of the country."

"Who do you work for?"

"I can't tell you that. You'll have to trust me. It doesn't look like you have too many other options."

Miranda stared at Lucy as if assessing her character. Her mouth hardened as she made a decision, then she said, "All right. I'm not that witch. Now what is in those documents?"

"First you answer my questions." Lucy looked hard at Miranda. "Honestly."

Miranda glared up at Lucy for a beat, then nodded as if her head had rusted to her neck.

"Did you send Nolan Taylor after the documents?"

"No."

"Did you know about the GPS device?"

"I didn't even know the account existed in my name."

Lucy shared a knowing glance with Betsy. "You don't run Pincer alone, do you?"

"It's my company." Her face remained white marble, while her voice burned with rancor.

"But you don't run it. Arachne calls the shots, doesn't she?"

Miranda's Adam's apple worked in her thin throat as if she were choking. "That witch thinks she's in charge! I'm the one who nursed it along for twenty years. I bought the gold mine and diamond mine and expanded Pincer into the telecommunications business. I put my whole soul into running it. Without me it would be nothing. Nothing, I tell you."

"How did you get involved with her?"

Miranda began to pace. "I answered an ad in an L.A. newspaper, of all things."

"For what?"

"The ad said a playwright in New York was looking for competent female actresses. So I sent in my photo and answered the ad. Acting had been a dream of mine." Her eyes blinked closed for a second as if some painful memory surfaced. "I lived in L.A. for eight years trying to establish a career."

"L.A. is not a cheap place to live," Betsy said.

"How well I learned that. I worked two waitressing jobs and still ended up owing loan sharks two hundred thousand dollars. They threatened to kill me if I didn't pay them. One of them worked me over so badly I ended up in an emergency room with a broken wrist."

"You must have been glad to get out of L.A."

"At first. Then when I found out this woman would only communicate with me through phone conversations, I knew something wasn't aboveboard. She finally confessed that she wasn't a playwright and was interested in finding someone willing to undergo plastic surgery and assume a new identity. I had second thoughts."

"Why did you agree to it?"

"I saw the loan sharks lurking in the lobby of my New York hotel and I was desperate to get away. Later, I wondered if she had tipped them off to blackmail me into the surgery."

"So you called her back?" Lucy said.

Miranda nodded. "Odd thing is, I've never seen her face."

"Not ever?" Lucy frowned.

"No."

"That means you can't identify her."

"Correct. She's made certain of that. I imagine so I could never testify against her."

"Clever woman," Lucy said, her voice flat.

"Yes, well, she's proven that." Miranda pursed her lips in a sour look.

"What was your real name when you lived in L.A.?"

"Jan Strafford."

"She had you change your name to Miranda N'Buta?"

"She wired me a lot of money to undergo plastic surgery and change my name. Then she sent me here to assume my role at Pincer. She had just opened the company in some tiny office downtown. I'm the one who grew the company, made it into what it is today. I gave it everything, gave *her* everything…"

Lucy thought a moment, then said, "And now she wants to kill you."

Fear swam in Miranda's eyes as she glanced up at Lucy. "I don't understand why. What's in those documents?"

"Different identities in countries all over the globe. They

all had your picture on them. I don't think you're the only decoy. We found at least twenty different names in the documents with different addresses. And I bet all those women have had the same plastic surgery." Lucy looked at Miranda. Was she looking at Arachne's face? "She set you up, along with the other women. It's brilliant, if you think about it. If she ever needs to disappear, all she has to do is pick one of the twenty women living all over the globe, murder her, then assume her identity—"

Miranda had turned whiter when Lucy mentioned the "M" word. She swallowed hard and said, "Why turn on me now?"

"We've been tracking her for months. She's bound to know about the bank job and knows we're close to finding her. She's covering her tracks by taking you out of the picture."

"She wouldn't dare." Miranda wrung her hands, then collapsed on the sofa.

"She destroyed your office." Lucy gestured to the room, warming to the subject. "My bet is, your intruder tonight was a contract killer."

Miranda hung her head and shook it in self-pity and doubt. "What am I going to do?"

"Get out from under Arachne's radar."

Miranda raised her face, her expression growing calculating again. "Who do you work for?"

"Someone who wants Arachne destroyed."

"No authorities will be involved?"

"You have my word, if you tell us all you know."

"I'll do one better than that, I'll give you the underbelly of her empire here in South Africa."

"You can tell us on the way to the airport." Lucy thought of the killer she'd battled at Pincer. "It's not safe here."

"Fine, I'll get my things."

"Hurry."

Lucy knew getting Miranda out of the country wouldn't be easy. Her body still ached from having fought that she-thing at Pincer. Lucy couldn't figure out how the woman deflected bullets. Or how she was involved with Miranda or Arachne. One thing was certain—she had to get Miranda out of the country, and soon.

Nolan peeked around a corner of the house and watched them leave. Ms. N'Buta was going with them willingly. She had two suitcases; the hellion struggled to get them in the Jeep. The dogs had paused near the door, waiting for a command.

"What about the dogs?" the hellion asked. "You can't just leave them unattended."

"I'm leaving them here. My gardener has always wanted them. I called him and they'll be taken care of."

One of the dogs caught Nolan's scent. The Doberman raised his nose high, then started growling and walking toward him. The second dog followed. He ducked back behind the house when he heard a whistle.

Then Miranda's voice saying, "Dogs, come."

At the snapped order, the dogs stopped and turned. "Inside, you two," Miranda ordered. Then the front door slammed.

Nolan let out the breath he'd been holding. He stayed hidden as the doors closed on the Jeep and it sped away. He decided to see what they were up to rather than confront them just yet. He ran to his car to give chase. He didn't see the head-lights following him until it was too late.

Chapter 12

Lucy watched Betsy shift in the seat beside her, gripping the Jeep's steering wheel, and snapping yet another glance out the rearview mirror. Lucy was catching Betsy's edginess. Since they'd left Miranda's home, Lucy had felt as if eyes were on her. Betsy must be getting the same vibe. Another five miles, and they'd reach the airport and meet Tommy and Cao. It couldn't come soon enough.

Lucy glanced along both lanes of the N2. A few lonely trucks and cars moved along the highway, their headlights meeting the waking sunlight. It was close to 5:00 a.m., and the sun was burning swatches of blue and yellow and fluorescent orange behind the stretch of mountains east of them.

Miranda sat in the Jeep's backseat, squashed between her two suitcases.

Miranda had been quiet a moment, but now she spoke over the road noise. "Besides the gold and diamond mines, Arachne traffics in people."

"How so?" Lucy asked, making sure the cell phone was above the backseat so Delphi could hear and see Miranda. They had interviewed her for the past twenty minutes. She'd given them the location of a gold mine in the Drakensberg Mountains and a diamond mine near Kimberly. The information wouldn't lead directly to Arachne, but it could prove the downfall of her African empire.

"Slavery, child prostitution, forced labor, selling of body parts."

"No way," Betsy said, incredulous.

Lucy swallowed hard at the cold reality in this part of the world and said, "It's true. The sale of body parts to witch doctors for traditional medicine is an export in this part of the world. They also mistakenly believe having sex with a virgin cures AIDS, and that's why there is so much child prostitution and rapes. My mother has been trying to educate the people about this for years and she fights for children's rights."

"The rest of the world knows this is happening?" Betsy asked.

"The U.S. State Department is aware of it. They have a Human Rights Practices report on Zimbabwe that contains thirty-nine pages of missing persons, murders, abductions, beatings, torture, rape, home invasions."

"Unfortunately, these events are commonplace," Miranda said. "The uprising of lawless regimes and unrest in Zimbabwe and many other areas of Africa have people struggling for survival. They've been relocated to camps where they starve to death or die of AIDS or are sold into prostitution by their captors. Infanticide exists because mothers can't feed their children and rather than see them starve to death, they let them die. Some sell one child into prostitution to feed the rest of their children. Arachne buys these children to work the mines."

"How despicable," Betsy said.

Lucy thought of the children and her hand tightened around the cell phone until the tendons in her knuckles turned white. "How many work in these mines?"

Miranda nodded. "Four hundred or so."

Delphi chimed in. "Where do they live?"

"In houses near the mines."

Lucy could imagine the type of living conditions these children were forced to endure. Righteous indignation gripped her chest, and she wanted more than ever to destroy Arachne and the tainted empire she ruled. Lucy stared hard at Arachne's accomplice, Miranda N'Buta. She seemed uneasy beneath Lucy's gaze and wrung her hands in her lap.

Delphi's electronically altered voice chimed in, "How does Arachne move the gold?"

"Railroad. Pincer owns Matope Railworks. It runs from Zimbabwe, through the Eastern Cape, and ends at Cape Town's shipyard." Miranda put her hands in her lap, the sound of her charm bracelet irritating in the small space of the Jeep.

Delphi asked, "You knew all of this and let it continue?"

Miranda lowered her head and sighed. "I know it was wrong. When I first learned of it, I was sickened. I even questioned the witch about it, but she was adamant that Pincer wouldn't make the kind of profit she insisted upon without these business practices. I turned a blind eye to it because Pincer was doing so well."

Lucy said, "Couldn't see the poison oak for the lilies."

Miranda looked at Lucy through her lashes, then bobbed her head. "I hope God can forgive me for my sins."

Lucy looked at Miranda N'Buta with a jaundiced eye. The whole remorseful performance seemed staged for Delphi.

Lucy didn't believe Miranda cared about anything beyond her own self-interest, and Arachne had to have sensed that when she interviewed Miranda all those years ago. Lucy hoped Delphi could see through this act. She hated that she'd promised not to hand Miranda over to the authorities in order to find out what she knew. In the end the information would save countless lives, and Lucy knew she'd done the right thing. Still, the tradeoff came at a high price.

Delphi hesitated a moment, then said, "If Pincer's practices come to light, Arachne will find a way to solely blame you."

"I know. And I had electronic videos on my hard drive of her threatening to kill me if I didn't follow her orders. They could have exonerated me, but she destroyed them."

"Have you recounted all you know?" Delphi asked.

"Everything."

Delphi said, "I'll speak privately to Lucy now."

Lucy put the phone to her ear. "Yes."

"Lucy, good job on getting to Miranda before Arachne. The mines she mentioned check out on South Africa's geological survey map. She's given us invaluable information and a good way to begin to bring down Arachne's empire," Delphi said, cold calculation in the metallic voice.

"How's that?"

"We're going to hit Arachne's finances. Take out all of it, including the railroad."

"That will be a pleasure." Lucy smiled inwardly at the prospect of meting out a bit of Athena Force justice.

"We need to hit hard and fast before she suspects what we are up to."

"Right."

"And be careful."

"We will."

There was a moment of weighted silence between them,

where Delphi seemed to read Lucy's mind. "Once it's known Miranda worked for Arachne, she'll be hard-pressed to find sanctuary in any country."

"Good." Lucy eyed one of the gold slippers on Miranda's bracelet.

As soon as Lucy closed the phone, Betsy said, "There's a Volvo that's been following us for a stretch." Her eyes were glued on the rearview mirror.

Lucy glanced behind them and pulled her gun from the ankle holster.

Nolan kept his gaze on the Jeep's taillights and on the sedan that had followed him since he'd left Miranda N'Buta's home. He had a good idea where she was heading now. The airport.

Questions plagued him and made his head hurt. Top of the list: was Ms. N'Buta somehow involved with Red? Had Miranda known where the bank documents were the whole time and used him? Had she bombed her own office and almost killed him? And what did she hope to gain by it all? The more he thought about being used, the more he could feel his anger brewing. Someone owed him some answers and he wouldn't mind taking a pound of flesh from Red.

He opened his computer to check on the GPS tracking device and he couldn't find the Web site on the Internet. It was as if it had disappeared or had never existed. He slammed the computer shut, gritting his teeth in frustration.

The Jeep began to speed up.

Had they made him?

He pushed down on the accelerator…seventy, seventy-five. The sedan stayed with him. For a moment all three vehicles sped down the highway, one chasing the other.

The Jeep zipped into the airport exit.

Nolan pulled into the exit lane.

He glimpsed the sedan's license plate with the name Cleaner on it, and a man's silhouette at the wheel. The sedan sped up and came abreast of him. The man lifted a pistol.

Nolan ducked.

Gunshots blasted the air.

Chunks of security glass rained down on Nolan's neck and chest as he held the wheel straight and braked.

The driver of the sedan shot past him, and Nolan popped up.

The sedan barreled toward the Jeep. Wheels screeched as the sedan took the sharp off-ramp curve. The driver stuck his hand out the window and fired at the Jeep, the end of the muzzle blazing red in the darkness.

The shot blasted a hole in the Jeep's rear window. The Jeep swerved, almost hitting the guard rail, then corrected.

The redhead stuck her arm out the window and fired at the sedan.

Nolan floored it.

The sedan was in mid-circle, hugging the pavement, when Nolan hit the sedan's rear bumper. The impact was at the right angle to send the sedan careening over the exit ramp.

It sailed, airborne, for a few seconds before it flipped and crashed to the ground.

Nolan saw Red turn in her seat, watching him, and he stuck his head out the window and saluted her.

"Damn, it's Taylor," Lucy said, the relief at seeing him at odds with the irritation in her voice. "He's okay. He should be in a hospital."

"Can't keep a big man down," Betsy said wryly.

"Why's he following us?" Miranda sat up in the backseat.

Betsy grinned at the rearview mirror. "Probably to get his wallet back."

"Stay down." Lucy pushed Miranda's head back down.

"I caught a glimpse of the man driving that sedan," Miranda said to her knees. "I'm certain he's the same man who came to my house and tried to kill me."

"We don't have to worry about him now." Lucy glanced at the Volvo. It stayed close on their bumper. "We got bigger fish to fry."

Betsy sized up Lucy for a moment. "You were worried about leaving Taylor at Pincer, weren't you?"

"No." Lucy frowned at Nolan behind them. That little smug salute still gnawed at her.

"Can't say that he isn't welcome at the moment," Betsy said. "He saved us some trouble. And damn, that boy can drive. He's right on our taillights."

"I don't trust him," Miranda said.

"Why?" Lucy asked.

"For one thing, Arachne hired him. For another, he appears straightforward and honest, but there's a price on his head. He came to Cape Town to hide out. And he had a run-in with one of my employees, and I haven't seen my employee since."

Why were hit men after Nolan Taylor? So he really was working for Arachne? But why had he tried to save her life when the bomb had exploded? Bad guys didn't do that unless they had something to gain. And he hadn't known at the time if they'd survive the explosion. And why had he run the shooter off the road? Bad guys were supposed to stay in character. She didn't like it when they wore white and developed a conscience. Where Taylor was concerned, she didn't know what to believe. She was leaning more and more toward Miranda's opinion of him.

Lucy thought of the two dead men she'd glimpsed in the hallway outside of Miranda's office and said, "What'd your employee look like?"

"A large blond Norwegian."

"He's dead. I think the woman who set the bomb in your office killed him and left the body there to dispose of it in the explosion, along with a security guard." Lucy might have suspected Taylor, but the killer had threatened him, too. So if Taylor was working for Arachne, who was the killer working for? None of it added up.

"I'm sorry to hear it," Miranda said. "Anfinson was the best bodyguard I'd ever had."

There wasn't an ounce of feeling in Miranda's voice, and Lucy wasn't surprised. She had a feeling Anfinson was more than Miranda's bodyguard. A hired gun? She wanted to be done with Miranda N'Buta as much as she wanted to be rid of Taylor.

It took only a few moments and several signs to reach the private hangars. They pulled into hangar number three. There was only one other corporate jet parked several bays over. Tommy and Cao stood near Tommy's Cessna 406 Caravan II, a twin-engine cargo plane that could seat twelve passengers. It was Tommy's pride and joy. He was doing the preflight check, while Cao stored the team's luggage from the safe house in the airplane. Tommy and Cao stiffened when they saw the Volvo pull in behind the Jeep.

Tommy wore a pair of sunglasses, but they didn't cover the blue and purple areas below his eyes and his swollen nose. When it registered on his face who was in the Volvo, he dropped the coffee cup in his hand and ran toward Taylor's car.

"We're looking at a perfect example of male stupidity," Betsy said, eyeing Tommy as he fought to open Taylor's door.

"Tell me about it." Lucy leaped out of the car.

Cao had been watching Tommy, too, and he jumped in

front of him and shoved him back. Tommy came across with a right. Cao easily dodged it and said, "Hey, cool it."

"Stay out of my way," Tommy growled.

Lucy jumped into the fray and grabbed Tommy from behind and caught his arms. "Tommy, not now."

Tommy's body strained toward the Volvo. "I'm gonna rearrange that sombitch's face. I've never had my nose broken. He's gonna pay." Tommy struggled to get free, but Lucy had his arms so tight they would come out of the sockets if he moved. And Cao was trying to block his view of Taylor. Tommy strained to glance past Cao at the Volvo.

Nolan stepped out of the car, his massive frame dwarfing the space around him. Lucy was certain Tommy wouldn't have a chance against Taylor, even though Taylor didn't look so good. His face was as pale as the Cessna's white paint job. His black jogging pants were burned in spots and torn up to his knees. The wind whipped at the ragged and singed sides and back of his jacket. Even in his current state of dishevelment, he looked good. Hunk material. Lucy couldn't believe that thought had popped into her head.

Tommy glared at Taylor and said, "Me and you, chump. Right now."

Betsy walked up to Taylor. "Gotta frisk you for weapons."

"Jolly good, have a go." He held up both his arms.

"You Brits are so accommodating."

"We try."

As Lucy watched Betsy's hands moving over Taylor's body, a touch of envy made her chew on her lower lip. She noticed she wasn't the only person watching them. Cao's expression was warring with Tommy's to see who could glare at Taylor the best.

"We meet again, love," Taylor said to Lucy while Betsy frisked him.

"Unfortunately," Lucy said, yanking on Tommy so he would be still. She might have yanked a little too hard, for Tommy grunted in pain.

"Is that any way to thank me for helping you?" Taylor rolled his broad shoulders.

"I didn't ask for your help."

Betsy stood, grinning with innate pleasure. "He's clean."

Taylor said, "I could have told you that."

"Where would the fun be in that?" Betsy threw back at him. Her hips swayed more than usual as she strode over to get Miranda's luggage out of the back of the Jeep.

"I'll show him fun," Tommy growled.

Taylor turned his attention back to Tommy. A self-satisfied expression molded his face as he held out his hand. "No hard feelings, old chap."

"Hard feelings! I'm gonna kick your ass back to England, that's what I'm going to do for you."

Lucy could understand Tommy's anger. Taylor had an air of superiority about him that could rile even an easygoing man. "Take a walk, Taylor," she said.

After a glance in her direction, Taylor said, "Very well." He strode over to Betsy and Miranda N'Buta.

Lucy leaned near Tommy's ear and said, "Tommy, one of Arachne's people just tried to kill Miranda. We don't have time for this. You can get even some other time. Right now, I'm counting on you to get her to Cairo."

Cao helped calm Tommy by saying, "Think what you are doing."

Tommy stilled, his heavy breaths drowned out by a 727 taking off. He seemed to come to his senses. "Let me go. I'm all right."

Lucy reluctantly dropped the hold on Tommy's arms, watching him closely.

Tommy straightened his flight jacket, adjusted his sunglasses that listed on his face. "Is she gonna give me trouble?"

"I don't think so," Lucy said. "She willingly came with us and she's eager to get out of the country."

"Fine." He prowled over to the Cessna. Before he crawled into the cockpit, he raised a finger at Taylor and yelled, "Later, man, your ass is mine."

Taylor saluted him, the blue ice in his eyes gleaming. He didn't look at all frightened, only amused.

Lucy forced her gaze back to Cao. "Before you left the safe house, did you get our gear and the explosives?"

He nodded toward the van. "Enough to blow up half of Africa, and I finished e-mailing the information in the microdots." Amusement gleamed in Cao's dark eyes. "I mailed the GPS to Hong Kong. We stopped at the Day Air office in the airport. It's probably on a cargo plane by now."

"That should give Arachne something to do."

Cao glanced past Lucy's shoulder at Taylor as he helped Betsy, who was struggling with the bags. Miranda was already climbing into a passenger seat in the Cessna.

Lucy and Cao both watched Taylor pick up the two heavy suitcases and carry them as if they weighed nothing.

"Look at him," Cao said. "He is trying to impress her."

Taylor might be the impetus that would finally push Cao over the edge in Betsy's direction. The devious romantic in Lucy said, "Looks like it's working."

Lucy watched Taylor murmuring low to Betsy as he stuffed the bags in the Cessna's cargo hold. Betsy's grin ran from ear to ear, clearly under Taylor's spell. Beneath those pastel blue eyes was a quiet intensity and cleverness that could fascinate any woman. And looking pale as he did, his white skin stark against the brown five o'clock shadow on his face, he looked too handsome. He could become a distraction, even to Lucy, one she didn't need on this mission. The sooner he was out of her hair, the better.

As if pulled by his anger, Cao strode up to them and stepped between them. "I'll do this," he said, scowling at Taylor, then Betsy.

Betsy jabbed her arms over her chest. "What makes you think I need your help?"

"He wasn't doing it properly," Cao fired back.

"So you know everything there is about cargo holds and suitcases now…"

While they argued, Taylor shot Lucy a knowing glance as if he understood the attraction between Cao and Betsy and the part he had just played in it. He walked toward Lucy, not taking his gaze from her.

His innate ability to read human nature irritated her. It seemed to be an amusing pastime for him, a game at which he excelled.

When he paused in front of her, he said, "I'd like some answers now."

Chapter 13

Cape Town International Airport

"All right, I guess you've got some coming."

"First, I want my wallet and identification cards back."

Lucy reached in her sweatshirt pocket and pulled out his things. She slapped them in his hands. His skin felt unusually warm, and she jerked her hand back. "I was going to give them to you."

"Really? Before you left me for dead or after?" He stuffed them in what was left of his jacket pocket.

"Unfair. Give me a little credit. I didn't let that killer cut your throat. And I didn't leave until I heard the cops. I knew they'd call an ambulance for you."

"You're just Mother Teresa in jeans." His gaze dropped, slowly inching down her body.

Lucy blushed down to the roots of her hair. She remembered the feel of his body against hers. A disconcerting awareness of him stirred warm in her belly.

"That schoolgirl blush is rather adorable on you, love."

"Forget the blush. I don't blush. I've never blushed in my life." Lucy cursed her fair skin and quickly changed topics. "How about we talk about what you were doing at Pincer before the bomb exploded?"

"One of the security guards called me about a break-in. I'm chief of security there. You should bloody well know that since you have my ID. Why were *you* there?"

"I was looking for information."

"Sure you weren't there to lift a few more wallets for your collection?" he asked, his voice heavy with derision.

"Look who's talking. I didn't break into *your* room."

"No, lending institutions are your specialty. Bank robber. Pickpocket. What other talents do you possess?" His gaze dropped to her breasts.

"You'll never know." She looked him up and down as he had her, then smiled.

"I'm quite disappointed." An infuriating grin twitched the sides of his mouth.

She wanted this conversation over, so she turned the topic back to Arachne. "When you were ordered to retrieve the bank documents, how were you contacted?" she asked.

"E-mail. Why?"

"Because you're taking orders directly from a woman who blackmails governments and deals in slavery."

"Bollocks! I took orders from Ms. N'Buta, who hired me."

"No, Arachne hired you."

"Arachne?" His handsome features shifted in surprise, then disbelief. "There is no Arachne. She's a myth, an intelligence community legend."

Lucy surveyed him warily. If he was acting, he was doing a good job of it. "Miranda knew nothing about the strongbox. It's Arachne's. She runs Pincer through Miranda. Arachne is the one who contacted you." His brow furrowed in disbelief and Lucy said, "Don't believe me? Ask Miranda. She's been her pawn for the past twenty years."

He looked confused as he said, "So it was Arachne who gave me the GPS Web site to track you down?"

"Yes. We found the device, by the way," Lucy added with sarcasm.

"Did you?" One corner of his mouth curved sardonically.

"Didn't take long." Lucy shot back a tight smile. "You still weren't communicating with Miranda."

He straightened his wide shoulders, his chest seeming to enlarge before Lucy's eyes. Then his brown brows snapped together as something dawned on him. "Wait one moment." In three long steps, he reached the cockpit.

Lucy followed him, checking out his butt. Not bad.

He stuck his head inside and spoke to Miranda. "So Arachne's the one behind the webcam in your office? And all the security?"

"Yes."

The gleam in Taylor's eyes turned sharp and he seemed deep in thought. She was beginning to wonder if he was just a pawn in Arachne's game.

Lucy said, "I'd like your computer. Maybe we can trace the e-mail site."

"Tell me who you and your lot are working for and I might consider giving it to you."

"We hire out our services."

"Mercenaries?"

Lucy nodded. "And I can't tell you who employed us."

"Someone who wants Arachne brought to justice?"

"Kinda like that."

His eyes probed her face for a long moment, then he said, "I'll give you my computer if you let me join you."

"You're kidding, right?" She made a move to step around him.

He blocked her way, a solid lump of man. "I'm dead serious. I won't be dealt out of this game." Genuine anger flashed in his expression. "Arachne has a lot to answer for—"

"Everyone wants a piece of her. You'll have to move to the end of the line."

Their eyes clashed again, the resolve in his handsome face coming out in the steely set of his jaw, the tight line of his lips, a pulse throbbing at the base of his neck. An air of danger oozed from him, and Lucy decided he might become more of a problem than she had anticipated.

She narrowed her eyes at him. "One thing you haven't answered is why Arachne hired you in the first place."

Miranda poked her head out of the plane and said, "I can tell you that. I believe she was testing Giger Anfinson's loyalty to see how far she could push him before it broke. She used to do that to me, too." Miranda's eyes gleamed with painful memories and she swallowed hard. "She also told me that Mr. Taylor was desperate for money and a place to lie low. She all but insinuated that she could use him as she had used Giger Anfinson."

Lucy jammed her hands on her hips. "Why are you so desperate?"

"Because I'm not filthy rich, and certain terrorist factions want me dead."

She searched his eyes for a lie, but they looked open and honest and way too unnerving. "I'm sorry to hear it, but that's not my problem," she said.

"Then you won't include me?"

"Not on your life."

"You'll find I won't be dismissed so easily." His voice softened, but a sharp edge punctuated each word.

Lucy stared up into his face—more like his neck. He was the first man tall enough to tower over her. It annoyed her that she had to look up at him. His very presence put her whole body on edge. "I don't deal well with threats. I blow them up."

He stared at her for a moment as if he could see inside her mind. "You really are easily baited."

She couldn't believe she had let him goad her. The more she was around him, the more he reminded her of her father— exacting, overbearing, a manipulative, English pain in the ass. She smiled through clenched teeth and said, "Stay out of my way, or you'll regret it."

Betsy had walked up to them. "Lucy, Tommy won't be back for at least two days. We're going to be down by one. We could use his help." She slowly perused Taylor's body, boldly implying the help she wanted wasn't all work related.

"Not from him," Lucy said, another pang of jealousy shooting through her.

"He did save your life when the bomb went off and both our lives back there on the highway. And he's willing to give us the computer. If he steps out of line we can always get rid of him. Like that." Betsy snapped her fingers.

Lucy shot Betsy a look for arguing Taylor's case. "We don't know him from Adam."

"I'm ex-SAS. I can keep up with the best of you." Taylor's voice lacked its usual mocking tone, as if he were just stating a fact. His eyes took on a sly glint as he said, "And I downloaded information from a PDA that you might find useful."

"What kind of information?"

"It came from Giger Anfinson. He must have been working for Ms. N'Buta and Arachne."

"Where's this information?"

"On my computer."

Lucy looked hard at him. "Where's your computer?"

A sardonic grin twitched one corner of his mouth. "Tell me I'm on board, and it's yours."

Lucy clung to the last threads of her patience. "Then we don't have a deal."

"I'm sorry to hear it," he said with cold English politeness.

Cao threw the bags into the cargo hold, closed it and looked at Betsy. His face screwed up as if he didn't like what he was about to say. "Betsy's right. We could use his help."

Lucy sized up Nolan Taylor. It galled her that he'd tried to bribe her, but he had enough resentment for Arachne that he might be of help to them. She knew he was telling the truth about his wealth, and it could be possible there was a price on his head. But could she trust him with the team members' lives? Talk about an emotional chameleon. His expressions changed like television commercials, moment by moment, and she found it hard to read him. But he somehow read her, knew exactly what to say to push her buttons. Totally unfair. But Betsy and Cao were right. They could use his help and she wanted that computer.

It galled her but she said, "We'll see."

She pulled out her phone to call Delphi. She hoped Delphi was against bringing Taylor in on the mission. When she saw Taylor watching her, she turned and walked around to the back of the hangar, feeling his probing gaze on her back.

Fifteen thousand feet over the Indian Ocean

Jamesi Titoto sipped coffee from a travel mug and looked at the gauges in the Basler BT-67 cockpit. He'd just taken off from Cape Town International Airport. The twin-engine cargo was tracked on course for Hong Kong, the autopilot doing all the work. He liked flying this route from Cape Town. Twelve hours up and back, if he had a tailwind. Three days a week. Working for Day Air, flying cargo and mail, he made enough salary to maintain a beach house in Rockland's Bay and have only two roommates. They were pilots, too, for Day Air.

Jamesi thought of his fiancée. Beautiful, sweet, celibate Hane. Hane who drove him crazy when he was near her and in his dreams and refused to sleep with him until their wedding night. God, would he last another month until they married?

A strange feeling prickled along Jamesi's neck, as if he were not alone on the plane, though he knew it was just his nerves. Probably from not having real sex, just two-minute trysts with the soap in the shower. That could drive a man nuts. He shifted in his seat. The feeling grew acute, as if he could feel someone behind him, hear his breath. He jerked around.

A woman with short blond hair, tanned skin and the cruelest green eyes he'd ever seen attacked him from behind. She chopped him in the throat. Pain seared his neck. He gasped for breath.

She struck with adder reflexes, grabbing his wrists and securing them with handcuffs. He hadn't even had time to put up a struggle.

"Play nice," she purred, "or you die. Don't move." She wagged a finger at him, then sat in the co-pilot seat.

He noticed she wore black leather pants, matching vest and white shirt that opened in a wide V down to her waist.

She seemed to feel his eyes on her and smiled over at him. "Like what you see?" The smile was that of a black widow, watching her next victim.

Before she decided to strike his throat again, he shifted his gaze to the package in her hands. She must have stowed away in the cargo hold and searched for the package in the mail bags. It had a Hong Kong address.

She ran a handheld scanner over the package and it beeped

loudly. She grinned, then opened the box with quick methodical yanks. When she had the brown shipping paper off and opened the lid, an electronic board fell out into her lap. She seemed to be looking for something else. She screamed in frustration when she found nothing.

The sound cut through Jamesi like a knife and he flinched. He also knew it wouldn't take much to piss her off.

She threw the box on the floor, grabbed her cell phone and hit a speed dial number. "The bank documents are not here, only the GPS transmitter. We've been played."

There was a long pause, then she said, "Have you heard from the Cleaner?" A beat. "In the hospital. Are you sure Miranda N'Buta escaped? It's not my fault you sent me on this fool's errand, it could have turned out differently. I can't work with this faulty intel. I'm out of the picture. This is your problem now, deal with it." Her face screwed up in an ugly mask.

He heard a raspy female screaming through the phone that she'd have the woman killed if she left the job unfinished. This only amused the blonde, and she smirked at the phone before she slapped it closed and stuffed it in her pocket. With one quick movement, she pulled a switchblade from inside her vest.

Click. She smiled at him as she opened it, her eyes narrowing, pinpointed with malicious intent.

Jamesi knew what was coming. "Please, don't."

"Sorry, but you're my last untidy end."

"No, please. I'll do anything. I'll take you anywhere. You need me to fly the plane. Please…."

"That's where you're wrong. I don't need anyone." She threw the knife.

The blade went straight through his neck and stuck out the other side. A scream caught in his throat. When he tried to swallow, all he could feel was the blade, the excruciating pain. Blood spewed from his jugular vein, ran hot and greasy down his neck. He watched as she took the controls and put in a co-ordinate for Hong Kong, then darkness knifed through him.

Chapter 14

KwaZulu-Natal Province, South Africa

Lucy reached for her father, but something held her back. He dangled over the side of the cliff, inches from her. His fingers slipping, slipping. She couldn't reach him.

"Dad, hold on." Lucy dropped to her knees, beating on the invisible force separating her from her father.

A woman's laughter made her turn around. Miranda N'Buta, or someone with her face, stood behind her. Lucy sensed it was Arachne. She was laughing, her mouth open and three times wider than normal. All Lucy could see was teeth.

"Lucy!" her father shrieked.

She turned as his fingers disappeared over the edge.

"Dad! Dad!"

Lucy woke to someone shaking her, a deep English voice calling her name. "Lucy, Lucy."

She swallowed a scream and realized whose voice she was hearing and where she was. She made a face and sat up in the seat. She glanced over at Nolan Taylor driving the Jeep.

"Bad dream?" he asked.

Lucy turned away, aware of the tears streaming down her cheeks. She wiped at them with the back of her hand and hoped he hadn't seen her moment of weakness. "Something like that," she said, her voice still unsteady from the terror of the dream. She cleared her throat.

"You have them a lot?"

"Only since we met." She shot him a brazen snarl of a grin.

That put him off his prying, and he stared straight ahead at the road.

Lucy was glad for the respite. God, how many hours in the Jeep had she spent with Taylor. It seemed like an eternity. Cao and Betsy had driven to Kimberly to destroy the diamond mine. Lucy had been forced to take Taylor with her to raze the gold mine. Delphi suspected Taylor wasn't on Arachne's side and that he would be an asset on the team.

At the moment, he didn't seem like an asset. More like an intrusion. He kept looking over at her with those ever inquisitive eyes of his, not missing a thing, the way a cat watches a mouse. She had deliberately not spoken to him, other than to give one-syllable answers about where to stop for food or who would take over at the wheel. It had kept her irritation to a minimum. But he was starting to annoy her just by being in such close proximity. That wasn't the only thing annoying her.

She glanced at the empty foam cups he'd stacked and left in a little pyramid by his seat. She'd deliberately thrown her coffee cups behind her seat, helter-skelter, letting the cups have free rein. But he'd picked them up and added them to his growing pyramid. His candy bar wrappers were folded and put in numerical order in the ashtray. And she'd seen him fold his napkin after he'd eaten. She wondered if he did the same thing with his underwear. Talk about anal. The man was just one irritation after another.

She realized something else: he had long lashes and streaks of gold ran through his short, sandy brown hair. He'd changed into jeans, T-shirt and a navy sweatshirt that was too short for his long arms. She could see the thick brown patch of hair on the back of his forearms and his long-fingered, large hands. His wide shoulder was almost touching hers, and she could feel the strength of his nearness like no man she'd ever felt before. She remembered when he'd broken into the safe house and every hard plane of his body had pressed against her.

She shifted uncomfortably in the seat and asked, "How long did I sleep?"

"About four hours. And I feel it's my duty to inform you that you snore." Amusement danced in his eyes.

"I do not." Not entirely true. She knew she snored. The girls in her dormitory at the Athena Academy had always complained of it. It didn't lessen her embarrassment about doing it in front of Taylor. A blush burned her neck and crept up to her cheeks.

"With your mouth open. I had to wipe away a little drool on the seat. Rather charming, really."

His insincere flattery was driving her nuts. Did all Englishmen use those trite phrases? She hadn't realized how annoying the words *rather* and *really* and *quite* could actually become. Water torture with words. She refused to let him know he was getting to her, so she took a few deep breaths and looked at her watch. Almost 4:00 p.m. She quickly changed subjects. "How far to the mine?"

He reached for the folded map in front of him on the dash. She was sorry now she'd asked her last question. He had tracked every mile of their progress on that damn map. She was tempted to throw it out the window. All she needed was her cell phone and the GPS tracking site she always used.

After a few glances at the map, he said, "We've got another fifty miles to the Tazara Mine. We should reach it by nightfall." He slowed the Jeep to take a sharp curve and laid the map in the exact spot it had occupied before.

Lucy held back the desire to grab it and litter South Africa. Instead, she glanced at the jagged snow-covered peaks of the Drakensberg Mountains all around them. Winter grasses covered the craggy rolling valleys. Dark clouds shifted and stirred the sky behind them. It didn't seem as if she were in Africa, for there was not one sign of the big five: lions, rhinos, buffalo, leopards or elephants. Wild animals that had roamed free at one time had long since disappeared from South Africa's terrain. Sadness tugged at Lucy when she saw the barren landscape.

She had always believed the very things that made Africa the cradle of civilization, wholly untamed and unspoiled, apart from every other country in the world, were its wildlife and indigenous hunter-gatherer cultures like the Bantu, Khoina, Xhosa and Zulu. Thanks to development and industrialization, very few groups practiced their traditions. They had moved into crowded, crime-ridden cities, absorbed into urban ethos. And the big five existed now only on game preserves, where poachers hunted rhinos to the brink of extinction. It was a sad testament to how Africa had been abused by modern man.

She looked at the gathering clouds and hoped they reached the mine before the storm.

"This part of South Africa is rather spectacular," he said. "Did you know the Drakensberg escarpment is the highest mountain range in Africa, south of Kilimanjaro?"

"Yeah, I knew that. My mother and I hiked these mountains."

"Really. So I guess you also know the Drakensberg Mountains trail down from the end of the Great Rift Valley in Mozambique, jutting through the eastern coast of South Africa."

Lucy looked at him as if he'd grown two heads. "What's with the geography lesson? When did you become a tour guide?"

"Since I read the placards along the roadside."

"You must have been bored driving." Lucy rolled her eyes.

"You were belting out snores." He shrugged. "I had to entertain myself somehow."

Lucy stared out the window, refusing to take the bait. Maybe he would stop trying to make polite conversation. She was fresh out of polite. To the right of the R34, the highway they were on, she could see railroad tracks. Beyond the tracks a cluster of Xhosa huts dotted the mountainside. They were basically tourist traps. They passed a sign promoting Zulu arts and crafts three miles ahead. Another sign whizzed past for "The Grange, World's largest golfing resort," only twenty miles west. Lucy grimaced.

As if Taylor read her mind, he said, "A country club in Africa? Seems a bit out of place."

"Development has eaten away at Africa's wilderness for years."

"I know apartheid was obsessed with building roads."

"Apartheid made sure every area in South Africa was accessible so they could suppress uprisings and exploit every square inch of land. It's a shame the unspoiled beauty and wilderness of South Africa turned into diamond, gold and coal mines. This area here," Lucy swept her hand over the mountainous horizon, "belonged to the Bushmen and Khoikhoi before European settlers arrived. They lived here for thousands of years. But they've disappeared as an identifiable group."

"You sound passionate." His deep voice held a note of skepticism, as if he couldn't believe she cared about anything.

"I lived in Africa for most of my childhood, until I went to America to attend school. And yes, I do care about ethnic groups. Not only Africans, but American Indians and the Aborigines. Nations all over the world. When we systematically take land and destroy whole societies because they're in our way, or they don't share our beliefs or they don't live as we think they should, then we destroy a part of ourselves. We all share the same DNA in the fifty-second generation. That makes us all related."

"I'd read that somewhere, and I agree with you about preserving man's diversities. How did you happen to live here?"

"My mother's a doctor for the WHO. When I was a kid we lived in Kenya, Somalia, Ethiopia, the Sudan."

"A lot of places."

"That's only half of them. My mother never stayed long in one place."

"What about your father?"

Lucy glanced at him. He had such an intense expression in his light blue eyes, as if he'd steered the conversation to this point. She realized he'd done it on purpose. To take her mind off the nightmare? It had worked. Was it his way of trying to comfort her?

She really didn't want to talk about her dad, so she said, "Let's change the subject. What about your childhood? What was it like?"

"I never traveled anywhere when I was a kid. I guess that's why I picked the Air Service. I couldn't wait to see other places besides London."

"You don't like it?"

He was silent a moment, then said, "London's a wonderful city if you happen to live in the affluent area and you have a means of escape."

Lucy picked up on the detachment in his voice and what

he wasn't saying. His childhood must have been a struggle. "Are your parents alive?"

"Both."

"What does your father do?"

He suffered a moment of uncomfortable hesitation, then said, "He was a bricklayer, but he is ill. My mum cleans houses. We never had much growing up. Me mum always managed to have fawd on thuh table, though." His accent had slipped into cockney. He caught it, cleared his throat and continued. "As you can guess I ate rather a lot as a kid."

Lucy glanced at his frame taking up the entire seat, his long legs bent up under the steering wheel from lack of room, and she said, "I can imagine. Do you have brothers and sisters?"

"Only me. My mum always said they couldn't afford to feed any more children. What about yourself?"

"My dad wanted sons, but after I came along my mother had a hysterectomy and he was stuck with only me."

"And you don't think he was happy about that?"

Lucy realized he'd adroitly turned the conversation back to her father, and she said, "Let's just say I'm a disappointment to my father and leave it at that."

She waited for him to ask another question but he lapsed into silence, staring straight ahead at the road. His silence should have been welcome, but for some reason a pang of disappointment nagged her.

She put her hand to the neckline of her camouflage T-shirt and pulled out her lucky charm. The metal felt smooth and cold on her fingertips, but warmed instantly at her touch. She thought of her father.

Even though he was a stickler about his expectations and guidelines on how she should live her life—the engineer in him lashing out—he would have volunteered for this mission to destroy Arachne. Though her father lived by a set of rigid moral principles—he'd be the first person to tell you that—he would follow his heart in a blink, like Lucy, if it came down to protecting his family or the world from an evil like Arachne. And he would have considered destroying Arachne a priority. Lucy had to admit he might not have broken as many rules as she had so far, but he would have done it nonetheless. And he would have enjoyed it, if he let himself.

Her father might complain about her mercenary career, but he liked marching to the tune of his own drummer and taking risks, too. He always had. Like father like daughter. He wouldn't have built bridges and tunnels in the most dangerous parts of the world if he didn't. Maybe one day he would see how similar they were and accept her for who she was, flaws and all.

The uncomfortable silence settled between them, with only the road noise thundering inside the Jeep.

Northern Cape, South Africa

Betsy drove along R313, talking to her granny on the cell phone. "Yes, ma'am. I'll be careful. Don't you worry 'bout me. I want you to get better."

"I'll be just fine, soon as I know you're home. Come home soon." Her grandmother's voice lacked the durable, resilient quality that so defined her.

Betsy felt the sting of tears in her eyes. It was always this way when she spoke to her grandmother, who was in the hospice. She never knew if this would be the last time she heard her granny's voice.

"Love you, Bets."

"Love you, too, Granny."

Betsy blinked back tears, hung up and dropped the cell phone into her pocket. She chewed on the inside of her lip and glanced over at Cao, sitting in the passenger seat of the van.

He hadn't seen her struggle with emotion. In fact, he hadn't taken his eyes off his computer this whole trip. He was receiving Wi-Fi from the mobile satellite dish he'd mounted on top of the van. His black straight hair fell down along the sides of his face and his head was cocked at an angle as he studied the screen. Talk about the cold shoulder. Since they'd left the airport and he'd found out he'd have to go with her to destroy the diamond mine, he'd been nothing but withdrawn, a real stick in the glue pot. That's why she'd called her granny.

They had just crossed the Orange River and were heading north. First Water Diamond Mine was near Niekerkshoop, about thirty miles away. She glanced at the flat terrain, unwilling to break the code of silence between them. He started this. He would have to be the one to break it.

They were driving through the red dune wilderness that bordered the Kalahari Desert. Nothing but red earth as far as she could see. The setting sun had painted the thick gray clouds with purples and pinks and golds. The clay-colored dust, which whirled and wisped through the air and seemed to cover everything, felt as if it had somehow seeped inside the Jeep and covered her. She could feel it gritty in her teeth. The air was so dry and cool here, her skin felt like cardboard. She'd guzzled half of the bottled water they'd brought on the trip. She looked over at the full bottle of water resting near Cao's thigh. That was his only one. How'd he do it? Did he have an endless font of water in him, like his endless supply of spiteful comments?

Bored, she shifted her attention back to the terrain. This would be the perfect place to film a movie about Mars. Devil's claw plants, cacti and scrub vegetation dotted the dunes. Farming fences formed latticework patches for miles. She passed a group of meerkats standing guard over their boroughs near the road. A family of six, sitting up on their hind legs, their little brown paws clasped as if they were praying. They reminded Betsy of America's prairie dogs. It was the only sign of African wildlife.

He wasn't as involved in his computer as she had surmised, because he typed as he said, "I hope your grandmother is all right."

"As good as expected. Thank you for asking." Betsy raised a surprised brow at the inquiry. He sounded genuinely concerned.

"I never knew my grandmother."

"I'm sorry. My granny practically raised me. I can't imagine my life without her." Betsy felt that familiar tightness in her throat, already feeling the inevitable. Then she realized Cao had disclosed something personal about his own life. Since they had worked together, he had never been forthcoming about his childhood. He always changed the subject when it came to his private life. She prodded him a little. "Why didn't you know your grandmother?"

"I grew up in an orphanage."

"I'm sorry."

"Don't be. You do not miss what you never had."

There was something so desolate and lonely in his words that Betsy felt for him. She couldn't imagine living in an orphanage, never growing up in a loving home. It made her appreciate her grandmother that much more, and the tears came again. She blinked them back and turned her attention back to the red road.

Quiet settled between them for a moment, then Cao said, "My life there wasn't so bad. The orphanage master, Shoiming, and his wife liked me."

"So you were close?"

"Shoi-ming would never show an open preference toward me, because he was our teacher and taught all the children. But we had a mutual respect."

"He must have seen how smart you were."

Cao glanced at her and a hint of a smile played along his

lips. "He recognized how bored I was, so he took me under his wing and let me have access to his private library."

"I bet that kept you busy."

Cao nodded. "Books became my friends. So you see, I really didn't miss having a family."

Betsy didn't believe that for a moment, but she held her tongue.

Cao seemed lost in his work and said no more.

Betsy listened to his fingers tapping on the computer and said, "What are you working on?"

"Two things. I'm tracing the data miner that stole the information we sent to our boss to a wireless server in Hong Kong."

"Wasn't the signal encrypted and scrambled?"

"Yes, WPA encryption."

"Hey, English for us microchip illiterates."

His brows snapped together and he looked annoyed as he said, "Wireless Protected Access encryption."

"You said you're doing two things."

"I'm also running a cloaking program through the NSA computer, while a separate sniffer program discovers the origin of the GPS signal. I've already located three routers for the signal, one in Hong Kong, one in Volgograd and one in Kestonia."

"How many more do you think there are?"

"I think Arachne is clever and arrogant. Arrogant people make mistakes. Think they'll never be caught. Underestimate the power of the zeitgeist of cyberspace. With patience and proper binary sequencing, nothing is hidden."

A chime prompt sounded. "You've got mail," blurted into the van's silence.

"Damn it!" Cao's fingers pounded the keyboard. When it didn't help, he pounded on the dashboard in frustration.

"What is it?"

"See for yourself." He turned the laptop screen so she could view it.

An image of a black spider filled half the screen; the web covered the other half. Then the screen went blank.

"I hit a firewall. I've lost my trace."

Betsy didn't want to rub it in, and deep down she admired Cao—he was the smartest person she'd ever met—but she couldn't pass this one up. "Maybe *you* shouldn't have been so confident."

"No firewall gets the better of me." Cao glowered at her as if she were Arachne and hit Control, Alt, Delete.

KwaZulu-Natal Province, South Africa

Nolan noticed the closer they drew to the mine, the more Lucy fidgeted and seemed agitated. Her left leg bounced up and down as she pulled her thick, shoulder-length, auburn hair into a ponytail and secured it with a rubber band. The austere, school marm hairdo, fettered to her head, looked un-natural on her. She was the type of woman he liked to see with wild and free hair. He had to rein in the urge to reach over and shake it loose.

She undid her seat belt.

"What are you about?" he asked, watching her crawl into the backseat.

"Getting the ammo out." There was a loud crunch and pop, and she said, "Uh, oh, there goes your tower of cups. Sorry."

Before he could take his hand off the wheel, she grabbed what was left of the smashed cups and rained them into the backseat. White chips went in all directions. He looked in the rearview mirror and saw her grinning like a kid playing in sand, then he caught an enticing view of her rear end as she wiggled into the backseat.

"You enjoyed that," he said.

"You're right."

"You don't like order, do you?"

"Only when it comes to explosives. Even then you really aren't completely certain of the outcome."

"I don't like being blown off course by surprises."

"You need to step out of line a little, Taylor. You're strung tighter than a tennis racket."

Was he really that rigid? He'd never thought about it before. Sarah had been in the communications end at SAS, and she was a stickler for organization and cleanliness like he was. She'd even stacked the towels in her apartment the way he liked. Though something had bored him when he'd been with Sarah. When she had tried to put them on a bloody shagging schedule, Fridays and Wednesdays, he'd called it quits. He was beginning to wonder how he'd stood Sarah for so long. He recalled feeling Lucy beneath his body and he wondered how she was in bed. He glanced at her and knew there was nothing cold about Lucy. She was all fire and crimson and cinders.

He heard her opening the boxes they had taken from the van. She pulled out an infantry army belt, found the small pistol at her ankle, checked it, then began reloading several extra clips.

Nolan could see the lights of the Tazara Mine lighting up the whole base of a mountain, burning in the darkness like eyes. It was a huge complex. Massive conveyer belts spewed out like tongues. Workers picked stones and rubble from the belts and dropped them in buckets near their feet.

Lucy slipped the clips in a pouch on her infantry belt, then buckled it around her waist.

He turned as she reached for the duct tape, tearing it with her teeth. When he saw her taping sticks of dynamite and homemade hand grenades to her waist, he asked, "You're quite serious about wearing those explosives?" He blinked at her in disbelief. What kind of woman was she? She wore dynamite like diamonds.

Her amber eyes shifted over to him. She had a direct, brazen way of looking at him that sent his heart pounding.

"Why? Would you rather wear them?" Her face lit up in a grin.

"What are you afraid of, Lucy Karmon?" He stared at her in awe.

"Running out of ammo when I need it." She picked up two Kevlar vests and threw one at him. "Better put that on."

"We need a plan of attack," he said, donning the vest.

The humor left her face. "Why? Plans change."

"Bloody hell, woman, you can't just go in there half-cocked."

"If I have a target I'm prepared." She motioned to the dynamite.

He gazed at her in disbelief. "How have you stayed alive this long?"

"Easy. I assess as I go. Use my wits and split second decisions in battle." Her voice grew heated. "Planning and rules are for the armed services. They have all these rules and planning. For what?" She shrugged angrily. "People still die. This isn't the military. I don't run my missions that way. You want a plan, here it is." She reached in her goody box and threw him a bone mic. "We'll stay in touch this way. You don't like it, then stay here." She gave him a hard, unflinching look.

He was certain she'd go in alone and he couldn't let her do that. "I'm in, but for the record—"

"Who's keeping a record?" She fitted the bone mic over her right ear until the tiny microphone touched her mouth.

He did the same.

"What's your call name?" she asked.

"Tango bravo echo."

"Too long and too military. How about Churchill?"

"It'll do. What's yours? Let me guess. Terror. Dynamo. Hurricane."

She grinned at him. "Not even close. Chaos."

"Fits you." He watched how the smile lit up her face.

She opened another long box, extracted an AK-47 assault rifle, and said, "Know how to handle one of these?"

Nolan ignored the dig and said, "Too bulky. I work better with this." Nolan pulled the push knife from his belt. He watched her shrug of acceptance and laid the weapon back in the box. "You were in the military, weren't you?" he asked.

"Am I so transparent?" She grinned again, but there was no amusement in it, only a veiled pain that she struggled desperately to hide.

"And you lost someone?"

She tried to hold the expression, but her lips quivered slightly. "Do you really want to know, or are you dissecting me like you do with everyone else?" She reached for a can of camouflage paste. She took out a large dollop, then handed the can to him.

Nolan watched her hand slide the dark paste over her cheeks, nose, chin, forehead, and couldn't argue with her on that point. Human nature had been a study of his since childhood and he'd had to survive first Tower Hamlets, or the Tower, as he called them, and then Her Majesty's Special Air Service and terrorist assassins. "You're not like everyone else," he heard himself saying as he spread the black paste on his face.

For a moment they stared into each other's eyes. He wanted to reach into the backseat and capture her mouth in a kiss but she broke the moment and picked up a small box of C-4 explosive. She crawled back up into the front and paused next to his seat. She was on her knees, the explosive between them, and staring him straight in the face. He stopped spreading the black paste on his cheek.

"Is that a good thing or bad thing?" she asked.

"Better by the moment, actually," he said, finding her position sexy in the extreme. His body reacted to her closeness.

She leaned toward him. Nolan thought she was going to kiss him and twisted toward her. She leaned back and ran two fingers over his nose, spreading the black paste on her fingers. "Forgot a place."

Nolan frowned in disappointment, but enjoyed her touching his face and asked, "So was he a boyfriend? Husband?"

He waited for her answer, his heart throbbing in his chest. Was that jealousy he was experiencing?

"A close friend."

"What happened?"

"Basically the army happened." Her hand moved away from his face and she crawled into the passenger seat. "We worked EOD—"

"Explosive Ordnance Disposal?" Nolan was impressed. Even he didn't have the guts to dismantle bombs for a living.

She nodded. "We were in Iraq, dismantling a Russian bomb. Our commanding officer said we had to use an American-translated manual to dismantle it. We told our CO there was a mistake in the translation. But he ordered us to follow the manual by the *book*. While I was arguing with the general, my friend—" She gulped and paused. After a moment, she shook her head as if to shake off the emotion. "Well, you know. He clipped the wrong wire, and…I left the army."

Nolan couldn't think of one thing to say to comfort her that wouldn't sound trite. He'd seen enough deaths in the SAS. Words were no comfort when it came to the memories.

She continued, "It was a long time ago. I don't like to talk about it. We'd better move out. I'm going to walk along the railroad tracks and set charges. Cover me, then we'll move in."

He nodded as she hopped out of the Jeep. He didn't like going on a mission without scouting the area, planning strategies of attack, but he decided he'd try it her way and see how it went. One thing was certain—keeping up with her would be a challenge.

Northern Cape, South Africa

Cao brought up the computer again and switched directly to MS-DOS and algorithms. He isolated the firewall that had allowed a virus into his computer. The virus spewed out before him in binary language. To his trained eye, it stood out like a nest of bees. Behind the last virus command, an image of a spider glowed black on the screen.

Cao admired the program as he read it. A new breed of insidious programming he'd never encountered before. Effective and very inspiring.

"What's wrong?" Betsy asked.

"Nothing," Cao said, as he carefully pressed the Delete key until he'd wiped out the virus. How would he track Arachne now? Had the whole mission tanked? He didn't want Betsy to see how upset he was. She'd rub it in, and he couldn't stand it.

He felt his gut tightening. *Think.* Easier thought than done. How could he think with Betsy so close? He could smell her perfume and see that cute little way she cut her eyes at him. A moment ago when he opened up about his childhood, he'd seen warmth in her eyes. It had made him ache inside. He should come right out and tell her how he felt, but they were on a mission. And he had other problems to deal with.

Like finding a trail he could follow. Arachne had to have made a mistake. Cao just had to discover it. Shoi-ming's proverbs came back to him, "Look at the problem so you cannot see it. It is *formless.* Listen to it but do not hear it. It is soundless. Grasp it but do not hold it. It is incorporeal. Fuse the forms into one and you shall find the unfathomable."

Then it dawned on him. He had the information from the microdots. He also had the data Nolan Taylor had downloaded from Giger Anfinson's computer.

"Uh, I hope it's not too bad." Betsy looked over at him from beneath her lashes.

Every time she looked at him, Cao felt his chest constrict, as if her eyes were electrified and they were hitting him with ten thousand volts. So he glanced back at his computer. "Nothing I can't solve."

Her expression melted into seriousness. "We're getting close to the mine," Betsy said, her tone a warning.

"I know. I'll be ready." Cao opened Windows and began combing the data for his own electronic attack.

Chapter 15

Lucy felt sleet hitting her face as she finished setting the last charge on the tracks. She shivered to keep warm beneath her sweatshirt and jeans and crept back toward the shanties that were a hundred yards from the tracks. The decrepit buildings, made of scrap wood, metal and cardboard, formed scattered rows like wide waving arms. Fires burned outside the doorways in an attempt to keep the inhabitants warm. Some shanties didn't even have doors. She could see bodies, on dirt floors, huddled under blankets. A barbed wire fence surrounded the area. The wind brought the smell of the ditch used for human excrement and Lucy grimaced. This desolation, built on misery, fed by greed, needed to be blown back to hell, and she was going to enjoy doing it.

She saw guards walking the north fence line and whispered into her bone mic, "Chaos to Churchill."

"Copy, over."

"I make two along the fence, over."

"Got them. Over."

In seconds, Taylor appeared out of the shadows and made quick work of the two guards, then he crept to the engine and crawled up inside. He hit the engineer with a karate chop to the back of the neck and caught him as he collapsed. Lucy saw his feet being pulled back through the stairs on the side of the engine. Taylor was such a large man that one blow sent his opponents sprawling. Lucy had to admit he impressed her. She had thought he would be a hindrance, but he was proving to be as competent as any of the other team members.

Bright lights burned over guarded towers stationed along the mountain ridge and throughout the mining camp. The mine itself was a huge pit burrowed into the mountain's bowels. A sloped wooden trough channeled water and gravel from the mine's mouth and dumped it into holding basins. At least thirty women and children bent over the sluices and panned the gravel for gold with handheld screens. An overseer, a tall African in khakis and an army-issue parka, walked behind the workers. He held out a bag for the gold nuggets picked from the screens. Then the overseer tossed the bag into a metal box.

Four young teenage girls struggled to load a full box into a rail car connected to an ancient-looking steam engine. A man she assumed was the engineer sat on the engine steps, smoking.

All the workers looked abused, cold, spiritless and weary. Dirt smudged their ragged clothes. The only thing of warmth covering their bodies were ill-fitting, torn sweaters that appeared as if they'd come from a charity box. Old rags covered their hands and legs.

Several of the younger children worked in teams, unable to hold the screens by themselves. They looked about six. An older child, who was shivering and looked ill, dropped a nugget as he tossed it into the bag. The overseer smacked him and made him pick it up. Anger boiled in Lucy's gut.

Lucy pulled out her cell phone and began snapping pictures of the whole deplorable scene, then she e-mailed them to Delphi, with a little text message: Let's surprise Arachne with some bad press.

"I count five guards, over," Lucy whispered into the bone mic, then slipped her cell phone back into a pouch on her belt.

"I'll take the blokes on the north side. Also claim the one who just brutally struck that child, over."

"Break an arm for me."

"My pleasure," Taylor said with a dangerous edge that sounded at odds with his deep refined voice.

"Keep offensive on the QT if possible. Probably more guards in the mine. I'd like to surprise them, over."

"Right. I've got a surprise for them."

"Roger that." As an afterthought, she added, "Be careful, Taylor."

"Nice of you to care, love."

"On my team, if two go in, two come out. Don't want the complication of rescuing you. Over," she said, before he could come back with a rejoinder.

Did her concern for his safety go deeper than merely keeping him alive because they were working together? Lucy found herself frowning as she palmed her Colt. She watched Taylor move off from the fence and stay in the shadows.

The sleet had turned to a mix of ice and snow. Frosty bits pinged against her skin. The heat of her breath blew a white cloud around her face. She blinked away snow from her lashes as she crouched and ran, veered left and pressed her back against a gravel and sludge pile. The mound was at least twenty feet high, and she had to creep to the edge and peek up.

The guard's booted feet showed between the slats of the

platform. He danced to keep warm. He wore a parka, the hood over his head, and held an Uzi. Lucy thought of the women and children who wore only tattered sweaters and rags as she slowly crept toward the platform and began climbing the timbers of the tower. A sharp intake of breath and a thump in her ear signaled that Taylor had just taken out his first guard.

Lucy couldn't let him show her up and in seconds, she was over the railing. She grabbed the man from behind in a choke hold, clapped her hand over his mouth and squeezed his carotid artery with the crux of her arm. He struggled for a few moments, the white cloud of their breaths meeting, clashing, then he fell limp.

Lucy dropped him, slipped over the side and moved on to the next platform fifty yards away. This platform was built into the mountainside, the highest view of the whole mining camp.

Another thump and a muffled sigh came over the mic.

Taylor was up by one.

Lucy hunkered down and followed a well-worn path to the guard tower. She stayed in the shadows of boulders and gravel piles.

This guard had earphones on, his head bobbing to music. Lucy slithered up to the platform and came up behind him. As if he felt her nearness, he turned.

Lucy elbowed him in the face, kicked him in the groin, then grabbed his Uzi and cracked him over the head with it. He looked at her as if she were a *Chibanda,* an evil, uncontrollable African spirit, then collapsed.

From her perch on the tower, Lucy could see the whole camp. Snow came down in earnest now, a thick blanket falling within the bright lights. She squinted and saw Taylor creeping out of the shadows toward the guard collecting the gold.

The women and children saw him, too. He raised his hand

to his lips to signal their silence, but the younger children, frightened by his sudden presence, let out screams and pointed.

At the disturbance, four guards came running out of the mine, weapons drawn.

Then all hell broke loose.

Telecommand Control Station, Arachne's lair

Monitors ran floor to ceiling in the wide rectangular-shaped room that occupied only a small section of the whole complex. Hundreds of images on the monitors throbbed an aberrant light into the windowless room. The on-screen images came from webcams, communications satellites and the National Reconnaissance Program satellite KH-14, the mother of all satellites, which communicated with NSA (National Security Agency), NGIA (National Geospatial Intelligence Agency), CIA (Central Intelligence Agency), DIA (Defense Intelligence Agency), and the U.S Strategic Command. On the room's ceiling, integrated SIGINT (intelligence-gathering) interceptors filtered and decoded broadband and fixed sound waves that accompanied the images. The sound bites were recorded digitally and stored for further inspection.

The light from the images seemed to reach a vortex in the room's center, where three people sat at a table shaped like an *S*. At the head of the table, Demos Kostas readjusted his wireless earphone. He glanced at his two subordinates, Blake and Zinzendorf. Blake was a short brunette. Her features looked more male than female. She had thick eyebrows and wore heavy black glasses that magnified her eyes like a fishbowl. When he looked at her, all he could see were these gargantuan green eyes. Zinzendorf was a dark-haired, tight-lipped German, who could sit at a computer screen for twenty hours without blinking. They both wore earphones, too.

Demos Kostas stretched and took pleasure in his work. This whole room had been his brainchild. Arachne had given him free rein to plan it and execute it as long as it didn't invade her space. She held court in a much larger area of the compound. She liked having her privacy, and Demos liked giving it to her. It made him uncomfortable when they met in person, her hooded gaze flaying him alive. No, he liked the inviolability of his own room, yards of steel separating him from her.

He had learned to deal with her mood swings and tirades. It had tried his patience to be sure. It was the only drawback. But she'd made him a rich man, and over the years he'd learned how to placate her. She was like his pet boa constrictor. Keep her contained and fed with information and she was happy.

As if she had heard his thoughts, a screen lit up with Arachne's webcam image, her head cut off, only the torso showing. When she spoke to the control room, her image filled up all of the screens, a thousand images of her coming at him all at once. Those long thin fingers always holding a cigarette, and that spider ring hazed over by smoke.

Blake and Zinzendorf snapped to attention.

Kostas sat up straight, too, and stared at the hand holding a cigarette. He disliked talking to an image with no face. He always wondered what she looked like.

"Kostas, what have you discovered?" she snapped.

Kostas glanced up at the search program he'd been running. He'd taken a copy of the bank robber pictured on a local newscast in Cape Town, cleaned it, copied it and entered it into a program he'd designed that cross-referenced photo IDs through hundreds of databases throughout the world. The only trouble with the program was that it took time to cross-reference all those images.

"I'm sorry, it's still running."

"I am surrounded by incompetents. If you are the best MIT has, then we're all doomed." The hand holding the cigarette started trembling with rage.

"I'm sorry. I can't make the program work any faster."

She inhaled hard as if to calm herself, then a cloud of smoke swirled in the webcam lens. "I'm losing my patience, Kostas. First, we lose the documents. Then Miranda N'Buta disappears. Now you can't tell me the identity of the criminal responsible, when his picture was on a local television station. Get me a name, or else." She angrily hit a button and her picture disappeared.

The many satellite transmissions flipped back on the screens in a flash of blinding lights.

Kostas stared at the program still running and hoped he got a hit soon, or he'd soon find the boa constrictor around his neck.

KwaZulu-Natal Province, South Africa

Lucy watched as the guards opened fire. Taylor grabbed the gold collector and used him as a shield.

The collector's eyes bulged in disbelief and fear as his own comrades tore his body apart with bullets.

The workers scattered in all directions.

Lucy swept out her Glock. She couldn't get a clean shot. The workers were running and yelling, dodging bullets. Children screamed, paralyzed in place by terror.

She bounded over the railing, hit the ground running and sped down the path toward Taylor. He'd thrown the collector's body to the side and was zigzagging his way directly to the guards, hollering a battle cry.

"Taylor, go back! Don't have a clear shot. Can't cover you!" Lucy yelled into the mic.

"No plans, remember?"

Lucy's heart raced as she reached the mine entrance, yanked a little boy and girl to the side, and took a clear shot.

The guard closest to her buckled.

Lucy plowed through more women and children, firing at openings. Two more guards dropped.

The last guard gave up trying to hit Taylor and turned to fire at her.

Taylor charged the last guard, knocking the Uzi out of his hands. Then they both fell to the ground. Lucy watched as Taylor wrestled with the man, hit him with a right, a left.

The guard's eyes rolled back in his head.

Taylor leaped off the man and grimaced, holding his arm. He pulled the bone mic from his head, then looked at his arm. Blood oozed down the sleeve of his jacket.

At the sight of blood, Lucy was back in Iraq, seeing John's hand cutting a wire on the bomb.

She rushed at Taylor, paused before him and punctuated her words by banging on his chest with her fists. "What kind of crap were you pulling?" she yelled. "Charging the guards without any cover. Were you trying to get yourself killed? People don't get killed on my watch. You hear me? They don't!" Snow hit her hot tears and stung her face.

He knocked the bone mic from her mouth as he grabbed her, squashing her to him, her arms trapped against his solid chest. His expression remained hard as he probed her face, only blinking when snow fell on his lashes. He leaned close, his handsome face inches from hers, and said, "See, love, you are afraid of more things than you thought." Then his mouth covered hers.

Chapter 16

Lucy felt Taylor's warmth envelop her. She tried to hang on to her anger, but it was as if all her senses had tunneled and she could only think about his lips against hers, the feel of his coarse whiskers brushing her smooth skin, his hard body pressed along the length of her. She leaned into him. His mouth tasted like bittersweet chocolate, smooth and spicy and exotic.

He groaned and pressed her so close she could hardly breathe. She found his massive strength wildly sensual, utterly encompassing. She felt him everywhere, pressing against her, touching her, wrapping her in masculine warmth. The feeling was similar to the contentment she felt when watching her own explosions, only this was hotter, tighter and tangible as only the physical could be. She wanted to drown in the feeling and never surface.

He kissed her as if he wanted to drink her in. Lucy opened

for him and his tongue slid inside. She leaned farther back, offering him all of her mouth.

His hands slipped to the small of her back and he pulled her closer. Lucy felt his erection against her. Regions in her lower body clinched, moistened and turned to liquid fire. She moaned softly into his mouth.

The sound of children laughing and clapping brought Lucy out of the sensual haze. Some of the older children were calling in Afrikaans, *"Soen, meisie. Soen, meisie."* Kiss girl. Kiss girl. Oh, my God! What was she doing?

She brought her hands up and shoved him back, panting, trembling, her senses overloaded from the contact.

For a moment, he seemed unable to speak. Then he said, "You can't fight this, love." His eyes smoldered as he reached to touch her cheek.

Lucy leaped back before he made contact. "Don't ever tell a rebel that."

"Attraction isn't a cause, Lucy. It's something that should be savored. Stop fighting everything that comes into your life."

"I don't. I'm not."

His expression lightened as if something dawned on him. "You're afraid. You're attracted to me and that scares the bloody hell out of you."

Lucy laughed, her voice void of amusement. She looked straight into those swirling blue eyes that glistened now as if he'd found the key to a cache of gold. She shrugged, struggling to remain casual. "So we shared a kiss. Big deal. That's all it was. One kiss." She held up a finger to make a point. "Not a very good one, either."

"Something had you trembling in my arms."

"Your unbelievable arrogance probably. And if I want your advice about how to live my life, I'll let you know."

"We'll discuss this later, when we're alone."

"Forget it." She wheeled and walked toward the crowd, but not before seeing the dogged resolve on his handsome face. Something told her it would take more than words to put him off. Blasting powder and a lot of detonation cord might work.

Why did she let him get to her? Why had she kissed him back? As she walked, her lucky charm thumped against her breasts, feeling heavy, like a rock around her neck. Was he right? Deep down, was she afraid? Afraid that like with everything else in her life, the limits of a relationship would make her want to revolt and get out of it. What about those vows she and Val had made of turning down proposals and having kids some day? She was a closet romantic when it came to other people, like Cao and Betsy, but when it came to her own life…?

If she were being honest with herself she'd admit she'd never seriously looked for a man. Had she pushed men away and not even realized it? He was making her question herself and she hated that. The old DAME was the standard by which she measured everything. And so far, she was riding high scores. She owned her own ranch in Montana. She loved her work. Her life couldn't be better. Then the English inquisitor had come along and flogged her with questions.

She frowned at the workers running from the shanties, yelling they were free. The crowd before her grew by the moment, two hundred strong. Seeing the passionate kiss between Lucy and Taylor must have dispelled the younger children's fear, because they crowded around them now.

She felt them touching her legs, patting her, saying, *"Dankie, dankie."* Thank you, thank you.

She hugged the children, their little bodies small and frail against her. Some were so young they probably didn't remember their parents or their homes; all they could remember was this horrible work camp. Lucy asked a little girl hugging her waist, "Who is in charge among you?"

"Shiwan takes care of us."

Lucy called to the crowd, "Where is Shiwan?"

The crowd parted. A tall thin girl, who looked in her twenties, emerged. She had a baby in her arms, covered by a moth-eaten blanket. Some of the younger children moved in around Shiwan, and she tenderly touched their heads as if they were her children and she loved each of them. Her eyes gleamed at Lucy with the kind of apprehension that came from growing up under oppression and fear. She had managed to hang on to some of her pride, for she raised her chin and said, "I am Shiwan."

Lucy looked at the baby. "The child is yours?"

"Forced on me." She covered the baby's face with the blanket as if she wouldn't give it up.

The guards must have taken turns with the older girls. A perk Arachne had offered them for their loyalty? Lucy stared at Shiwan. How old had she been when the guards started using her? What's a good age to be molested? Lucy couldn't begin to imagine the misery Shiwan had suffered. Or any of the children, for that matter. She looked into the eyes of the crowd. Other girls held babies and gripped the hands of toddlers. She blinked suddenly.

When she spoke, indignation choked her voice. She cleared her throat and began again, "This mine belongs to a very bad person. I am going to destroy it and the camp. Can you round up all of the children? Make sure they have what little belongings they wish to carry with them."

"Where are you sending us?" She looked at Lucy with alarm. "We've no wish to enter orphanages in Johannesburg. They are as bad as this camp, or worse."

Lucy knew the South African government still struggled to keep order after the uprising and apartheid had ended. There were places like Johannesburg where gangs dominated, crime abounded and poverty flourished. "Those of you who wish to go back to your parents can go. We'll have to find someone to care for those of you who have no parents. But all of you will have your freedom back."

"Freedom?" She shrugged. "What will we do with it? We have nothing but what you see here." She waved a hand toward the shanties.

"All the gold in the train is yours."

"Ours?" She gazed at Lucy in wonder.

"Yes. You all will ride the train into Cape Town. I'll see that someone helps you and helps find suitable living quarters for you. There should be enough money to take care of all of you." Lucy knew she couldn't be seen around the children or the authorities could track her back to the mine destruction. She'd have to call Delphi and ask for help.

"We could have a farm." A glimmer of hope sparkled in Shiwan's eyes. "My father was a farmer, before he died in the civil war."

"We can find someone to help you get started and enroll the children in school."

"We cannot ask for more than that."

Another older girl stepped forward, pulling a toddler with her. "I will help. We'll all help. It's more than we could ever have dreamed of having."

Few heartfelt moments presented themselves in mercenary work. The job was about force and destruction and walking a tight line between good and evil. But every now and then a golden moment like this one came along, and Lucy grabbed it and held it and knew that she was making a difference in a crazy world.

"Could you round up all the children?" Lucy said. "Get the belongings they wish to carry with them. We're leaving tonight."

Another cheer went up.

"We need to hurry before this snowstorm worsens."

Shiwan barked orders at the children and they went running for the shanties to collect their things.

"I'll see if I can rouse the engineer," Taylor said. He held two small children, one in each arm. The sight of such a bear of a man tenderly holding two toddlers, one patting his face, made him look so damn handsome a dull ache twisted in her chest.

Don't look at him. He probably knows how adorable he looks holding children. "I'll make sure the mine is clear and set the charges."

Lucy glanced away, unexpectedly uncomfortable and knowing why: Nolan Taylor frightened her. The only man who had ever come close to it. She'd rather run through a field of land mines than be near him. She couldn't wait to end this mission and see the last of the overconfident, intuitive Englishman.

Lucy's team cell phone rang. She pulled it out of her pocket and answered, "Yes."

"Madonna, here." Lucy recognized Betsy's voice and she sounded tired.

"Hey."

"The diamond mine is finito."

"Everyone okay?"

"Ten four on that. Dragon's tracking our target on the Net."

"Keep me posted on his progress."

"What shall we do with these poor kids forced to work at the mine?" Betsy asked. "If you could have seen the conditions they were living under—"

"I've seen it. It was the same here. Put them on a train bound for Cape Town. We'll arrange for someone to meet them and help them." Lucy kept Delphi's name out of it.

"Great. We'll rendezvous with you and Tommy at Beaufort West."

Beaufort was a small town near the Karoo National Park. "Roger that. I'll be in touch if plans change." Lucy hung up, feeling an overwhelming sense of relief at an accomplished mission with no injuries. Next on the agenda: make sure the children got to Cape Town, then get rid of Nolan Taylor. Something told her the last goal wouldn't be so easy.

Cairo, Egypt

Miranda glanced out the tiny window at the Cairo International Airport. From the air it looked like a space station surrounded by a sea of dark foaming sand and lighted tarmac. Moonlight bounced off the silver roofs of the terminals as if it were a tiny city shaped like a spider.

Miranda could actually see her freedom. She congratulated herself on breaking free of Arachne. For the first time in a long time, she was her own woman, free to live as she pleased. No more taking orders or nasty humiliating calls from the witch. And Miranda had gotten off scot-free and a lot richer than she'd ever imagined. Pincer was no longer hers, that was hard to accept, but she hadn't made out so badly in the end. Swiss accounts and freedom awaited her. A new start, somewhere. Maybe Russia. She had heard it was easy to get into the smuggling and drug trade there and make millions. As soon as she was rid of this pilot, she'd book a ticket to Saint Petersburg.

She heard the pilot speaking low over the radio to the tower. He was mumbling. The only words she could catch were "Roger, one-niner-four-six."

He hadn't said two words to her the whole way. All he had done was eat aspirin like candy. Not that he didn't need it. His face looked as if he'd gone twelve rounds in a boxing ring, his nose crooked and purple and swollen to the size of a clown's. She wasn't complaining about his reticence. Idle chatter had always been an irritation to her.

The plane banked and they were circling around the airport.

"What's the matter?" she called up to him. The unexpected turn didn't feel right.

"Waiting for runway clearance. Shouldn't be but a few minutes."

"How long are a few minutes?"

"I don't know, ma'am, but if you wanna pilot the plane, be my guest."

Miranda glowered at the back of the pilot's blond head for his rudeness. She wanted off this dumpy plane and away from these mercenaries who were after Arachne. By now, they would have found the mines and seen how the workers were kept. Arachne had bought the children on black markets and Miranda had been responsible for their preservation. It had been an area in which Miranda could skimp and stash away some of the mine profit without Arachne finding out. The way Miranda saw it, she'd kept the little beggars in better living conditions than they were accustomed to. Still, to an outsider, the camps looked bad. Miranda wasn't afraid of the other mercenaries, but the person with the altered voice on the cell phone, who called the shots, that person worried Miranda. It had been like talking to Arachne without the nasty overtones—just quiet reserved steel behind the voice. And the redhead, the one known as Lucy, she was someone to fear. Her eyes held an unpredictable light, the radiance of a firebrand. Given half a chance, Lucy might rethink Miranda's freedom.

Miranda shifted in the seat, pulled out her purse and found the Derringer she kept there. She leaned back in the seat and waited. The next few minutes would feel like an eternity. Until she landed she wouldn't be able to relax.

Beaufort West, South Africa

"Right here will do." Lucy held her Colt to the back of the engineer's head as he slowed the engine. He was a middle-aged wiry man, and his hand trembled as he gripped the throttle lever.

The tracks ran parallel to the N1 highway, and she could see the Jeep's headlights stopping alongside the train. Taylor was driving the Jeep, while Lucy kept an eye on the engineer. The lights of Beaufort West, a small tourist town, gleamed in the night. Karoo National Park was within walking distance and it brought in most of the revenue for the tiny towns near it.

Two teen boys had been shoveling coal into the steam burner and they paused. Shiwan had left her baby in the care of another girl and ridden in the engine, too.

Lucy turned to her now, and said, "Do you know how to use a gun?"

Shiwan nodded. "My father taught me."

Lucy handed her the pistol. "Take this. Keep it pointed at him." She motioned toward the engineer. Lucy didn't trust him. He looked ready to bolt at any minute. "Someone will meet you in Cape Town and take care of you." Delphi had already called, and it was arranged that someone trustworthy would be there to help Shiwan.

"How can we thank you?" Tears swam in Shiwan's eyes as she hugged Lucy.

"Take care of yourself and have a good life. That will be thanks enough." Lucy hugged her tightly.

"And please don't tell the authorities who blew up the mine and released you. It wouldn't be good if they knew what I looked like. Can you do that and make sure the rest of the children keep quiet?"

"Certainly."

Lucy leaned close to the engineer and whispered in his ear,

"You talk to the authorities, or these children don't get to Cape Town, I'll come back for you."

"No talk, no talk, missy." He stared straight ahead, his hand still trembling.

Shiwan jammed the gun into his neck. "Like she said."

Lucy smiled. She had created a female Dirty Harry. She was certain the children would be okay in Shiwan's hands. She touched the heads of the two boys shoveling coal, then leaped down off the engine.

A door opened on one of the cars and hundreds of faces peered out at her, the children calling goodbye and thank you. Lucy waved to them, then noticed them gesturing to someone behind her. Taylor stood in the headlights of the Jeep. His long legs cast giant-like shadows on the pavement, and he looked about ten feet tall. A genuine white-toothed smile tugged at his lips, at odds with the dark camouflage paint still on his face. It didn't take away from his attractive features. She'd never seen him smile like that before, and her breath quickened.

What was wrong with her? She could barely stand him. With his stacked coffee cups and folded chocolate wrappers and his arrogance. And that audacious kiss… Oh, God. The kiss of the century. How could she forget it? Giving in to it, letting it take over her body. It was as if his lips were laced with Rohypnol and she'd lost her inhibitions and her ability to think. It had been humiliating, and, damn it, the most awesome kiss she'd ever experienced in her life.

She quickly glanced away and forced her attention back on the engine as it puffed and hissed and the huge wheels creaked into motion. He might be hunk material and a roofie kisser, but she dreaded being alone with him, having him analyze her. She just wanted him gone. True, he'd helped her with this mission, but when he'd run out into the line of fire without cover, that had been the ultimate in heroic stupidity. She wasn't about to work with him again, and the sooner she let him know it, the better.

By the time Lucy reached the Jeep, Taylor was waiting at the passenger door. He was actually playing the English gentleman and holding the door for her. "You don't have to do that. My hands work just fine." She stepped around his wide shoulder to get in.

He deliberately leaned close and whispered against the back of her neck, "I'm aware of that. I'd like to see just how skilled they are."

His hot breath sent a tingle down the back of her neck and she couldn't stop the tremor that went through her. She sat down in the seat, trying to control her pounding heart, and looked at him in as unruffled a way as she could manage. "They know how to break a man's neck in ten seconds. Shall I show you?"

He grinned. "Such sexy words. You really know how to turn a bloke on." Before she could reply, he slammed the door.

She watched him walk through the headlights, wide shoulders swaying, his short blond hair glistening. And the smug grin on his face. As soon as he opened the Jeep door and sat behind the wheel, Lucy decided to deal with his self-satisfied expression. "When we get to Beaufort, our arrangement is over."

"Be careful, you're acting scared of me again."

"I'd appreciate it if you'd stop second-guessing me. You haven't gotten close yet."

"Prove it."

"How?"

"Go out on a date with me."

"Is this your shtick with the English ladies? Pretty lame, if you ask me."

"I don't need lines for other women, love. They tend to use them on me. You're my one and only challenge."

"Bully for me."

"Right, hide behind that tough girl exterior. It's charming."

"Hey, I wasn't born yesterday. I'm not letting you manipulate me into a date." She rolled her eyes.

"Coward."

"I have nothing to prove to you." She crossed her arms and stared at the white lines flashing by on the road.

"It's one date, Lucy. I'm not asking for your hand in marriage."

Was she afraid? Not of this overconfident, controlling Englishman. So why not sleep with him and shut him up once and for all? Maybe take his ego down a peg or two. She couldn't believe she was actually contemplating a one-night stand with him. It wasn't as if she'd have to face him in the morning. She could slip out early and leave with the team.

"We don't have time," she said as if still trying to convince herself it was a bad idea.

"Your friends won't be back until morning, if that. We have the rest of the night, more than enough time." He glanced over at her, his face glowing like a demon's in the red dash lights, a handsome devious specter.

She hesitated, thinking about the call she'd gotten from Cao and Betsy. Mission accomplished on their end. They had destroyed the diamond mine and were to rendezvous with Lucy and Tommy in Beaufort West. Lucy wished they had been quicker about it and she didn't have so much time to kill with Taylor. After a moment of indecision, she said, "All right. One date. On one condition."

He looked sideways at her. "I assumed there would be strings attached. What now? You want me to disappear from your life entirely?"

"Something like that. I can't work with you any longer."

He mulled that over for a moment, then said, "Right, then. I'll find other work."

They lapsed into silence, the road noise growing loud in Lucy's ears. The Jeep suddenly felt like a two-foot box and they were both stuffed inside. Tension pulsed in the air like a heartbeat. A vein in her temple throbbed. She felt his gaze on her, boring into her, and her insides churned with uncertainty. What had she just done? Agreed to a date with him? Had she lost her mind?

Cairo, Egypt

Miranda watched the pilot open the hatch. He shot her a sour look and said, "Hope you enjoyed the flight."

Miranda wouldn't dignify him with a comment. She snatched up her purse and said, "Hurry with my bags."

"Yes, ma'am. Your wish is my command." The pilot saluted her in a sarcastic way, then stepped down through the hatch.

When Miranda's feet hit the pavement, she let herself relax. Almost free. Time to plan her new life. She breathed in the dry night air, so different from the humid air of Cape Town. The smell of jet fuel and asphalt clung to the night. The pilot had docked the plane close to a terminal for private flights, and only one other small plane was beside them. There was no ramp like on commercial flights and she would have to walk twenty yards to the airport doors. Several spotlights burned above them. From her vantage point, she could see through the tall windows that ran the length of the terminal. Several passengers checked their watches, while another talked on a cell phone. Miranda didn't see guards milling about. A good sign.

The pilot had pulled out her luggage from the cargo hold and now handed the two hard-sides to her. "Here you go."

Miranda shot him an indignant look. "You don't expect me to carry those?"

"Look, lady, you can carry them, or I can leave them right here. I'm no bell hop." He smirked at her, the purple and black bruises under his eyes from the broken nose making him look like a rude raccoon.

"I'll take them." She jerked up the handles, locked them in place, then she rolled them toward the door.

Before she reached the doors, they opened. She stared into the faces of three men, one in a suit, the other two in brown uniforms, carrying rifles. Turbans covered their hair. Fear knotted her stomach.

She drew up short and said, "Oh, hello."

The suit held out his hand and impatiently clicked his fingers. "Your passport."

"Yes, of course." She fished it out of her purse.

He stared at it a moment.

"If it's about my sudden appearance—"

"You are Miranda N'Buta?"

She nodded.

"I see you're from Cape Town."

"Yes."

"Did you know there's a warrant out for your arrest?"

"For what?"

"Murder, fraud, embezzlement." He looked her over with a critical eye. "You'll have to come with me."

Miranda reached in her purse for the Derringer, the charms on her bracelet clacking.

He grabbed her arm and jerked on the bracelet. The clasp gave way and it fell to the ground with a final thunk. "I wouldn't do that." He snatched her purse off her shoulder.

Miranda reached for the bracelet, but the policeman forced her to stand, wrenching her arm.

The suit surveyed the pilot, taking in his broken nose. "How was it you brought her here?"

"She needed a charter. That's what I do for a living."

"He's lying," Miranda screamed. "He's a mercenary. I was promised immunity. Who tipped you off? You can't do this to me."

The suit nodded and the two guards grabbed her. "Take her away."

"I'm innocent. Leave me alone. It was all Arachne. She did it." Miranda's screams faded as they dragged her through the doors.

Tommy shook his head, then smiled as he turned and walked back to the plane.

Telecommand Control Station, Arachne's lair

Kostas stared at the face on the screen. He'd gotten a hit on a Montana division of motor vehicles photo. The face the program had matched wasn't that of a male. It was a female. A pretty woman with shoulder-length hair and sparkling ginger eyes. Lucy Karmon was smiling for the camera. He brought up the original picture, pasted it over the image. Identical. She must have been in disguise for the bank job.

He addressed Blake. "Got that background information yet?"

"Almost there." Blake kept her big fish eyes on the monitor in front of her. "I have it, thanks to the Defense Department."

Kostas glared at her goldfish eyes. "On screen, please."

Blake looked dejected that she wouldn't be praised and hit a button. The file appeared on one of the big screens so they all could read it.

Zinzendorf whistled and said, "Ouch, that's gonna hurt."

Kostas knew just what Zinzendorf was referring to. He was reluctant to tell Arachne, because he knew she wouldn't be happy. "Keep your comments to yourself, Zin, and get back to work," Kostas snapped, taking out his own frustration on his staff.

Zinzendorf glowered at him and returned to monitoring the satellite screen.

Kostas straightened in his chair and with one keyboard stroke Arachne's image filled the screens. She wasn't smoking this time. She was filing her long black fingernails. The sound went down Kostas' neck and made him bite down hard.

"Yes," she snapped.

"I've got a name for you."

"About time. Who is he?" she asked, then had a coughing attack.

"It's a she. Lucy Karmon."

"A she?"

"Yes."

"Who?"

"A mercenary. Ex-army. EOD Division." He'd saved the worst for last. He hesitated, inhaled, and fired the words. "And she's an Athena Academy graduate."

Arachne froze, the emery board trembling in her grip as her fingers strained to hold it. "I should have known."

Kostas gathered enough courage to say, "Even if they have the documents, there's no way they can find you. I've made certain of it."

"Well, we do have that, now don't we? But they came close this time. Too close. I won't have all I've worked for destroyed."

"It won't be."

"Find out if this girl works alone or with someone. I want to know everything about her. And I mean everything. What she eats. Her blood type. Family connections. Who she's screwing. And I want to know who hired her." Her image went blank.

Kostas was glad Arachne's enmity had another target besides him.

Chapter 17

Beaufort West, South Africa

"Why are we in this game preserve?" Lucy finished wiping the last of the camouflage paint off her face, then she shot Taylor a suspicious glance.

"We need to find a motel for the night." He stressed the last word and made it sound like the sexiest word in the English vocabulary.

Lucy rolled her eyes, tossed the towel in the backseat and said, "We've passed about ten motels. What are you looking for, the Waldorf-Astoria?"

"I'm hopeful."

"Forget about it around here."

He had already wiped his face clean, but there were tiny dark smears left in his five o'clock shadow, making him more of a hunk if that was possible. His profile was toward her and she watched the corner of his lip curving into a resolved line.

"So when are you going to stop? We've driven eight kilometers from Beaufort. It's nowhere land out here." Lucy glanced out at the dark terrain. They were at the base of the Nuweveld Mountains in the Great Karoo Veld, the interior of South Africa. Sheep country. Farms scattered the plains and buttes and parts of the mountains. They were currently inside the Karoo National Park. About two miles back, they had passed a herd of wildebeest grazing near the road.

A wicked grin slid lazily across his lips. "Soon. Be patient." His baritone dropped to a rich sensual huskiness as if he were imagining what would happen as soon as they arrived.

Lucy was imagining it, too, and she was back in his arms, feeling his lips against her. Her body warmed and turned liquid deep inside. A fine sheen of sweat broke out on her palms. She found herself wondering if he made love with the same thoroughness as he approached everything. She swallowed hard, remembering the stacked cups, the folded wrappers, the map he had studied. The thought of getting near a motel with him frightened her and excited her. She swallowed hard and said, "Don't worry. I'd just as soon sleep in the Jeep."

"We can do better than that." His grin widened as a sign appeared in the headlights. Ka-Koa Tsera Bush Camp splayed across the sign. He turned right into the drive.

The way he maneuvered the turn made her ask, "Did you know this was here?"

He nodded. "It was a long trip following you on the train. I looked up the bush camp on the computer. Perfect out-of-the-way place to lay low. I've even checked us in."

Lucy twisted and glanced into the backseat. She realized she'd left her computer in her backpack. She looked at his full-of-himself expression and narrowed her eyes. "I hope you got two rooms."

Taylor didn't answer her and jerked the Jeep to a halt so hard Lucy's head hit the seat rest.

She glanced up. They had stopped in front of Highgate Lodge. Solar-powered spotlights cut through the darkness and beamed along the main office and walkways. The office looked like a huge log cabin with a wide porch on the front and a peanut-shaped pool that was covered over with a tarp for winter. Ten A-frame chalets, built post-and-beam style like the office, fanned out behind the main building. It might have been a picturesque place if Taylor wasn't along.

He grabbed the keys and leaped out of the Jeep.

Lucy followed him.

His strides were so long that he'd already made it inside the office. There was a discernible objective to his strides that Lucy didn't like. When she stepped inside, the clerk, an elderly woman, peered at them through her glasses.

"May I help you?" the woman asked in a gravelly voice.

Taylor sauntered up to the counter. "I have a reservation." He turned and winked at Lucy. "Mr. Taylor."

The elderly woman wasn't immune to his charm and her grin widened. "Ah, yes. We received your reservation an hour ago. I've made ready a lovely chalet. Number 10, on the end. We call it the Honeymoon Suite." The woman smiled deliberately at Lucy, giving her one of those age-old glances between females, part commiseration and part knowing amusement.

"There's been a big mistake. We need two rooms."

"Sorry, all booked up."

Lucy saw Taylor's smug smile. She wanted to pick up the pamphlet holder near the door and throw it at him. Instead, she forced a rubbery smile.

"Jolly good." He took the key. "Is room service available this late?"

"Of course."

"We'll have two steaks, baked potatoes, salads and a bottle of your best champagne."

"No champagne." Lucy shook a finger at the clerk to get her point across.

"Give us the champagne," Nolan said over his shoulder as he walked toward the door.

"Right away. Checkout is at eleven."

Lucy said, "We'll be out *long* before that."

"Come on, love, stop making jokes." He grabbed Lucy's hand and pulled her toward the door.

As soon as they were outside, Lucy jerked her hand out of his grasp. "I want the Jeep keys. Now!"

He dangled the keys in his hand above her head. "Come and get them."

Lucy lunged for them.

He grabbed her, pulled her to him and kissed her.

Lucy fought him, but his arms held her like iron bars. He captured her mouth in a punishing kiss, crushing her lips against her teeth. Oh, God, his lips, those powerful mind-numbing lips…consuming her. His tongue slid into her mouth and along her teeth.

Lucy's resolve warred with her need for him, and she opened her mouth to let him inside, while she wrapped her arms around his neck.

He explored every inch of her mouth, lazily, carefully, his tongue slipping beneath hers, twining, weaving. His hands slid slowly down to her hips. Then he was easing her backwards, never letting up on her mouth.

Lucy clung to his neck, lost in the feel of him. Before she knew it, her back hit something hard. He fumbled with the room key, opened the door, eased her inside, then closed the door with his foot.

Lucy opened her eyes and caught a quick glimpse of the chalet. A lamp had been left on and she could see the post-and-beam construction of the triangular-shaped walls, the bare wood and rough-hewn beams exposed. Two full beds. A table. A small bar and kitchenette. A ladder led to a loft with another twin bed. It really was perfect for a wild night of sex. Somewhere between the office and the room, her body had decided she needed this. Wanted it. Why fight the attraction? She'd never have to see him again.

"Alone at last," he whispered against her lips, his fingers slipping off the rubber band holding her ponytail. He ran his hands through her thick hair, shaking it loose. "I've wanted to do that for hours."

A shiver went down her neck, then he trailed tiny kisses all over her face, while he pulled her sweatshirt off.

"And I've wanted to do this." Lucy tugged off his jacket and opened the buttons on his green shirt, exposing his chest.

He was all lean chiseled muscle, abs so ripped and hard they could crack an egg. A small patch of golden hair fanned out across the center of his chest and made a tiny line down to the waist of his jeans. At the sight of his large naked chest, she gave a sharp intake of breath. Guys weren't supposed to look that sexy and hot. "Your body's a woman's dream," she murmured.

"I'm glad I please you."

"You do more than that." She jerked his shirt down his arms and let it pool at his feet. Then she was feeling his pecs, splaying her fingers over his abs.

He stiffened and caught her hands before she went for his jeans. "A bit of a rush, love. My turn now."

He pulled off her T-shirt. He reached for her lucky charm hanging from her neck and rubbed it between his fingers.

"Do I want to know why you're wearing a shell casing around your neck?"

"A lucky charm."

"You won't need it tonight, love. We've both gotten lucky."

He dropped his hold on it and turned his attention to her shoulder, trailing kisses along her skin as he eased off first one bra strap, then the other one. A shiver went through Lucy. Her skin felt on fire where he touched her.

He unhooked her bra, freeing her breasts. His gaze moved over her. "Beautiful," he said. Then he was teasing her right nipple between his fingers.

His controlled slowness was driving Lucy crazy. She wanted to see him out of control with desire like she was, so she slipped her hands down the inside of his jeans and briefs. She found his erection, thick in her hands, pulsing.

He gasped and tried to grab her hands. But Lucy was determined this time. She stroked the sensitive tip and kissed him, thrusting her tongue in his mouth.

He jerked, his hands dropping, his body straining against her hand. She could feel him using all his self-control to hold back his desire. His whole body trembled from it.

"I want you, now," she said against his lips.

"Bloody hell." The last thread of his restraint melted and he was pushing her back against the bed, jerking on her jeans zipper.

Lucy was doing the same with his pants.

They fell together, then they were kicking off their jeans. He pulled a condom from his pocket and slipped it on. When they were completely naked, he mounted her and thrust deep inside her. She was wet and ready for him and she felt his hardness filling her. He grabbed her hips, groaned and moved faster and faster, slamming his hips against hers, his eyes moving over their naked bodies.

Lucy matched the motion, needing all of him inside her. She raked her nails down his back.

"Oh, God…" He stiffened, then thrust several more times, touching her womb.

They both cried out as they came.

For an instant Lucy felt herself slip into that strange quiet place she experienced after setting off a bomb, that place where nothing could touch her and time moved at her own perfect pitch. Oh, God, she didn't think she'd ever feel that during intimacy with a man, especially this man.

He kissed her, then looked down at her. "Is that smile for me?"

"No, for me." Lucy grinned up at him.

He continued to stare into her eyes as if peering into the deepest depths of her. "You're so bloody beautiful. You unhinge me."

No one had ever called Lucy beautiful before and she reveled in the compliment before she said, "I'm glad something does, Taylor. I was beginning to worry." She grinned at him, feeling their sweaty bodies hot and damp against each other, her body pulsing with him still inside.

"My Christian name is Nolan. We know each other well enough now for you to use it."

"Okay, Nolan." Lucy tested the name and liked the way it lingered on her tongue. "Let's push your limits and see how unhinged you can get." Lucy gave him a wicked, teasing look and ran her leg up the back of his long, corded thigh.

"You may regret it." He grinned back.

"So I've found something you're afraid of."

"What's that?"

"Me."

His eyes gleamed like blue marbles down at her and she could see her reflection in his eyes. "The only thing about you that frightens me is not getting enough of you. I don't think

I ever will." He dipped his head to capture one of her nipples in his mouth.

Lucy bucked beneath him as he suckled, and she wondered if it was the other way around.

Northern Cape, South Africa

Cao could smell the strong scent of sheep wafting through the open window of their accommodations. The morning sun streamed in through the windows. He could see the flat red veld stretching out for miles around. He'd been up all night and had made coffee. He sipped it now from a complimentary mug in their room.

It had taken until midnight before they'd seen all the young workers at the diamond mine aboard the Blue Train, a public transport rail service that ran from Cape Town to Pretoria. Cao had been appalled by what he'd seen, even for an orphan raised in rural China. It had been long past midnight before they'd happened upon the Mellon Wold Guest Farm, not far off the N12. So they'd stopped for the night. The problem was they'd only been able to get one room.

Betsy was sleeping in her own full-size bed. He liked to catch glimpses of her asleep as he worked. Her arms were buried beneath a pillow and her full lips were slightly parted. Her long thick lashes cast a semicircle above her cheeks.

He had tried not to wake her with his work. An alarm on his laptop dinged. He'd been waiting for this hit. His cloaking program had pinpointed the location of revwave.org. It had been the Web site that kept appearing on the information Nolan Taylor had downloaded from Giger Anfinson's computer. Cao had thought it looked strange when he'd first seen it. And then it had hit him. It was an anagram for vweaver.org. His eyes widened in disbelief as he read the location of the source: the computer at the National Radio Astronomy Observatory in Green Bank, West Virginia.

He searched Google for NRAO and the Web page appeared. The National Radio Astronomy Observatories were the world's most premier research facilities for radio astronomy. The NRAO operated powerful, advanced radio telescopes spanning the western hemisphere. The Web page said the telescopes were used by astronomers and physicists. What a perfect spot for a blackmailer. If Arachne had somehow tapped into the listening ability of the radio telescopes and their satellites, she could eavesdrop on anyone anywhere in the world. The implication was staggering.

There were four sites throughout America—Arizona, New Mexico, West Virginia and Virginia. Cao clicked on the site for Green Bank, West Virginia. It was only a couple hundred miles from Washington.

Cao closed the window and glanced at the Google hits again. One was about bunkers located in the Blue Ridge Mountains, not far from Green Bank. He clicked on the site and read that the bunkers had been built in 1962, during the Cuban Missile Crisis, a nearby safe haven for Washington politicians.

"Well, well, well," Cao chanted softly to himself. It was all coming together.

Betsy stirred and said, "Would you stop with that keyboard tapping? It's worse than a woodpecker on a drainpipe. What are you doing, anyway?" She raised her head and looked at him. Her short hair was lopsided, and her eyes had a sleepy-sexy, half-opened appearance. "You didn't sleep, did you? You've been up all night with that damn thing." She pointed a limp finger at his computer. "If I didn't know better, I'd think you were in love with it." She dropped her head on her pillow as if she couldn't hold it up any longer.

He wanted to say, "I'm in love with you more." But he didn't. Her attitude annoyed him. He was on the trail of the most wanted criminal in the world, a ghost who had eluded the authorities for years, and she was telling him to stop annoying her.

"Well, maybe I am in love with it," he said. "It does not give me half as much grief as you. Go back to sleep," he said.

"Lord, save me from geeks," she said, pulling the pillow over her head.

"Don't worry, you won't need saving." Cao picked up the cell phone and walked out of the room to call Lucy. Betsy had ruined his triumph, tainted it, and his conquering spirit had taken a nosedive.

Highgate Lodge, South Africa

Lucy heard the television in the room turn on. The last guests in the chalet must have programmed it to come on in the morning. She cracked open an eye and saw the empty champagne bottle on the nightstand, along with two empty plates. The musky smell of sex still hung in the air.

She felt Nolan spooned against her, his arm over her side, his breaths deep and even, the stubble on his chin pressed against the back of her neck. She reveled in the feel of him beside her and thought of last night. They had made love again, before room service had arrived. Then they had taken a shower, soaping each other, exploring each other's bodies. Lucy had never felt such a warm after-sex glow. It had lingered between them, making them unable to take their hands off each other. True to form, Nolan had gone back to his thorough exploration of her body, driving her crazy with his lips and tongue in all the right places. Lucy gingerly stretched like a sated cat after a long night of sleep, and she felt the tingling still between her legs. She was living proof that inflexible, fastidious men made fantastic lovers.

One of Lucy's cell phones vibrated on the nightstand and she reached over to answer it. "Lucy, here," she whispered so as not to wake Nolan.

"It's me," Cao said. "I think I've tracked down Arachne."

"Where?"

"West Virginia in the Blue Ridge Mountains."

A burst of excitement brought Lucy fully awake as she listened to Cao's explanation and how he'd pinpointed the area.

A familiar vibrant voice caught Lucy's attention. She gazed at the television set. Reporter Shannon Conner filled the screen. Her shoulder-length blond hair waved in the wind, her brown eyes straight on the camera. Shannon's face glowed as if she loved her job. Shannon was renowned as a reporter, but she also had another distinction: the only student ever to have been expelled from the Athena Academy. Shannon had carried her grudge against the school like a badge and never missed an opportunity to try and ruin Athena Academy's reputation.

"Dragon, hold on a minute," Lucy said, listening to Shannon's report.

"I'm standing here in South Africa with a story that encompasses corporate espionage and murder. The destruction you see behind me is the only thing left of a gold mine owned by Pincer Industries." The camera panned wide, showing the destruction of the mine and the tracks and the rubble of the shanties Lucy had destroyed.

Lucy smiled at her work.

"A Pincer diamond mine was destroyed almost simultaneously. Two days prior, a bomb went off at the Pincer building in downtown Cape Town. The CEO's office was destroyed." Cut to the Pincer building, a corner of the top floor hanging in ruin. "All three are believed to be the work of the same bomber."

Lucy frowned at the screen. She would never have left

something so sloppy. What was Shannon trying to prove with this story?

"Remains of two bodies were found in the first explosion. The coroner's report confirmed the two males were dead hours before the explosion. Sources say the CEO of Pincer, Miranda N'Buta, has disappeared and is wanted for questioning." A picture of Miranda N'Buta flashed up on a corner of the screen. "Pincer's stock has plummeted and stockholders fear bankruptcy. Stay tuned to ABS for the latest breaking news on this story. I have leads on who might be behind the destruction of this corporation and the murders."

Who was Shannon going to blame? How did she get to South Africa so quickly? Who tipped her off? Shannon must not have proof that Lucy and her team were behind it, but Shannon was close to finding it. Too close if that shrewd smirk on her face was any indication.

Lucy put the phone back to her ear. "I'm here. Do me a favor. E-mail what you've discovered to Delphi."

"What will you be doing?" Cao asked.

"I've got to see a reporter about a story. I'll let you know where we'll meet up." Lucy clicked off the phone.

She looked at Nolan still sleeping peacefully. Last night had been like some sexual fantasy, hot and erotic and perfect. But the world was invading now, reality biting her on the ass. Time to break ties with Nolan Taylor and find Shannon before she implicated Lucy and the team for those murders, or worse, connected it all to the Athena Academy. Then they'd have to check out this site Cao had discovered.

Lucy eased out of bed, carefully resting Nolan's arm on a pillow. He moaned softly, then snuggled up to the pillow. Even in the morning, he looked good enough to drool over, a sleeping hunk. The covers only came up to his waist, leaving his large chest and one sculpted long arm exposed. She sighed wistfully and wished for a couple more hours in bed with him. But she needed space to clear her head, and duty called. She went in search of her clothes.

Mount Wellington Hotel, Cape Town

Lucy pulled the Jeep up in front of the hotel. The bricks had been painted bright gold and the Romanesque structure stuck out like a huge golden goose on Orange Street, in the heart of the City Bowl District.

A valet, wearing starched white pants, a black jacket and a black cap, bolted toward her and opened the door.

The cool Cape wind swooshed through the inside of the Jeep and flipped the hem of her cardigan dress. As she stepped out, she gave him a good view of her legs. She'd hit a shop on the outskirts of Cape Town, and the black and white striped dress had caught her eye. It was tighter than she preferred but the cashmere wool wasn't a tight knit. She'd bought a black cashmere bolero to wear over it, black pumps and a black large-brimmed hat that covered most of her face. A matching striped scarf hid her red hair, and huge black sunglasses concealed her eyes. It felt great to shed jeans and army fatigues and feel feminine again. She'd had fun picking out the *Breakfast at Tiffany's,* Audrey Hepburn disguise. And after the uninhibited sex she'd had she was feeling a lot like Holly Golightly.

She smiled at the valet and handed him the keys. "I won't be long."

He returned the smile, holding her gaze longer than was necessary. "Yes, ma'am."

Did she have a brand on her forehead that read: Experienced Multiple Orgasms Last Night? Was the valet trying to intuit how many? Her secret. And she let him know that with a mysterious grin.

He watched her walk up the steps and through the lobby doors. Thinking of orgasms brought back thoughts of Nolan Taylor. He would have already found she was gone. She hoped he wasn't too angry at her. So what if he was? Why should she care? She wasn't going to see the Englishman again. They were over. Finito.

That thought made Lucy's brows furrow as she strode through the lobby. Baroque furniture, potted ferns and succulents filled the lobby. In the center sat a huge cage housing five parrots, preening, two squawking and looking bored.

She passed an elderly English couple leaving the hotel, a porter pushing a mountain of luggage behind them. Lucy stayed behind the luggage, out of sight of the desk clerk, a woman, about thirty with dreadlocks, and wearing the same white and black uniform as the doorman. Her head was buried in a newspaper. Lucy saw the sign for the stairs and slipped through the door.

After several calls to the local station, an ABS affiliate, Lucy finally had to tell the producer's secretary she was Shannon's sister and their mother had died and it was imperative she know her whereabouts and phone number.

The hotel was only two floors. Lucy's heels ticked on the stairs and echoed in the stairwell. She reached the second floor and slipped into the hallway. Number 206 was at the end of the hall.

Lucy hoped it was early enough to catch Shannon Conner before she'd left her room. She had to find out what Shannon knew. She paused and knocked.

Nothing but the sound of a television.

Lucy knocked again and was about to find the lock pick she'd stuffed in her purse when the door opened.

Shannon appeared, wearing a plain navy suit and white silk shirt. She eyed Lucy up and down. "You must have the wrong room."

"No, I'm pretty sure I've got the right one." Lucy stepped past Shannon into the room.

"Hey, I'm just leaving. You can't waltz in here—"

"Cut the crap, Shannon." Lucy turned, her dress whirling around her long legs. "Close the door so we can talk."

"Why should I?"

"I can give you the truth behind the Pincer story."

Shannon stared at Lucy's face. "Do I know you?"

"I don't know. Do you?" Lucy kept her face blank.

Shannon seemed to struggle between her yearning for a lead and throwing Lucy out. The reporter in her won out, and she closed the door. "Make it quick and it better be the truth."

Lucy glanced at the dark-headed male announcer on the television. Shannon saw her watching it and said, "My competition."

"I hope he reports the facts rather than twists them."

"I only report the truth," Shannon said, her voice growing heated with emotion.

"Your past broadcasts don't reflect that."

"How dare you."

"I dare because one day you could hurt a lot of people."

"I can't help it if the truth hurts." She narrowed her dark eyes on Lucy, then said, "Wait a minute. Are you an Athena Academy graduate? Did Allison Gracelyn send you here to stop my prying into the Pincer story? That's it, isn't it? She doesn't want the truth to get out."

"Are you going to implicate her in the story?"

"Someone tipped me off that she's involved, up to her eyeballs, in the bombing and mine destructions." Shannon crossed her arms over her chest in a defensive stance.

"Did your source give you proof of this?"

Shannon hesitated, a moment of insecurity passing over her face, then she said, "Not yet. But I'll have it."

"You won't because it's a lie." Lucy shook her head at

Shannon's petty bitterness. "It would behoove you to check the background of this source of yours. Who is it?"

"I can't tell you that."

"Listen, Shannon, I know Allison and so do you. And we both know she's not involved in this, and she didn't send me here to plead her case. She's not as vindictive as you want to believe. No one at the Academy is. But you've held a grudge against AA for years. And you should ask yourself why your source feeds you tips that are always detrimental to the Athena Academy and anyone tied to it. Better yet, ask yourself who is behind Pincer's destruction."

Shannon frowned in thought and for once her self-possession looked threatened.

The announcer's voice broke into the room. "We have a special report from Tory Patton."

Tory's chin-length hair, striking face and glistening green eyes filled the screen. Lucy knew she and her husband, Ben Forsythe, had recently had a baby. Motherhood seemed to be agreeing with her. In fact, she glowed.

"No way, she can't be here." Shannon's face screwed up in a frown, then she walked toward the screen as if some invisible force was drawing her to the television. "She always does this to me."

"This is Tory Patton reporting live from Cape Town. Standing behind me are over four hundred children who were held prisoner and forced to work in Pincer's diamond and gold mines." She turned to Shiwan, who looked nervous but not afraid. She was beaming at Tory.

Lucy had a feeling Tory was the person Delphi had sent to help them.

"This is Shiwan," Tory said. "She was taken from her family by slave traders at age eight, and forced to work in the mine." The images of the deplorable shacks Lucy had sent to Delphi via her cell phone appeared on the screen, then it cut back to Tory. Lucy was certain now Delphi had sent Tory to help the children. "Can you elaborate on your experiences there?"

"It was horrible drudgery. A lot of children died from cold and overwork and little food. We are all lucky to be alive. And I thank the people who rescued us and destroyed the mines." Shiwan smiled at Tory, a secret hidden behind her lips.

"Can you tell us who they are?"

"They asked not to be identified, but they are heroes in our eyes and hearts."

Shannon reached over and angrily flicked off the television set, a mask of jealousy covering her face. "She always steals my thunder."

"Maybe because Tory gets the human interest side of a story." Lucy turned and walked toward the door.

"Wait!" Shannon followed her. "Who are you?"

"A friend, if you ever need one. I hope you get the story right this time." Lucy left Shannon frowning at her back.

Lucy had a feeling Arachne had been feeding Shannon tips for years. She might finally realize she had been one of Arachne's many puppets.

When Lucy made it back to the Jeep, her cell phone rang. "Yes."

"I received the information Cao sent," Delphi's electronic voice said. Even though it was disguised there was a clear note of excitement in the tone. "This lead is well worth investigating. Your team's next assignment is to check out the NRAO facility. I know the director there. She's been briefed on what Cao discovered and she's eager to meet with your team. Her name is Irene Blanchard. Keep me updated."

"All right." Lucy wondered if Irene Blanchard was an Oracle agent, too.

"As usual, Lucy—"

"I know, be careful." Lucy hung up and called Cao and Betsy to inform them of a new meeting place, Touws River, rather than Beaufort. She'd changed the meeting site because it was about sixty miles east of Cape Town, and the airfield was smaller than the one in Beaufort West. Chartered planes carried tourists to Beaufort so they could tour the Karoo National Park, and that airstrip had more traffic than the one in Touws River. But the major reason she'd changed it was to avoid Nolan—if he decided to try and renege on their deal. She'd have to call Tommy, too.

She couldn't hold back the excitement coursing through her. If this lead panned out, Arachne would be history.

Touws River, South Africa

Lucy pulled the Jeep up to the airfield in Touws. The out-of-the-way airstrip looked like a perfect deserted spot for drug runners and illegal-weapons dealers. Four private planes formed a line along the short runway—none were Tommy's. An airbrushed metallic green viper coiled around the tail fin of his Cessna. Hard to miss.

Her gaze moved to the lengthy metal building running adjacent to the landing strip. The structure had been turned into a hangar. One end of it served as the office. The building looked as if it had seen better days. A coating of rust covered its roof, and dried winter grass tufted around the edges of the foundation. The large bay doors were open on the hangar, and she could see a mechanic working on an old biplane. She could only see his green jumpsuit, his head hidden in the hull of the craft. Several ancient-looking vending machines hummed near the office entrance.

Half an hour ago, Cao and Betsy had checked in, and they were only ten minutes from the airstrip. Tommy had been fifteen minutes of air time away. Lucy fished out a pair of black jeans, a T-shirt and sweatshirt she'd bought when she went shopping. She needed to change before they took off. She didn't want to face the team in her *Breakfast at Tiffany's* outfit. Holding the clothes made her recall Nolan having taken off her clothes last night. The image of him, as she'd left him that morning, lying in the bed and hugging her pillow, stole into her memory.

Lucy almost made it to the office to find the bathroom, when a pickup truck came barreling down the road. The wind whirled a cloud of crimson dust behind the vehicle. A film of filth covered the windshield and she could only see two dark silhouettes inside. Something about the size of the passenger bothered her. The wide shoulders that dwarfed the cab of the truck. The head that almost touched the roof.

The truck pulled up beside her. Even through the dirty glass, she could see the pair of frosty blue eyes glaring back at her. A balding man had driven Nolan. After a moment, Nolan turned to him and money exchanged hands.

She swallowed hard, not knowing if she was happy to see him, or mad as hell.

He got out of the truck, thanked the driver, slammed the door, then walked toward her. He snapped an iPAQ closed.

She stood her ground against those frigid eyes. They scoured her from head to toe and paused at her breasts. "Dresses suit you." He reached out to touch her cheek.

Lucy knew she couldn't let him touch her, or he'd manipulate her into getting his way. And God, he looked good. He hadn't shaved, and his hair still looked wet from where he'd recently washed it. Tiny golden brown tendrils curled around his temples. She leaped back as if he was about to hit her and said, "How did you find me?"

"My cell phone has a GPS device. I dropped it into your backpack. Never hurts to be prepared."

Lucy glanced toward the Jeep. She recalled not returning his cell phone. "We had a deal. One date and we don't have to see each other again."

"You only said we wouldn't work together in the future." He winked at her. "We didn't agree I was no longer on this mission."

Lucy racked her brain and remembered what she'd said. Had it been a subliminal blunder? Had she wanted him on the team? She sighed loudly and said, "Okay, you can see this through to the end. But then that's it."

"Right."

Lucy saw the full-of-himself smirk on his lips, before she glowered at him and stomped off to change her clothes.

Chapter 18

National Radio Astronomy Observatory, Green Bank, West Virginia

Lucy trailed behind Cao, Betsy, Tommy and Nolan as they all followed Irene Blanchard through the control room at the Jansky Lab. A gray carpet met the institutional white that covered the lab walls, adding to its sterile look. Different work stations and monitors formed a maze through the room. Some of the desks were occupied by astronomers who looked up only for a second before turning their attention back to their work. Lucy knew from Cao's research about the site that astronomers and university students from all around the world came to use it.

Lucy walked past processors that ran floor to ceiling. Telemetry meters and wires covered them, and they hummed with a confident pitch. The scent of coffee and donuts wafted from a snack bar across the hall, the only scent that broke the clinical, sterile air. The room reminded Lucy of the physics and astronomy lab at the Athena Academy, sans the headshots of Einstein and planetary models of the solar system.

Irene Blanchard chatted happily with Nolan as she guided them to a long desk with three monitors. She had a ruddy complexion, hid her excess weight with a long lab coat and kept peering at Nolan through gold-rimmed spectacles. She looked ready to salivate. What was it about Nolan that made women fall all over him—just the hunk attraction? Was it his James Bond accent? Those light blue eyes that probed every inch of a woman? Maybe it was the charm he used as a weapon to ingratiate himself into someone's good graces. He seemed to be pouring it on now.

"How was your flight over?" Irene asked.

"Lovely," Nolan said. "Your airfield made it quite convenient."

They had cleared a landing at the NRAO airstrip in the town of Green Bank with Irene. It was about thirty miles away, since there was a no-fly zone over the NRAO site. If they knew how many explosives Cao and Tommy had taken from the safe house and stored in Tommy's plane Irene might have axed their landing. Lucy smiled at the thought.

Betsy wasn't immune to Nolan's charms, either. She walked beside him, vying for his attention, saying, "It really didn't take long at all to get here."

Cao looked like a man in a dental chair about to have work done, and Nolan was the dentist. Betsy and Cao hadn't spoken much on the trip over. No progress in that area, Lucy thought ruefully.

Lucy had kept to herself and read on the trip in an attempt to curb interaction with Nolan. Luckily he hadn't spoken of their one night together, which suited her. She wished she could forget it as easily.

Tommy wasn't too thrilled about having Nolan accompany them on this mission, either, and he kept shooting him pitchfork looks behind his back. To say the least, Nolan's presence had caused so much tension that it felt like a pall over the team, one Lucy hoped to alleviate very soon.

Lucy glanced back at Irene Blanchard. She seemed to be having fun. Nolan had just whispered something to her and she was laughing, a mule-type braying that echoed around the lab.

She sobered, hit his arm playfully and remembered the rest of the group. She raised her voice, catching Lucy's and Cao's and Tommy's gazes—she made a point to avoid Betsy. "The Jansky Lab is the brain center behind our masterpiece." She pointed out a window to the monster dish telescope that looked like a small city on stilts. It was half a mile away. "We compile and store data here. Also we can move the drive motors and wheels to adjust the telescope to where we want it."

She walked them to a long curved desk that looked like something out of a NASA Control Center. Telemetry data spewed across five monitors.

Cao leaned over a monitor and said, "Ah, your Digital Control System is Modcomp with DCS Task Software."

Irene lit up with amazement and said, "We're currently testing WIDAR."

Cao's head bobbed. "Bypassing Modcomp and going directly to an EVLA processor. MVME-162FX embedded Controller, messanine connectors to four Industry Pack modules. Good idea. Much quicker."

"We're also installing two SBS Greensprings IPs."

"Sixteen Bit parallel I/O modules for interface?"

Betsy stepped over to Lucy and whispered, "Never thought

I'd see someone who understood that geek Greek." Jealousy snapped her brows together. She didn't wait for Lucy's reply and said louder, "I'm going to the water fountain. I saw one out in the hall." She walked back through the lab, looking annoyed and chewing on the inside of her lip.

Lucy watched the interplay between Cao and Irene. They connected as if they'd known each other all their lives, in higher realms of intelligence than an average person could ever comprehend. Lucy understood Betsy's sudden jealousy.

Cao asked, "Does it require python control scripts?"

"Yes." Irene smiled at Cao. "You have to be the one who found out our system was being corrupted?"

Cao nodded, an almost self-effacing expression.

"I could use someone like you around here. Need a job?"

Cao smiled and shook his head. "Thank you, but no thank you. I do not work for institutions any longer."

"How did you find the connection?"

"It was buried in the Memory Mapped Data block."

"Really? How diabolical."

"May I?" Cao motioned to one of the stations.

"Certainly."

Cao sat down and began typing, his eyes flashing across the screen. "I can show you its source in a moment."

Irene bent over Cao's shoulder, watching.

Lucy said, "Just don't do anything to alert Arachne that we're snooping, okay?"

Cao nodded. "She'll never know we've tapped into her cloaked line."

Nolan stepped over to Lucy and leaned in close to her ear. "We need to talk."

Lucy smelled the hot chocolate he'd drunk in a coffee shop in Green Bank. They'd stopped there before driving to the facility. Everyone else had gotten lattes or cappuccinos. Not that chocolate was a bad thing. It brought back memories of the taste of his mouth last night, the feel of it all over her body. A frisson of yearning tugged at her. She had to stop herself from leaning closer to his mouth as she said, "About what?"

"Plotting a strategy of attack."

"That again." Lucy shook her head. "You sound like an army general. I told you—"

He grabbed her arm, cutting off her words, the pressure almost hurting. "Listen, Lucy, I won't have you in danger because you're so bloody headstrong."

Lucy broke his hold on her arm and whispered, "This team has worked together for years. Without you, I might add. Don't try to tell me how to run a mission." He started to say something and she held up a finger. "I mean it. And don't think you can order me around just because we spent one night together." She pried his fingers from her arm.

"We'll have to rectify that." His hot breath burned her neck.

A tingle flew all the way up to the roots of her hair, and she felt a sudden dampness between her legs. Her body didn't seem to be her own when he was around. "Highly unlikely," she said, her voice cracking slightly.

"I'd say it was likely. You're *all* I think about, love."

The sensual way he was looking her over forced Lucy to fight a desire to pull him outside of the building and have him ravish her again. She'd never been this attracted to a man before, or this aroused. It was as if her body craved his touch. She needed some space to clear her head. She turned to go and join Betsy at the water fountain but was stopped by Cao's next words.

"I've found it. I've got the location."

Spring Knob, Allegheny Mountains

A full moon rode high in the sky and threw a bright silver veil over the treetops of Spring Knob Mountain. Lucy climbed through the underbrush, past trees, over boulders, staying in the shadows. Perspiration dripped down her back as she groped for purchase along the sheer mountain terrain. July in West Virginia was nothing like it was in South Africa. Whereas South Africa was in the middle of winter, West Virginia was experiencing the balmy humid streams of mid-summer. The elevation here, too, caused her to breathe heavier and made the work of climbing harder.

She felt a new .45 securely in the shoulder holster, rubbing against her left side, and her backup pistol hugging her ankle. Her backpack carried ten sticks of dynamite, enough C-4 to blow up half the mountain, and det cord. Four of her homemade grenades were strapped to her back. And still a feeling nagged at her that she may not have brought along enough firepower.

The damp smell of rich earth and rotting leaves clung to the air and caused Lucy to wrinkle her nose. The sky, void of reflections from city lights, would have been pure black if not for the moonlight. It reminded Lucy of nights on her Montana ranch.

Spring Knob Mountain bordered a secluded area in Monongahela National Park. Dense forests and mountain peaks surrounded the area for miles, not a sign of humanity save for several campgrounds seventy miles away.

Cao had traced the line to an old bunker buried on the mountaintop. He'd also discovered another data miner, attached to the same line that was sending information to a location in Hong Kong. He traced the spy filters in the computer data files, and the trails had led back to Hong Kong. Was someone in Hong Kong spying on the bunker? Had the spy received all of Arachne's data? The new discovery gave Lucy hope that this might be Arachne's epicenter.

Lucy had Cao e-mail this information to Delphi and they were given the green light to take the bunker, and hopefully capture Arachne alive—if she were, indeed, hiding inside.

Lucy knew nothing concerning Arachne was certain. Her unpredictability and cunning had allowed her to avoid capture for decades. Lucy didn't know what to expect inside the bunker. But if Arachne was there, Lucy wasn't leaving without her.

The team had fanned out. Cao and Tommy were on her right. Nolan on her left. Betsy had scaled the mountain on the southern side. It was agreed she'd take up a position from the mountaintop, a hundred yards from the bunker entrance, which was in a little vale on the east side of the mountain.

"Madonna to Chaos, over." Betsy's low voice came over the mic.

"Go, over."

"I'm clear on this end. Two bogies at the entrance. Two at the gate."

"Roger that."

"What's your ETA, over?"

Lucy pulled herself up on top of a boulder and saw that Nolan had already reached the ten-foot barbed wire fence before the rest of them. The fence surrounded the complex. NO TRESPASSING signs glimmered menacingly about every fifty feet. In seconds Nolan was up and over the fence.

"ETA five minutes. On the flip side, over," Lucy said.

She reached the fence just as Cao and Tommy hopped over. They used the M4 Colt Carbines they were carrying to crush the wire and leap over. The M4s were modified with sound suppressors and laser/infrared designators along with night vision. The only weapon Lucy could talk Nolan into carrying was a SIG-Sauer P226 "tactical" .40 caliber with a silencer. It held fifteen rounds, hopefully enough ammo to keep him alive. When Cao and Tommy had loaded the plane with explosives from the safe house in Cape Town, they'd also helped themselves to the storehouse of weapons.

Lucy was the last to scale the fence. On the way down, a piece of wire caught her arm and tore several deep scratches across her forearm. It stung for a moment, and Lucy knew it was only the first of Arachne's stings she was likely to feel.

Telecommand Control Station, Arachne's lair

Kostas had just poured himself a cup of coffee. The smell of it wafted beneath his nose as he glanced at Blake and Zinzendorf. Blake chewed on a nail while she plucked at the keyboard with one hand. Zinzendorf's lips smacked as he chewed gum.

"What did I tell you about gum?" Kostas said.

"It's no worse than your coffee."

"I can bring what I want in here." He snapped at Blake, "You found any intel on the redhead, yet?"

"Not who hired her. I've tapped her home phone lines. Nothing there but a housekeeper who keeps calling her son."

Kostas knew Arachne would eat him alive if he didn't get something on the redhead soon. Kostas went to sit in his chair when Zinzendorf's voice stopped him.

"I believe we've got movement outside."

"Animal? Or human?"

Zinzendorf hit a few buttons and the satellite transmissions of the bunker and surrounding area zoomed in, growing pixels before their eyes. Four dark figures skulked toward the bunker.

"Give me infrared," Kostas ordered.

Blake switched a button and the image turned negative, the green outline of the figures moving blurs.

"High def," Kostas barked.

Blake tweaked the image and Kostas clearly saw one of the faces. The redhead's.

Suddenly Arachne's webcam image bounced onto the screens. He knew she was seeing the same image that was being broadcast on the control room screens.

"Is that the woman we've been tracking down, Kostas?" she asked, strangely composed.

He didn't like that unnatural calm in her voice; there was something sinister and eerie about it. "That's her."

"Well, well, well. I'm glad to hear she'll finally get stuck in my web," she said in a satisfied hiss. "Alert the guards and launch the drones. Now!"

Kostas wished she'd stop ordering him about. He knew what to do. He'd been the one to design the contingency plan in case of invasion. In fact, he'd been waiting for years for this moment. He could finally test his handiwork on human subjects. It wasn't any fun killing birds and rabbits. He had a real challenge now. Excitement rippled through him as he hit the launch sequence for the drones. Then he grabbed a joystick and brought out a little surprise for the redhead and her friends.

Nolan had almost made it to the bunker entrance. He crouched and waited for Lucy and the others to catch up. The bunker had been hidden in a dell that was about two hundred feet lower in elevation than the summit. The rock and rubble that had been dug out of the mountaintop to bury the bunker thirty years ago lay in large mounds scattered near the entrance. Pines, mountain laurel and honeysuckle had covered the debris and it looked like part of the mountain. From the air, the entrance wouldn't have been visible, but he spotted a maintained path expertly hidden in all the underbrush.

Lucy, Cao and Tommy crept up behind him. Lucy said, "I'm going to blow the entrance, then we can storm it. Stay put until you get my signal."

Nolan grabbed her hand and said, "Be careful."

"You know the rule, five go in, five come out." She smiled at him, then crept into the bushes.

That's when Nolan heard the hiss of an electronic door opening. He realized it was being transmitted over the mic.

Betsy said, "You ain't gonna believe this."

"What is it?" Lucy's uneasiness resonated over the mic.

"Three portals buried in the mountaintop just opened. I'm not far from one of them. Oh my God! Something's coming out of them—"

"Take cover, Madonna," Lucy said.

Nolan pulled out a night vision scope and followed the high-pitched whirring noises. He tracked the mechanical whines skyward, over Betsy's position on the summit. He blinked in surprise as three dark masses disappeared into the night. Drone planes. The double-prop planes had a wingspan of about six feet, bigger than toy airplanes but not by much. They looked like the type of reconnaissance drones that the Air Service had been experimenting with right before he paid out. They were flying away in three separate directions.

"What the hell those things?" Tommy asked.

"Drones," Nolan said, "probably carrying information."

Lucy emerged from the bushes, having turned back. "Madonna, do you copy that? It's imperative we take them out."

"They're mine," Betsy said.

Three consecutive blasts echoed through the mountains from Betsy's Remington, Sugar. They sounded like cannon fire in the quiet of the mountains.

"Sugar can't stop them," Betsy said, the mic unable to mask

the shocked, anxious tone in her voice. "They have laser sensors like guided missiles or something. They dodged my fire."

"Keep trying," Lucy said.

Hidden spotlights in the ground suddenly blinded Nolan. He glanced over at Lucy and the others. They were caught in the lights, too. Sitting ducks.

"Oh, no. More drones launching," Betsy said.

Nolan watched through the scope as two planes headed straight for them.

Betsy's rifle blasts thundered through the mountains, but the whirr grew louder as the planes swooped toward them.

The next few moments were a crazy blur.

Two red beams speared out from one plane's wing tips. The beams cut through trees, burning trunks in half, tearing across rocks, bits of granite flying in all directions. The beam headed straight for Lucy.

Nolan drew his weapon as he knocked her down before the beam caught her head. He covered her with his body and fired at the drone. The bullets bounced off it.

"What the hell is that?" she said.

"A laser weapon of some kind."

The plane circled around for another pass, while the second plane zoomed toward them. Bullets pinged around them.

Tommy and Cao fired their M4s at the drones, taking cover in the trees and brush.

The first plane dived, the red beam zeroed in on Cao.

Nolan yelled at him, "Get down."

Too late. The beam grazed Cao's right arm. He dropped his weapon, grabbing at the open slice along his forearm. Blood spewed everywhere. Tommy continued shooting at the plane.

"Man down!" Lucy rolled to her feet, zigzagged toward Cao, avoiding bullets and the laser beam.

"Who's down?" Betsy spoke over the mic.

"Cao." Lucy reached Cao and yanked off her long-sleeve camouflage shirt, revealing a sleeveless T-shirt beneath. She wrapped Cao's arm in the shirt to stop the bleeding. He had turned pale, his face twisted in agony.

The planes attacked again. A beam hit an oak near Nolan. The laser cut through the three-foot trunk as if it were whipped cream, then the branches toppled. Half the tree fell straight at him.

He leaped out of the way and he heard Betsy's frantic voice, "Is he all right? Somebody answer me, damn it!"

"It's his arm," Nolan said, not knowing the extent of Cao's injuries. "But he's alive." Nolan scooped up the M4 Cao had dropped and covered Lucy and Cao.

Nolan and Tommy fired at the incoming planes as they made another pass. The drones swooped and circled, returning fire.

Nolan heard Lucy yell and saw Tommy fall.

Nolan leaped behind a tree trunk as the red beam sliced the air where his chest had just been. The planes zoomed past. He hit the dirt and rolled, avoiding a wave of beams flashing straight at him.

Nolan kept firing, his mind identifying a pattern in the defensive maneuvers of whoever was controlling the planes. He caught on to the turns and banks and swirls, then took aim and waited for the plane with the laser weapon to come into his sight.

Rat-a-tat-tat.

He fired at the propellers, feeling the kick of the weapon in his shoulder. Ten consecutive shots.

Metal tore apart, then the plane fell and crashed, exploding into flames.

Nolan caught the other plane as it came straight for him. He dodged a barrage of bullets.

The plane sailed past.

He darted out from behind a pine, raised the M4 and fired at the right propeller. It wavered and dipped.

Nolan tucked and forward rolled, weapon in hand, and fired up under the plane.

It nose-dived and crashed.

Nolan looked up to find Lucy, realizing she might have been right. You can't plan for every danger. You have to improvise your way through it. He expected to see her with Cao, but he only saw Betsy, who had left her position to help Cao.

Lucy pulled Tommy to his feet. Blood oozed from a wound in his thigh.

Nolan ran to help her lift him.

When they had Tommy standing, Lucy let Nolan take the brunt of Tommy's weight. "Can you handle him alone?"

Tommy didn't look pleased and said, "I can make it myself."

"Get over it, Tommy, and let him help you." Lucy's words, though a command, held a tone of familiarity and kindness shared between friends. She looked at Nolan. "Help Betsy get Tommy and Cao down the mountain and see they get to a hospital." Then she took off running toward the summit.

"Lucy, no!" Nolan growled into the mic, frantic because he couldn't stop her and drop Tommy.

"Someone has to cover you. Help them down the mountain."

He watched her running toward the portals, where the steel doors were opening for another launch.

Lucy neared the portals and hunkered down below them, taking cover behind a thick stand of honeysuckle. The portals were six-foot-by-six-foot openings, carved out of solid rock, spaced about fifty feet apart. They were embedded into the side of the summit. The automatic doors were halfway open in preparation for another launch.

She had to crawl up another twenty feet of boulders and

brush to reach them. She scrambled part of the way up, then gunfire erupted behind her. Bullets zoomed past her head.

She spoke over the mic. "Is everyone clear?"

"We're over the fence," Betsy said.

"Take cover."

Lucy spotted the red flare of gunfire coming from behind some trees as she found cover beside a boulder. The bullets thumped into the ground and rocks behind her.

Lucy stayed low and pulled out three sticks of good old dynamite from her backpack. She dipped into a box of C-4, molded the plastique around the tip of the sticks, then yanked off a grenade from her back. She found a spot where she could see around the boulder and still maintain cover. With a jerk of her fingers, she pulled the pin.

"Hello from me." She popped up, throwing the grenade as hard as she could in the direction of the guards. She sighted her Colt on the grenade as if it were a skeet. When it was ten feet from the ground, she pulled off a round.

The grenade exploded.

Trees, debris and men flew in all directions. The guards' screams filled the air.

She clambered the rest of the way to the portals. She lit the dynamite. The metal doors were almost open.

Lucy tossed the dynamite into the first portal and ran for the next one.

Gunfire followed her and she weaved and bobbed, avoiding the bullets. Another line of guards emerged west of her.

She kept running, hopping over rocks, stumbling, rolling. She reached the second portal and hurled a flaming stick through the opening.

The drone was about to take off from the last portal. Lucy tossed the stick of dynamite between its small tires, then she stumbled and sprinted down the rocks for cover, returning fire at the guards with her Colt.

The explosions went off at once, like perfectly orchestrated fireworks. The night sky blazed as if the whole world were on fire.

Lucy dove and covered her head, feeling the percussion of the explosions strumming through her body and the ground. Bits of fallout pummeled her back.

"Chaos, copy?" Nolan's English baritone sounded in her ear.

"Copy, Churchill. Mission accomplished. On to the next one." Lucy wanted to observe the devastation she had created, but she had dropped to a lower elevation, hidden by thick firs.

"I'm covering you."

"Madonna needs your help." Lucy grimaced at Nolan's high-handedness.

"Dragon to Chaos."

"Go." Lucy stood cautiously, glancing around her for unexpected guards to pop out.

"Plan change. I'm helping Madonna down with Viper." Cao's voice sounded ragged with pain.

"You're wounded, too."

"It's done," Nolan broke in. "I'm staying."

Lucy knew no amount of arguing would change Cao's and Nolan's minds. And she could use the backup, so she said, "Roger that. Keep me updated."

Lucy prayed Tommy and Cao would be all right. She'd seen how much blood they both had lost. She was wearing it all over the front of her camouflage fatigues and her T-shirt. Five go in, five come out—the mantra tolled in her mind. The irony hit her. It was not four this time. But five. Let it be five that survive, she mentally repeated, needing to believe the litany.

"Roger, over," Cao said.

Nolan's English accent came back. "I'm all yours, Chaos."

Lucy picked up on the subtext in his voice. "You might be sorry you said that. I'm going for the entrance."

"Right, meet you there."

Telecommand Control Station, Arachne's lair

Smoke poured into the Control Station. Kostas, Blake and Zinzendorf coughed and groped blindly to find a way out. The Control Station, with two feet of solid iron and steel, was hermetically sealed. Because the outside air exchange pipe had taken a hit, smoke instead of fresh air foamed in through the vents, creating a virtual gas chamber.

Kostas yelled at Arachne's image on the screen, "Open the door so we can get out."

"You know the rules."

He hated the frigid calm in her voice. "Please, we're dying in here."

"Poor planning, Kostas. Look at it this way, you've found the design flaws in all your labors."

"Damn you, Arachne," Kostas yelled, beating on the door, swallowing smoke. His eyes burned and tears ran down his cheeks.

"Too late. I've been damned for some time."

Through a blackening haze of smoke, he saw Arachne take a hit off a cigarette, watching them die. Were her pursed lips hinting at a bemused smile?

Blake and Zinzendorf fell to their knees.

Kostas' lungs tightened, strangling him from within. He gasped in smoke and let it burn his insides, then collapsed against the door. The room began to spin. The images on the wall screens whirled around him like a Ferris wheel. Then the smoke claimed him.

Chapter 19

Lucy and Nolan crouched behind a rise of firs growing along the rocky terrain. The entrance to the bunker was about fifty yards from them. They listened to guards' footfalls running past. Nolan's face looked so handsome in the moonlight. She could hear his breathing, practically see his brain calculating as he followed the four guards through the sights of an M4. He had the SIG jammed into his belt. Somewhere along the way he'd turned into Rambo.

She'd set the bomb at the entrance and now held her cell phone. She tapped Nolan on the shoulder, signaling with the phone that she was about to use it to detonate the charge. He nodded that he was ready. She dialed her favorite programmed code, 867-5309.

The explosion sent the guards scurrying in all directions.

In the madness of the moment, Nolan grabbed her and kissed her. Lucy felt the power of his lips down in her knees, and it made her shaky for a second. He broke away, squeezed her in a hug, and said, "You be careful, love."

"This isn't about being careful, it's about stopping Arachne," Lucy whispered back, feeling his hot breath on her face, his arms around her. She wanted to freeze the moment, stay in it, but she knew that was impossible.

He stepped back, all business again, and motioned for her to follow him. They sneaked up behind two guards. Lucy took Lefty. Nolan headed for Righty. He pummeled the guard with his fist. She used the butt end of her Colt on the guy's temple. Both guards ate dirt.

They cautiously made their way to the bunker entrance, picking their way through the metal shards of the mangled door at their feet.

Nolan covered her and waved her to go through.

Lucy spotted a security camera at the entrance. Without breaking stride, she shot out the lens. The silencer on her Colt muffled the report and it sounded like a heavy rock hitting glass.

She stepped into a long cave-like passageway that angled down at a forty-five degree angle. She breathed in cool damp air, laced with the smell of smoke.

Nolan followed her and sniffed the air. "Electrical fire?"

"Smells like it. We have to hurry and search this place."

"Lead the way, love."

Her senses on the alert for danger, Lucy hurried down the passage, their footfalls thundering in the thickening cave-like silence. The deeper the pathway drew them into the mountain, the more Lucy's gut tightened with unease. If this was a trap, this would be the perfect spot for it. "Come in, said the spider to the fly." The nursery rhyme sparked in her mind. A shiver slithered down the back of her neck.

They reached a set of double doors. Without warning, guards popped out as if they'd been waiting for them. Shots erupted.

Lucy somersaulted, returning fire. Nolan hit the ground, following her lead. In seconds Lucy rolled to her feet. She wheeled in Nolan's direction to see if he was all right. He was already standing, three guards sprawled at his feet.

Nolan stepped over them as he cautiously pushed a door open. He glanced back at her, the dim fluorescent corridor lights turning Nolan's eyes to honed gray glass. "Stay here. Let me do a little reconnaissance."

"The hell you will," she blurted. "You're not pulling that martyr crap with me again." As if she needed his protection. She should have felt offended. But she couldn't stay provoked at him seeing the concern in his eyes.

"Suit yourself." He shot her an annoyed glance and didn't argue, as if he knew better. He made sure it was clear, then waved her through.

The passage led straight down. The smell of smoke grew stronger. Finally they reached a dead end. Two steel security doors stood before them. They looked like bank vault doors, solid metal, and electronically controlled and sealed.

Nolan sniffed the air. "Smells like the smoke is coming from behind the door on the right."

"We'll search that way last."

She pulled out the C-4 and det cord from her backpack. She cautiously packed just the right amount of C-4 along the base, the sides, and the top of the door. She lit the cords.

Nolan grabbed her and covered her with his body.

Lucy counted the seconds to detonation, "Four, three, two, one…"

The discharge sent the doors tumbling. A whoosh of air brushed past Lucy as they crashed down.

Even before the smoke cleared, Nolan was stepping up to the entrance. Lucy avoided the felled door and followed him. A cacophony of sound emanated from the doorway. It reminded Lucy of walking through a television retailer who had all the televisions turned on at once, a chaotic yet well-ordered sound.

Nolan and she shared a look, then separated, taking opposite sides of the room. They kept their guns close, elbows locked, as they peeked inside.

What Lucy saw made her mouth fall open. It even gave Nolan pause. A cavity the size of a rotunda held huge plasma screens that ran floor to ceiling along the walls. Hundreds of satellite images played out before her eyes and formed a patchwork quilt of transmissions. It looked like a mission control room for NASA, multiplied by a thousand, set up for the ultimate spying web.

There was order to the turmoil of pictures in front of her. They were grouped in zones. Lucy instantly recognized the exterior views of government offices such as Capitol Hill and the White House. Connected to the peripheral shots were interior security images of senators' offices and representatives' offices. The main buildings of the CIA, NSA, FBI, the United Nations and many other intel agencies from across the globe. Offices of well-known CEO's and heads of state. She did a double take when she spotted the Athena Academy's main building, the familiar wraithlike image of the White Tank Mountains rising up behind it.

Lucy's gaze shifted to the center of the huge gallery. A woman, her emaciated body almost nonexistent beneath a black overshirt and pants, sat on a bridge. An evil female Captain Kirk, save for a body that looked wasted and bony arms so fragile they looked ready to snap if she moved the wrong way. Her lackluster chestnut hair fell in stringy disarray to her shoulders. She puffed on a cigarette and grinned at them. Her blue eyes gleamed, the dark circles beneath them emphasizing the desperate and haunted light in them. She could have passed as Miranda N'Buta's unhealthy twin. Was she Arachne, or one of her stand-ins?

"Do come in." Her voice resonated around the huge space, muting the sound coming from the screen images. "It took you long enough."

Lucy and Nolan walked deeper into the cavernous room, their weapons pointed at Arachne.

She didn't look at all alarmed, more entertained.

"Your game is over," Nolan said.

"I'm very disappointed in you, Mr. Taylor."

"Why? Because I didn't turn out to be your puppet?"

"Among other things. I was so counting on you retrieving my documents."

"You like playing with people's lives, don't you?"

"You have to admit it's fascinating. Like watching thousands of plays unfolding before your eyes." She emptied her lungs of smoke in one long blow. "Look before you, both of you. You'll never again see such cutting-edge technology. The radio telescope signals are filtered through a sound system scrambler and recorded on my computer network. No one is beyond my reach, and I can tell you this—human nature is an ugly, selfish beast if you study it. I can see the whole world in all its merciless colors sitting right here."

"But can you see yourself?" Lucy asked.

It captured Arachne's attention. "You dare judge me." Her pale face reddened with rage. "You, a pitiful automaton made by Marion Gracelyn's Athena Academy," she snarled as she spat out the last two words. "Do you know what she did to me? She betrayed me and caused the death of the only man I ever loved. I lost his child because of her…." Her voice had risen until she was screaming, and it brought on a coughing fit. She grabbed a handkerchief and put it up to her mouth.

When Arachne could breathe again she brought down the

handkerchief. A small spot of blood glowed stark against the white material. Lucy also saw tears streaming down Arachne's cheeks. For a moment, Lucy could see beneath Arachne's persona, to her humanity, driven by loneliness and bitterness and desperation. Had Lucy and Nolan found the true Arachne?

She gazed at Lucy. "Don't dare look at me with pity in your eyes. I'm dying. That doesn't mean you win. Because if you win, Marion Gracelyn wins." She smiled, her yellow teeth stained by blood and tobacco, an insane gleam alive in her eyes.

"Were you behind Marion's murder?" Lucy asked.

Arachne's smile told Lucy all she needed to know. "Who hired you?"

It was Lucy's turn to smile, a smile that was solid, unmovable. "You're the all-knowing Oz. You tell me."

Arachne's smile disappeared. "Watch your insolence. I can kill you in a blink."

Lucy didn't doubt her. She hid her fear behind a bravado she didn't feel as she asked, "You must have created your doubles and settled them around the world before you learned of your illness."

"That's correct." Arachne's gaze tightened on Lucy. "I never dreamed they'd be my downfall."

"Where did you dig up the super assassin you sent to blow up Miranda's office?" Lucy asked. "She human or what?"

Arachne merely smiled, her whole face seeming to glow from it. "She's a special protégée. Too bad she didn't finish you both."

Nolan said, "Now we're going to finish you." He made a move toward Arachne's image.

A laser beam shot out of nowhere and seared a line along the tip of his boots. He froze, smoke rising up from the burned rubber sole.

Lucy glanced up and saw four globe-shaped robots

embedded in each corner of the room. Two feet in circumference, protected by a glass shield, hundreds of embedded fiber-optic eyes blinked at her. A roving barrel protruded from the center of each robot, and they were aimed at Lucy and Nolan. Now she knew why Arachne seemed so confident.

"I wouldn't move," Arachne warned. "These little jewels guard my inner sanctum. Their laser weapons are ten thousandths of a second accurate. I've seen them destroy a fly in midair. Now drop your weapons."

Lucy threw down the Colt. Nolan tossed the M4 and SIG stuck in the back of his pants on the cement floor.

"Good." One of Arachne's bony fingers hit a button.

Nolan tensed and said, "What did you just do?"

"I pushed a self-destruct detonator. You really didn't think I'd let you take me alive, did you? No, I'm going out in a blaze of glory, and I'm taking both of you and the Athena Academy with me." An evil grin tugged at her thin lips as she began putting in a code on a keypad near her hand. "As soon as I punch in this number, a remote detonator will turn on and the Academy will be no more."

Fear clenched at Lucy's gut. She glanced around the huge room and saw the charges set below each robot, the LCD screens counting down the minutes and seconds.

1:52, 1:51…

Oh, God. Arachne wasn't lying. And if she finished that code, all the students and faculty at the Athena Academy were in jeopardy.

Chapter 20

Mountain base

Cao felt his arm throbbing with fire. Lucy's shirt had soaked through with blood. He fought the dizzy feeling in his head as he struggled to support half of Tommy's weight. Betsy held up the other half.

"Stop here a moment," Cao said.

"If you can't make it, it's okay. I can handle Tommy's weight," Betsy said.

"I'm sorry to be a burden," Tommy grumbled, breaking Betsy's hold on his elbow and leaning against a tree. He rubbed his bleeding thigh as if it helped the pain.

"It's not that." Cao reached for his backpack and struggled to pull out his laptop with one hand.

"This is no time to be stopping." Betsy stepped over and helped him extract it.

"It'll only take a second." He sat on the ground and opened the laptop. "I don't know if it will work, but it might help Lucy and Nolan get inside the bunker."

"What might help them?" Betsy folded her arms over her chest and frowned at him.

"When I was in the NRAO's control room, sifting through Arachne's cloaked portal, I added a self-destruct program that would shut down the whole computer system as a safeguard. I didn't want it to tip off Arachne that we were coming so I put a delay on it—if it got through the filters undetected, that is. There were some amazing filters in those cloaked programs. I'm not certain my program is even running now. I just want to check."

"Make it quick." Betsy let out an impatient sigh.

"Just a sec." Cao waited for the connection, but a window popped up saying he was out of range. "No Wi-Fi signal here."

Betsy peered over his shoulder. "Looks like you're out of luck this time. Check it later. Let's go."

Cao frowned at the computer, then slammed the lid shut. His arm hurt worse now. He glanced back up the mountain behind them and wondered if his program would have helped Lucy and Nolan.

Arachne's bunker

The seconds strummed against Lucy's ribs, along her face and throat. She glanced at the many-eyed robots, their flashing red orbs watching her. She wished now that she and Nolan had some kind of silent communication code. Nolan might have been partly correct: you *can* plan ahead for some things.

She glanced back at Arachne. She was still tapping in the

code. Lucy couldn't stand idly by and let Arachne finish putting in that number. Hundreds of people could die.

Lucy glanced at the timer: 0:41 seconds and counting. The robots' eyes were blinking red at her, daring her to move.

Oh, God. This was it. They had to do something. Make their move now.

Arachne stopped punching in the numbers and stared at the tiny LCD screen near the keypad. "Something's wrong. The code is not working." Arachne banged on the screen. "Why isn't it working?"

Lucy gazed at Nolan, then at Arachne.

As if he grasped the meaning of her glance, he motioned with his eyes toward the robots.

They both jumped at the same time.

Lucy went for the Colt in her ankle and dove for the floor.

Nolan grabbed the SIG where he'd dropped it and rolled, drawing the robots fire at him.

Lasers flashed in all directions, their killing beams everywhere in Lucy's vision. She felt a beam hit her leg. Pain seared her calf and ripped down her heel as she fell.

The beams suddenly stopped. Life drained from the robots, their orbs closing as if they'd gone into sleep mode. All the screens turned black. The power in the rotunda flicked off; only the emergency lights near the floor burned. An eerie silence blanketed everything.

Lucy could hear her own heartbeats sounding like drums in her ears. She didn't know what had happened, but she'd take the luck. Then she glanced at the timers.

Still running: 0:39, 0:38.

Her luck was quickly running out. She pulled herself up, pain shooting up to her knee.

"No, this isn't happening," Arachne screamed, then Lucy heard an electrical hiss and saw Nolan running for the door.

"Hurry, Lucy." Nolan spoke over the mic, dodging the laser weapon in Arachne's hand. It was shaped like a cell phone. She was shooting sporadically at him.

Lucy realized he was drawing Arachne's fire. She hobbled for the door. They were both running for their lives.

"No! You won't get away!" Arachne shrieked, her homicidal, resigned eyes narrowing on Lucy.

Nolan returned fire, covering Lucy as she came through the doorway.

A laser beam burned off a corner of the metal threshold. It flew against Lucy's shoulder. The heat burned her shirt and skin, but it was nothing compared to the pain in her calf.

Nolan tossed his weapon away, grabbed her hand, and they ran up the corridor, a race against time. Lucy could feel the seconds keeping time with her heartbeat.

She couldn't make her leg move fast enough. Her right calf was on fire. All she could do was limp, and each step took an eternity. She felt Nolan pulling her up the corridor and she knew she was slowing him down. It was too late for her.

"Go on without me. Save yourself," she yelled at him, feeling her lucky charm thumping against her chest. A lot of good it was doing her.

"Two go in. Two come out." He swept her up in his arms without losing a beat and continued running.

"Cheap shot, Nolan. We'll both die."

"I'm not leaving you."

She looked into his handsome brave face, strained slightly under her weight. Her future became instantly clear to her, as if she were peering at her whole life through the crystal weight of his eyes. And she felt the inner loneliness that had bound her heart for years. It became a boulder in her chest. Nolan's glistening blue eyes were the last thing she saw before the explosion.

Base of Spring Knob Mountain

The explosion rocked the ground beneath Betsy's feet, the aftershock quaking up her legs and settling in her chest. She and Cao had secured Tommy into the front seat of the Jeep, and they both paused.

"Dear Lord," she said. She glanced behind her and saw a plume of flames lighting up the night sky. It looked as if the mountain had suffered a volcanic eruption and the top of it spewed molten flames.

She and Cao shared a look, fraught with uncertainty and anguish.

"Hope that was one of Lucy's explosions?" Tommy mumbled, then closed his eyes as if struggling with the pain.

"I'd hate to think it was Arachne's." Betsy spoke louder over the bone mic, her voice tight with worry. "Madonna to Chaos, copy?"

Nothing.

Betsy, frantic now, yelled into the mic. "Damn it, Chaos, you there?"

No response.

"Churchill, you copy?"

"Maybe they're out of range," Cao said.

"We can only pray they are."

Cao kept staring up the mountain. "I'm going back."

"No, you're hurt," Betsy said, helping Cao into the backseat. "How far you gonna get bleeding like you are?" She looked at the bloody shirt wrapped around his arm. Blood had soaked his own shirt up to his shoulder. "You can barely stand. It was all you could do to help me get Tommy in the Jeep. If they're not okay, there's nothing we can do now."

Betsy had already called the nearest emergency hospital in

Charlottesville, Virginia, and they were sending a MEDVAC chopper.

The Adam's apple in Cao's throat bobbed and the pain she saw on his face wasn't all from his wound. "I guess my program didn't work."

"You tried. That's all that counts. That's all any of us can do." Betsy felt one of those dismal life-reassuring moments, where she was worried for Lucy, but she couldn't help feeling relieved it wasn't her up on the top of that mountain. Betsy would have gladly taken Lucy's place, and she knew Lucy would have done the same for her. That's what hurt so much. And she knew Cao was having the same thoughts. It made her bend down and touch her lips to his.

Cao wrapped his good hand around the back of her neck, and he deepened the kiss, not letting her go. She felt the warmth of his lips and realized heroes came in all shapes and sizes. Some were even geeks.

"'Bout time you guys finally got around to it," Tommy's weak voice came from the front seat.

They broke the kiss, both realizing they were not alone. Something dawned on Betsy and she said, "Oh my God. I left Sugar behind."

Passion and brightness she'd never seen before burned in Cao's expression as he said, "She's most likely destroyed by now."

"I've never left her anywhere before." Betsy sighed and said, "We'd better go." She slammed the door and ran around to the driver's side, realizing she wouldn't have left Sugar behind if she hadn't been worried about Cao.

She hopped in the Jeep and started the engine, then pulled out her cell phone. They had agreed ahead of time to call their contact if the mission didn't go as planned. Betsy sped down the dirt road and hit their employer's number. It was a call she dreaded. She wished Lucy was making it instead of her. Tears stung her eyes, and the shadowy dirt road blurred in the Jeep's headlights.

Chapter 21

Nolan couldn't breathe. He realized he was buried beneath rock and bunker debris. He slowly sat up, pieces of rubble falling all around him. He felt a bit like the undead rising from a grave. Several of his ribs ached. Probably broken. He just needed to find Lucy.

He glanced around. Smoke from the explosion was starting to clear, though it hung like cotton in his lungs. He stood up, shaking off the queasy feeling in his stomach, searching for Lucy. Where was she?

He turned to the closest pile of debris and tore into it. Jagged rocks and bits of metal cut into his bare hands as he dug through the rubble.

"Lucy, speak to me." Nolan's vision blurred and tears trailed down his cheeks. It could be the smoke irritating his eyes. He knew it wasn't. For the first time in his life he felt the steely hold on his feelings slipping from his grasp. Emotion churned and swelled inside him like a violent storm and there was no order to them. Just raging bedlam that he couldn't compartmentalize and contain. He'd never felt so adrift.

"LUCY!" He screamed at the top of his lungs.

"Stop yelling."

Nolan froze at the sound of her wilting voice in the mic. She was alive. He allowed himself to breathe again and said, "Bloody hell, woman, where are you?"

"Behind you."

Nolan turned and saw her just sitting up, throwing aside rubble and bits of brush that had covered her. She had landed on an edge of a boulder, on her side. Her fatigues were ripped and scorched. The laser shot on the side of her calf had torn through her pants and looked jagged and raw. The ponytail she'd worn had come loose and her red hair stuck out all over her head, layered with dirt and grime, singed in spots. She'd never looked more fetching to him. Seeing her alive set a fire loose in his chest.

He ran to her side to help her stand.

She touched his cheek. "You've been crying." Her voice softened. "Over me?"

"You unbalance me, woman. I'm nothing but a jumbled muddle around you."

"I kinda like you that way." She kissed him.

Nolan hugged her so hard she cried out. He broke the kiss and loosened his grip. "Forgive me, love. I'm just glad we both made it. Come on. You need to see a doctor."

"There's nothing wrong with me but my leg," she said, her voice lacking its usual bold confidence. "I'm not leaving here. The authorities will be climbing all over this place soon. We have to search it before they get here."

"You need a doctor."

"What I need is your help."

Lucy used his arm to support herself and said, "Oh, God.

I can still see her eyes. I'll never forget that look on her face. It'll haunt me 'till I die."

"It was the look of defeat."

"We need to check on the Athena Academy and update Delphi."

"We will."

"And Cao and Tommy."

"Right. Stop worrying about everyone else and worry about yourself for once."

At that moment, someone called Lucy's name. A form emerged out of the darkness. Nolan flinched, taking up a defensive stance in front of Lucy.

"It's me, Allison Gracelyn."

Lucy touched his arm. "Stand down. She's a friend."

"Can we trust her?" Nolan asked.

"Of course." Lucy wondered if Delphi had sent Allison. It was the only thing that explained her sudden appearance.

A flashlight flicked on and moved over both of them. "Do you think we found the real Arachne?" Allison asked.

Lucy said, "My gut tells me she was the real deal, but forensic evidence will confirm it."

"We better look for it in a hurry," Allison said. "An army of CIA, NSA and U.S. military agents are on their way here as we speak."

So Allison was on clean-up detail.

"Great," Lucy said. "How'd they get wind we found Arachne?"

"My guess? They have connections at the NRAO, too."

"Delphi send you?" Lucy asked to confirm her suspicions.

"Yes. Sorry, I couldn't get here sooner. I've had my own troubles." She paused near Nolan. All he could see was her dark shoulder-length hair behind the flashlight and hourglass figure. "Are you sure you're both up to staying?"

"Bitter end for me," Lucy said.

Nolan nodded. "You have us both."

Allison motioned toward the destroyed bunker. "What about the rest of your team?"

"We had wounded."

Nolan said, "Arachne launched three drones. We tried to destroy them, but they got away."

"It's anyone's guess where they were heading," Lucy said. "Probably carrying instructions upon her death."

Allison sighed. "That's unfortunate. It means she has a network."

"Cao e-mailed the information I'm about to tell you, but you should know it, too." Lucy tried to put weight on her leg and Nolan had to help steady her. "There were spy filters in the cloaked line Arachne had tapped into from the NRAO computer. Cao tracked them back to Hong Kong, but couldn't get an exact location. Someone was spying on Arachne's operation."

"It just gets worse and worse, doesn't it?" Allison said, sounding tired.

Lucy asked, "Is the Athena Academy okay? Arachne threatened to destroy it right after she activated the bombs to blow up the bunker. She couldn't finish putting in the code… I hope we stopped her in time."

Allison's eyes took on a haunted look. "Oh, no. That would be just like her to do something so vindictive." She pulled out her cell phone and walked away from Nolan and Lucy.

"What's the Athena Academy?" Nolan asked.

"A school for girls that we both attended."

Nolan picked up on the fear in Lucy's voice and he knew the school meant a lot to her. He hoped they had stopped Arachne in time before she took more lives.

* * *

Thirty minutes later, Lucy felt drops of perspiration falling down the sides of her face as she hobbled through the rubble, looking for evidence of Arachne's body. Her calf throbbed, but she was determined to help Allison. She leaned on a piece of plumbing pipe Nolan had given her as a makeshift cane and paused beside Allison, who squatted over something.

The bunker had been reduced to rubble. Parts of the debris still smoldered in spots. The corridor leading down into the bunker had acted like a pathway for the energy burst, causing it to maintain its intensity. Another bunker area, a room made of solid steel with walls two feet thick, had survived the blast. It was a smaller version of Arachne's bridge, a control room of some sort. When Nolan had opened the door, they'd found three bodies inside along with powerful computer processors untouched save for smoke damage. Surprisingly, the power lines to the room had been sealed inside the steel, and Allison had brought up the computer and downloaded whatever files were left in it, then wiped the memory clean.

Allison's cell phone rang. She and Lucy shared a tense look, then Allison answered, "Yes. In the gym. The locker room. Thank goodness."

When she said goodbye, Lucy didn't care about the pretension of eavesdropping and blatantly asked, "They found the bomb?"

"Yes. Arachne told the truth. She wanted to destroy the school."

"It's disarmed now?"

"Mrs. Warren came to the rescue. Seems there was enough plastique to blow up three academies hidden in a gym locker with a cell phone detonator."

Lucy's shoulders sagged with relief that it was all over.

Nolan said, "I think I've found something." He was

pointing the flashlight Allison had lent him at a pile of rubble near his feet. He picked up something. "Looks like a part of a human bone."

Allison shined her own flashlight on the bone fragment in Nolan's wide hand. "Looks like a femur." She held out an evidence bag. "Good work, Mr. Taylor."

He grinned at Allison as he dropped the fragment inside. "My pleasure, madam."

At the warm smile Allison gave him, Lucy felt a bite of jealousy.

Footsteps and voices sounded from the corridor.

Lucy saw Allison hide the evidence bag inside the waist of her jeans.

Guns clicked.

A voice said, "Hold it right there."

Allison turned and shined her flashlight on four men. Suits, as Lucy liked to call them. They looked like FBI or their cousins. She shifted the light back to one suit, a handsome tall guy with prematurely graying hair and dark blue eyes.

"Morgan Rush." Allison said the name as if it left a bitter taste in her mouth.

Lucy whispered to Allison, "Who's he?"

"The trouble I was having. He's an NSA agent and he's been a little too interested in my comings and goings lately. And I've had to keep the NSA from discovering our pursuit of Arachne."

Rush said, "Allison, what are you doing here?"

"I could ask you the same thing."

"I'm working."

"So am I."

Lucy felt as if she were watching two gunfighters facing each other, ready to draw.

"Who are these people?" Rush shined his flashlight on Lucy and Nolan. "This is a crime scene."

"Friends, helping me."

"Friends?" Rush slowly fanned the flashlight over Nolan's tall frame, his burned clothes, dirt and smoke all over him. Then to Lucy, who didn't look any better. "I'll need to question them."

"You know the protocol, Rush. I'm the first agent on the scene. That makes it my crime scene," Allison said. "If you have any questions, direct them to me. Better tell your friends there," she shined the flashlight on the other three men, "to be careful."

Rush's blue eyes shifted from Lucy to Nolan to Allison. Then frustration pulled at his brow.

Allison's gaze shifted to Lucy and Nolan. "You guys can leave. I can handle it from here. Thanks for your help."

Lucy smiled into Allison's confident brown eyes and had no concerns about leaving her alone with the authorities.

Nolan walked over and grabbed Lucy's arm. "Let's motor, love."

"Okay." Lucy hobbled on her pipe as she glanced behind her and saw Allison and Rush nose to nose, speaking in angry hushed tones. Rush was in for the fight of his life. Lucy's grin faded as she reached up and felt her neck. Tears came to her eyes, and she had a hard time blinking them away.

"What's wrong?"

"My lucky charm. It's gone. Must have lost it in the explosion." Lucy felt as if a part of her childhood had vanished with it, the best memories of her father. She looked over at him. "Do you have a cell phone that works? I lost mine in the blast."

"Of course, here. Are you calling to check on Cao and Tommy?"

"Yes, then I have to call my dad." After surviving the blast,

Lucy knew she couldn't go another day, another hour, another minute, without calling her father and telling him that she wanted them to be closer. He had to know that she loved him. She didn't care if he reciprocated her affections. He just had to know how she felt.

"There'll be a charge for the calls."

Lucy fixed him with a level stare. "There's always some kind of catch with you."

His eyes twinkled with a calculating gleam she knew all too well. "Don't worry, love, I'll collect when the time is right."

"I bet you will."

The shrewd grin never left his face.

Chapter 22

Allison Gracelyn sat in her office with the door locked, a preventative against one of Agent Morgan Rush's unannounced visits. He seemed to appear at the worst times, an annoyance that she knew wasn't going away anytime soon. In fact, he was still annoyed with her after catching her at the bunker. She refused to answer any of his questions because he refused to answer any of hers, such as how he knew about the bunker. They were at a standoff.

She hit the Page Down button and watched the file names scroll past. It was the information Cao had e-mailed her on the microdots recovered from the Cape Town bank vault. She had been reviewing the files for an hour now, mostly bank account data on Arachne's blackmail client list. She wanted information on the spy who'd intercepted Cao's transmission in Hong Kong and who'd been tapping into Arachne's network. It was a long shot, Allison knew.

Windows chimed and she received an instant message box. Thankful for the interruption, she clicked on the message:

Hey, Allison,
We had a hit on the femur DNA: Jackie Cavanaugh. Weird and physically impossible. Jackie Cavanaugh was some kind of rogue CIA assassin in the '70s and has been assumed dead for years. I plan to run the test again to see if I get the same results. I'll keep you posted.
Later,
Alex

Allison had given Alex Forsythe, a fellow Athena grad and FBI forensic scientist, the bone sample Nolan had found in the bunker. So Arachne *had* been Jackie Cavanaugh, a CIA assassin. That would explain Arachne's infamous cunning and inventive ways of murder and blackmail. It must not have been hard faking her own death out in the field, a rogue assassin that could have become an embarrassment to the CIA. The CIA had probably been relieved to pronounce her dead.

Allison should have felt elated about confirming Arachne's identity and her death. It should have made her happy to know that the threat to the Athena Academy and everything her mother had worked so hard to build was finally over. But she felt only unease. Lucy had told Allison that Arachne looked as if she was dying. What if Arachne had made a backup plan in case the bomb she had planted at the Academy hadn't detonated? Maybe Arachne's final coup de grâce was still out there, waiting to happen.

Allison shook her head and told herself she was inventing trouble. Tracking a nemesis like Arachne had made her overly cautious.

She continued scrolling. Minutes ticked by. She began to see double and was about to close the window when she paused at the file name: Mylek Gegs.

The anagram jumped out at her: My eggs. But what did the l-e-k stand for? She opened the file and soon found out.

A Lab 33 document filled the screen, written in Dr. Aldrich Peters' own hand. The powers that be at the NSA had let Allison review the files they'd recovered at Lab 33. She had read about Peters's sordid experiments in human genetics and test tube babies. Peters had been a madman.

Allison read the date. It was before the experiments were conducted on Rainy Miller. Rainy's eggs were taken by Dr. Peters without her knowledge or consent while she attended the Athena Academy. Lab 33 was in Arizona, not far from the school. Allison had often wondered how many other students suffered from Peters's experiments.

She read down to the donor line: Jackie Cavanaugh.

Her insides felt as if someone had kicked her. Allison struggled to breathe. Arachne had somehow donated eggs to Lab 33?

The eggs had been labeled alphabetically, E, K and L.

Had they survived?

Allison thought of the drones Arachne had launched. Three eggs. Three drones. What information had they carried? And where had they gone? Had one of them gone to Hong Kong? The possibilities churned in Allison's mind and made her dizzy.

Epilogue

Nolan felt the bass thumping in his chest. Colored lights flashed across the club as the heavy metal band pounded out a song he'd never heard before. The walls of the club felt as if they might collapse from the noise. People crowded the dance floor, jumping and bumping to the music.

Nolan kept his gaze on Lucy and Tommy dancing. Lucy seemed to thrive in the middle of all the commotion, smiling, pulling Tommy around the dance floor as if she owned it. Her calf had healed, and so had his ribs. Tommy still hadn't come to grips with having Nolan on the team, and every now and then his smile would fade when his eyes met Nolan's.

Nolan wondered again how Lucy had managed to drag him to this nightclub. What he really wanted to do was take her off to their quiet hotel room and make love to her. He noticed that his Long Island iced tea wasn't where it should be and he picked up the tumbler to put it directly in the middle of the coaster. The song ended abruptly.

Lucy came up behind him and grabbed his hand. "Oh, no you don't." She grabbed his drink and polished it off, missing the coaster entirely when she put the glass down. "Come on, let's dance."

The band struck up a slow song.

Nolan allowed Lucy to yank him out to the dance floor, smiling at her, aware his life would never be monotonous or dull with her in it.

"So, your mother and father are flying in to meet you tomorrow?" he asked, making small talk.

"Seems Dad and I are getting along better, and they both can spare the time. Mom says it'll be like a second honeymoon for them. Speaking of honeymoons, look at those two," she said, nodding to Cao and Betsy.

They were in the middle of the dance floor, slow dancing, seemingly oblivious to the beat of the music and everyone else around them. Cao had his good arm locked around Betsy's waist, holding her as if she were the most precious thing in his life. His other arm was in a full cast up past his shoulder.

"They've been inseparable since Cao left the hospital," Lucy said.

Nolan wrapped his arms around her waist. "They finally got around to being honest about their feelings. Which reminds me, I'm collecting on that debt you owe me."

Her brown eyes looked confused for a moment, then a memory dawned in her expression. "Oh, the phone thing."

"Right."

"Payback is hell. What do you have in mind?" Her eyes twinkled with a ginger light.

He grinned at her. "As you know, I have no job in Cape Town. I'm currently unable to go back to England—"

"You're staying on my ranch."

"Which works for me, but I won't be a kept man. I have my principles. I need employment."

"Uh-huh. I get it now. You think you're ready to become a mercenary? It's not easy work, you know."

"With you around, I'm certain it isn't." He looked deep into her eyes and pulled her close, dancing hip to hip. He could feel himself becoming aroused. She could stimulate him just by entering a room.

"I see that's not all you want," she crooned, her earthy brown eyes softening with that sexy cat-like look that drove him crazy. She wiggled her hips seductively against his and made his breath catch. "The list is growing by the second. Now you want two things from me?"

She laughed, throwing back her head. Her red hair hung loose around her shoulders. He'd never noticed before, but her hair was an extraordinary red. Gold highlights tipped the ends.

"As many as I can wangle out of you, love," he whispered back.

"Well, you'll have to think of something else as my payment besides being on the team." She wiggled her brows at him.

His hand moved up, delving into the softness of her hair. He pulled her face close, almost tasting her lips. "Why?"

"You already are part of the team. Jeez, you English can be slow." She teased him with a grin.

"But we catch on quickly." Nolan kissed her, letting her lead him around the dance floor. He deepened the kiss until he heard her sigh. It was all he could take. He swept her up and headed for the door.

* * * * *

Don't miss the next exciting Athena Force adventure!
BENEATH THE SURFACE
by Meredith Fletcher
Available May 2008!
Turn the page for a sneak preview.

The second time Shannon Conner talked with Vincent Drago, the freelance information specialist wrapped a hand around her neck, slammed her against a wall hard enough to drive the air from her lungs, put a gun to her head and told her, "I'm going to blow your head off for setting me up."

The first time she'd talked with him had been over the phone, and she'd used an alias. Maybe if she hadn't started everything with a lie, things might have gone more smoothly.

"Wait," Shannon croaked desperately. *Wait? He's pointing a gun at your head, looking like he's going to use it, and the best you can come up with is wait?* She really couldn't believe herself. Maybe something was wrong with her survival instinct.

Other reporters and friends, or what passed as friends—acquaintances, really—had sometimes said they suspected she had a death wish.

Shannon didn't think that was true. She wanted to live. She glanced around the small room in the back of the bar where Drago had arranged to meet her. Actually, he'd arranged to meet her up front. He'd just yanked her into the back room at the first opportunity.

Then he'd slammed her up against the wall and put the gun to her head. If she'd known he was going to do that, she wouldn't have shown up.

"Do you know how much trouble I'm in because of you?" Drago demanded.

"No," Shannon croaked around the vise-grip of the man's big hand. "How much?" She'd been trained for years to ask open-ended questions.

From what Shannon had found out about Drago, he had a shady career. Some of Shannon's police contacts had claimed the man sometimes worked for the government on hush-hush jobs. Others claimed he was a semilegal blackmailer.

Drago was six feet six inches tall and looked like a human bulldozer. His carroty orange hair offered a warning about the dark temper he possessed. His goatee was a darker red, and kept neatly trimmed. He wore good suits and had expensive tastes. He could afford them because he did business with Fortune 500 companies.

According to the information Shannon had gotten, Drago was one of the best computer hackers working the private investigation scene. The man was supposedly an artist when it came to easing through firewalls and cracking encryptions. He was supposed to be more deadly with a computer than he was with a weapon.

Shannon was pretty sure she wouldn't have felt as threatened if Drago had been holding a computer keyboard to her head. Of course, he could have bashed her brains out with it.

She held on to Drago's wrist with both of her hands and tried to reel in her imagination. Thinking about the different ways he could kill her wasn't going to help.

"Somebody found out about me," Drago snarled. Angry red spots mottled his pale face.

"You advertise in the Yellow Pages," Shannon pointed out. "People are supposed to find out about you."

"Somebody got into my computer." Drago looked apoplectic. "*My* computer! Nobody gets into my computer. Who are you working for?" Drago slammed her against the wall again.

The back of Shannon's head struck the wall. Black spots danced in her vision. She tried to remember the last time she'd had her life on the line, and thought it was during her coverage of the apartment fires that had broken out downtown. Nine people had died in that blaze. She'd very nearly been one of them.

Shannon held on to Drago's thick wrist in quiet desperation. Even standing on tiptoes she could barely draw a breath of air.

"I'm not working for anyone," Shannon said.

"You work for American Broadcasting Systems."

"I told you that. I also told you this wasn't a story I was covering for the news station." That was true. Oddly enough, throughout her years as a reporter, Shannon had discovered more people believed lies than truths. They just seemed to *want* to.

"Are you working for the government?" Drago asked.

"No."

"Because the Web sites I tracked felt like federal government sniffers to me."

That was surprising. Shannon didn't know why the federal government would have been feeding her the information she'd been getting lately. Or before, for that matter.

"I don't work for the government," Shannon insisted.

Her mind raced. She knew a physical confrontation with Drago was going to end badly. She was a foot shorter than he was and weighed about half of what he did. The room contained crates and cases of liquor. The single low-wattage bulb in the ceiling barely chased the night out of the space.

There was no help there, and nothing within reach that she could use as a club.

"I've seen you on television," Drago said. "I've seen you lie and wheedle your way into stories that other reporters couldn't get."

Despite being strung up against the wall, Shannon took momentary pride in her accomplishments. Getting recognized for something she'd done felt good. It always had.

"I knew I shouldn't have trusted you," Drago went on. He smiled, but there was no humor or warmth in the effort. "From the start I figured you were out to cross me up. But I bought into that blond hair and those doe-soft brown eyes." He leaned down, a long way down, and sniffed her hair.

Shannon cringed, and couldn't help closing her eyes. She hated being manhandled. She resisted the urge to scream only because she thought if she did, he might kill her outright to shut her up.

"You sold me, baby," Drago whispered into her ear. "Hook, line and sinker. You had me with that teary-eyed look—"

Shannon didn't use that one often, but she knew it almost guaranteed instant game, set and match when she did. She just didn't like appearing weak.

"—and the way you told me you needed help to find a cyberstalker."

Well, that was almost true.

Shannon had to struggle to keep from hiccupping in fear. The need to know what Drago had discovered almost leeched away the power her fear had over her. "Who did you find?"

nocturne™

THE FINAL INSTALLMENT OF
THE BLOODRUNNERS TRILOGY

Last Wolf Watching

Runner Brody Carter has found his match in
Michaela Doucet, a human with unusual psychic powers.
When Michaela's brother is threatened, Brody becomes
her protector, and suddenly not only has to protect her
from her enemies but also from himself....

LOOK FOR
LAST WOLF WATCHING
BY
RHYANNON
BYRD

Available May 2008 wherever you buy books.

Dramatic and Sensual Tales of Paranormal Romance

HARLEQUIN® Romance®

Western Weddings

Jason Welborn was convinced that his business partner's daughter, Jenny, had come to claim her share in the business. But Jenny seemed determined to win him over, and the more he tried to push her away, the more feisty Jenny's response. Slowly but surely she was starting to get under Jason's skin....

Look for

Coming Home to the Cattleman

by

JUDY CHRISTENBERRY

Available May wherever you buy books.

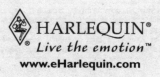

HARLEQUIN®
Live the emotion™

www.eHarlequin.com

HRI7511

REQUEST YOUR FREE BOOKS!

2 FREE NOVELS PLUS 2 FREE GIFTS!

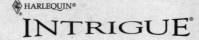
HARLEQUIN®
INTRIGUE®

Breathtaking Romantic Suspense

YES! Please send me 2 FREE Harlequin Intrigue® novels and my 2 FREE gifts (gifts are worth about $10). After receiving them, if I don't wish to receive any more books, I can return the shipping statement marked "cancel." If I don't cancel, I will receive 6 brand-new novels every month and be billed just $4.24 per book in the U.S. or $4.99 per book in Canada, plus 25¢ shipping and handling per book and applicable taxes, if any*. That's a savings of close to 15% off the cover price! I understand that accepting the 2 free books and gifts places me under no obligation to buy anything. I can always return a shipment and cancel at any time. Even if I never buy another book from Harlequin, the two free books and gifts are mine to keep forever.

182 HDN EEZ7   382 HDN EEZK

Name	(PLEASE PRINT)	
Address		Apt. #
City	State/Prov.	Zip/Postal Code

Signature (if under 18, a parent or guardian must sign)

Mail to the **Harlequin Reader Service:**
IN U.S.A.: P.O. Box 1867, Buffalo, NY 14240-1867
IN CANADA: P.O. Box 609, Fort Erie, Ontario L2A 5X3

Not valid to current subscribers of Harlequin Intrigue books.

Want to try two free books from another line?
Call 1-800-873-8635 or visit www.morefreebooks.com.

* Terms and prices subject to change without notice. N.Y. residents add applicable sales tax. Canadian residents will be charged applicable provincial taxes and GST. This offer is limited to one order per household. All orders subject to approval. Credit or debit balances in a customer's account(s) may be offset by any other outstanding balance owed by or to the customer. Please allow 4 to 6 weeks for delivery. Offer available while quantities last.

Your Privacy: Harlequin is committed to protecting your privacy. Our Privacy Policy is available online at www.eHarlequin.com or upon request from the Reader Service. From time to time we make our lists of customers available to reputable third parties who may have a product or service of interest to you. If you would prefer we not share your name and address, please check here. ☐

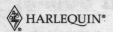
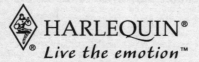

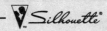

SPECIAL EDITION™

THE WILDER FAMILY
Healing Hearts in Walnut River

Social worker Isobel Suarez was proud to work at Walnut River General Hospital, so when Neil Kane showed up from the attorney general's office to investigate insurance fraud, she was up in arms. Until she melted in his arms, and things got very tricky...

Look for

HER MR. RIGHT?

by

KAREN ROSE SMITH

Available May wherever books are sold.

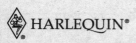

HARLEQUIN®

American ★ Romance®

Three Boys and a Baby

When Ella Garvey's eight-year-old twins and
their best friend, Dillon, discover an abandoned
baby girl, they fear she will be put in jail—
or worse! They decide to take matters into their
own hands and run away. Luckily the outlaws are
found quickly…and Ella finds a second chance
at love—with Dillon's dad, Jackson.

LOOK FOR

Three Boys and a Baby

BY

LAURA MARIE ALTOM

Available May
wherever you buy books.

LOVE, HOME & HAPPINESS